The
Golden
Rooms

The
Golden Rooms

BY VARDIS FISHER

The Vanguard Press

NEW YORK

Manufactured in the U. S. A. by H. Wolff, New York, N. Y.

FOR GRANT AND WAYNE
AND BOB

The
Golden
Rooms

I

SQUATTING, with the hams of his rump against his heels, his forearms resting at ease across his thighs and his big hands hanging limply as if broken at their wrists, Harg was gazing at a grove of trees. He was not thinking of the trees. For him they were little more than things that stood upright and tried to walk away when the wind was on them and changed color in time of cold. They were turning yellow now.

Beyond the trees, beyond many hills, were strange creatures whose appearance resembled his own and that of his people; but they were much taller—almost twice as tall, it had seemed to him—and they ran as swiftly as the deer and hunted with the kind of weapons he had never seen before. Only yesterday he had wandered far from his family group and had seen these tall men; he had crawled noiselessly through a thicket of birch and alder to spy on them, as he had spied many times before. Upon peering out, he had seen a man sitting in a pile of sticks and stones and had watched him rub sticks and stones together.

3

At first Harg had supposed the man was choosing a weapon. Harg had his weapons, too, pieces of flint and jasper and quartz, some of which he used for cutting and scraping and some for striking blows. But he had never rubbed two of them together. He took his weapons as he found them, choosing from piles of broken stones the natural axes and knives that would serve him best.

He now remembered the man and felt there was purpose in what the man had done. The man had rubbed things together and from time to time had interrupted his labor to do something, but Harg had not been able to tell what the man did when not rubbing. The man had sat so long that Harg had become impatient for a closer view and had crawled forward a little, trying to see what the man did with the pile of stuff around him. But he had not been able to tell; and when at last the man rose and went away, taking some stones and sticks with him, Harg had been perplexed. There lived in him the unhappy belief that the man's weapons were better than his own, and were better because the man had changed them.

Harg found stones and rubbed them, though nobody in his group had ever done anything like that. Nor did Harg understand at all why he was doing it. Obscurely, persistently, he felt there had been purpose, some kind of higher cunning, in the stranger's labor. Harg employed no method in his rubbing, having no clear purpose in mind, nor the faintest notion that by rubbing the stones he would change them. Like one obsessed by imitation, he merely rubbed pieces of flint together; stared at them and perceived no change; became bored and impatient; and then threw them away.

Today he was trying to think of the matter. Some

4

pieces of stone were better than others. Some had a sharp cutting edge with which he could cut the hide on a rabbit and get at its flesh. A few were roughly shaped to fit his grasp, and these he could hurl. And still others were long and slender, with sharp points that he could thrust into his prey. But he and his people had always taken stones as they found them, discarding weapons when they came on better ones but never trying to improve the ones they had.

Harg was only a youth entering puberty, but he was by far the most intelligent member of his family. Many times he had spied on the strange people, and he had learned with the shock of astonishment that they used fire. At least they sat close by fires much smaller than any Harg had ever seen and did things with the fires; and little by little he had come by the notion that these people, in a way utterly mysterious to him, were able to make fire.

Harg lived his life by impulses and whims and dark intuitions, and he felt now that the man was still beyond the grove of trees, doing things with stones and sticks. Softly, like the hunting creature he was, he approached the grove and entered it and on hands and knees crawled to the far side. When he peered out he was disappointed; there was no living thing in sight. He thought next that perhaps the pile was out there from which the man had chosen certain weapons. A thought for Harg or any of his people instantly became a certainty, and so in haste he left the grove and searched. But he found no stones or sticks, and with the disappointment in him becoming pain, mixed with fear and anger, he wandered aimlessly until he came within sight of his people. Upon seeing them, he withdrew, because he was a solitary youth who in daylight hours liked to be alone with his thoughts and designs. He spent each night with them at their squatting place by a stream but during the day he went off by himself to hunt for food; and so now he slunk away, still intent on learning what the strange man had been doing.

A week passed, and the perplexed unhappiness lived in him. Another autumn had come. For Harg and his people autumn was a difficult time of rain when they were chilled through and wished they could seize and occupy a cave possessed by beasts. After the rains came bitter cold and snow. Food was scarce then, and they starved and shivered, and the weaker ones among them died. They had not learned that the bleak time of life was always followed by a warmer time. When spring came they felt there could never be cold weather again; and so always they were dismayed and angered and afraid when leaves turned yellow, frost carpeted the earth, and terrible snow fell deep around them.

Harg sensed that a period of cold was coming and he continued to search for something that eluded his recognition. He thought he was looking for better weapons; and when he came to a pile of stones he would patiently examine them and never find anything more dependable than what he already had. He had a big axe, the head and the handle all of one piece, and he had flint knives with sharp cutting edges. But it was his way, and the way of all people, to believe there were better things—in weapons, in food, in shelter—if they could be found. And, besides, unknown to himself, he was seeking fire because now and then in the past his family had been warmed when a forest or a prairie burned.

One day while searching he came to a more fascinating

6

pile of splintered stones than any he had ever seen. Before him in a shattered heap lay iron pyrites and flints in all designs and sizes. There were slender lances two feet long; bludgeons that could be grasped and swung or hurled; short broad blades with rough handles; and an unbelievable wealth of chisels and daggers. The pile lay scattered near a chalk cliff and was hidden on all sides by tall grass.

With the unreason typical of him and his people, Harg thought these were the stones where the strange man had sat. He did not look round him to observe that there were no trees near. He saw only this wonder heap of weapons from which anyone would gladly choose; and with delight that was audible he sat among the fragments. Here were tools with which he could dream of crushing the skull of the cave bear or ripping open the belly of the mammoth. Such a glory of priceless things had never fallen to his lot before, and one by one or several at a time he drew them to him, uttering guttural cries of joy.

After a while he chose all he could carry and staggered off with them but he did not go far. In him was the feeling that he ought to sit with them and rub them as the stranger had done. When some of the flints slipped and fell from his grasp, he sat with his armful, deep in tall, dry vegetation where he was almost hidden. He felt safe here and was glad; now he could rub the flints and learn what rubbing would do.

First he chose at random two long blades and rubbed one against the other; but these were very hard, and when, from time to time, he interrupted his labor to examine them, neither seemed to be any sharper or more pointed. But he did perceive with surprise that both were warm. He tested an edge with a finger on which the skin was as brown and tough as the hawthorn quill; he gently prodded an arm with a lance. These tools, it seemed to him, were sharp enough. They were better than any he had used, and he would have been content with them if he had not learned that rubbing gave them warmth. Without knowing what he sought to do or how he could do it, he bent to his task.

He chose other stones and rubbed them, now rasping with one across another's face, or now sawing an edge across an edge, striving by trial and error to change them. When he sawed across a blade, sparks flew off, but of the sparks he was only dimly conscious, if indeed at all. Sparks he had seen many times, and for him they were only bright, momentary things that flashed and vanished.

Fire he had seen—dreadful fire that swept across prairies of grass or forests of dead trees. He and his people were afraid of fire, yet attracted by it, too, because they had learned that in cold weather fire could give them comfort and warmth. They had eaten beasts that had burned to death. And now, below the level of his conscious mind, Harg was moved by a feeling that the strange people used fire and controlled it and made it serve their needs.

But Harg did not know that sparks were fire. They were only sudden bright things that flew off the stones; and he paid no attention to them until, in a moment of astonishment, he saw a blade of grass turn golden and curl and slowly darken. Leaving his squatting position, he fell to hands and knees and stared at the stem of grass, a tiny fragment of which had burned. He touched it fearfully, and the ash crumbled. But he could feel no warmth. Nevertheless, in the amazed wonder of his mind was the thought that fire had touched this leaf.

8

Rising to his feet, he looked round him to learn if there was any fire in sight. There was none. There was only this hillside of grass that spread away to a stone ledge or downward to wooded hills. He gazed at the sky, but there was no sign of fire there and no sound of it. Kneeling again, he gently broke off the stem of grass and laid it across an open palm. When he touched the burned part, the ash flaked off in his hand, and with a long fingernail he traced the edge between the burned and the unburned part. That fire had lived for a moment within arm's reach of him he no longer had any doubt.

But where had this fire come from? Trying to think of the baffling matter, he again squatted on his heels and stared at the ash on his palm, at the stones, at the world around him. Had the man on whom he spied been making fire? If Harg had clearly remembered that experience, he would have realized that the man had made no fire, that he had merely rubbed stones together for a while and had gone away, taking a few of the stones with him. But Harg's memories were confused; his mind was a dark little world with few certainties in it. It seemed to him now that the man had been making fire, and with this belief in him he set to work again.

For a while he labored aimlessly, choosing stones and rubbing them furiously, and with disappointment laying them aside. Sparks flew off, but these did not mean fire for him. Like the sun and stars and moon, like so many other things of which he was only vaguely conscious, they had no meaning in his life. Like all his people, he experimented blindly, darkly, hoping for a miracle.

After more than an hour of futile labor, he sat with his pile of stones and strove to think of the matter—and, in

9

an effort to fix the materials of thought so that he could grasp and use them, he stared at the grass or the flints, or at both of them together, trying to see a relationship between the two. He gathered a handful of grass and rubbed it against a stone. He took a stone in one hand, a bunch of grass in the other, and rubbed them with all his strength; and presently he became aware of a sensation of warmth in the palm that clutched the grass. He examined his hand. He studied the grass and saw that it was falling apart and turning brown. Again he rubbed the grass, and held it to his cheek and felt the warmth in it. Excited now, he gathered a huge pile of grass between his knees, and with both hands he seized a large stone and rubbed it back and forth across the pile. He worked for several minutes before, in despair, he gave up.

He forgot about fire and fixed his interest on the tools. He did not intend to take all of them with him; but like a child trying to choose among toys, he could not tell which to leave and which to take. One and another he would pick up to test its edge, its point, or to learn how well the handle fitted his grasp. Among the larger stones was one that resembled an axe. It had a good blade, but the handle was large and heavy and rough. Harg laid the handle across a big rock, and with another rock he smote it. Failing after repeated efforts to knock off a part of the handle, he grasped the blade of the axe with one hand, laid the handle across a rock, and used another stone as a maul. He was squatting on his heels with dead grass piled round him to his waist when he began to pound the handle. Sparks flew off in showers, but he paid no heed to them. His whole interest was fixed on chipping the knots off the handle and making it comfortable in his grasp. When it resisted his blows he became angry; and in searching around him for other stones with which to chisel and hammer he came upon a piece of dead but well-seasoned wood. Returning, he knelt and sawed across the handle with the wood; and he was so absorbed by his labor that he did not know the grass near him had caught flame and was burning. He did not realize this until the hair on his body was singed and his flesh smarted in the heat; and when with a cry of astonishment he leapt up, there was fire all around him.

Leaving his tools, he ran but he did not go far; and upon turning with amazement to look back, he trembled like one overcome by fear. It seemed to him, then, that he had been trying to make fire; and here fire was, moving in a yellow sheet away from him and down the wind. He began to shout with shrill triumphant cries and to dance up and down with his short bowed legs; and he flung his arms wide to the sky and pointed at the fire and called upon all people to look.

The fire was moving away from him, and Harg followed it, trotting across the warm ashes until he came into the heat. He was now driven by a wish to capture this fire and control it, to gather it somehow in his arms and take it to the squatting-place of his family; and so, howling like a crazy fellow, he ran back and forth behind it, or he tried to outflank it and head it off and stop it and make it behave.

Behind him, and quickly approaching, were three men from his family group. At first they were merely curious about the fire, but upon drawing near they were amazed by Harg's behavior. Like one bereft of his senses, he was still loping back and forth, gesturing and shouting, and trying to possess and control the fire he had made. He was making such wild outcry that one of the men began to shout; and upon hearing him Harg turned. At once he raced over to the men, pointing back as he ran, and babbling and slobbering from the excess of triumph in him. He tried to tell them things for which he had no words.

Harg's people had a simple language of a few verbs and nouns, but these few they used singly, never putting a verb and a noun together to make a sentence. Indeed, each single word served as many sentences, the differences in meaning being conveyed by intonation; and in talking they used not only words but also a multitude of ejaculations and gestures.

When Harg came up, he pointed at the fire and shouted, "Look!" He was so excited that he shouted the command many times and made impetuous gestures and moved back and forth as if restraining in himself an impulse to run.

"Fire," said the oldest of the men; and he looked at the others as if to see what they made of this.

Another man said, "Fire," and the third said, "Fire," all of them speaking as if the matter were commonplace.

But Harg was shaking with excitement and trying to tell them that this fire belonged to him, that he had made it, that he knew how to make fire; and when he saw no understanding in their big dull faces, he shouted at them the word which they all used for weapon. "Weapon!" he cried; and after visibly struggling with the new knowledge that was like a song of triumph in his whole being, he put two words together. "Weapon-fire!" he said. Then, despairing, he rubbed his palms together, his eyes meanwhile watching their faces. He fell to his knees in the grass, continuing to rub his hands, moving about and rubbing against the grass; but for the men who watched him his behavior was meaningless.

The oldest man, Gugg, who by right of age and size was leader of his group, became impatient and a little angry, and he moved toward Harg as if to strike him and make him stop his frenzied babbling. But Harg saw him coming and leapt back. He rose to his feet and for a long moment he looked at the men and they looked at him. Harg's gaze beseeched them to understand what he had done and what a remarkable young man he was; but they thought he was in some kind of tantrum. They stared at him, each wondering in his own way what was wrong with the boy.

When, at last, Harg turned and saw the fire burning in a golden arc two hundred yards away, he strove again to explain the thing to them. "Come," he said, and started toward the fire. Gugg hesitated, but after a moment he thought perhaps Harg had killed an animal and wanted to give it to him. And so the three men went with Harg and came to the burnt earth, and Harg rushed back and forth over the ashes, searching for his wonder heap of tools. The men thought he was looking for food and hunted with him. When Harg found his pile of stones, he burst into a terrible song of joy. He squatted on his heels and grasped two stones and rubbed them together, interrupting his labor now and then to point at the fire or the burnt area, still trying to make these men understand. In fact, Harg himself had only the dimmest notion of how he had made the fire. He did not know that burnt grass would not burn again. He thought if he worked hard with the stones he would somehow, miraculously, make another fire; and he hoped the men would be patient and wait.

But the men became more and more impatient. Gugg growled, and his growl was a threat. He had expected to find food; but here, squatting before him, was a boy rubbing stones together, and that made no sense at all. Gugg had never rubbed two stones together and saw no reason why anybody should. Harg sensed the impatience in the man and worked all the more furiously; he talked to the men; he pointed at the fire, only the smoke of which he could now see; and he prayed in the only way he could for another triumph. But the foolish fellow was merely sawing one stone across another without directing the sparks to dry grass or even realizing that the sparks were fire.

Gugg was on the point of striking the lad when one of the men diverted his attention. Yawg had been looking at the stones. After a while the thought had come to his dim mind that better weapons lay here than any he owned, and he dropped to his knees and pawed over them, choosing a knife and a lance for his own use. When the other men saw what he was doing they became interested, too; and Gugg, who always had his way in such matters, growled at them and made it plain that he would choose first. When he squatted among the stones the other two men moved back, and for several minutes Gugg tested the points and the blades before making up his mind. He chose three of the stones and turned away, heading back to his family, and the other men selected weapons and followed him.

When Harg was left alone he felt dejected. He felt so defeated and misunderstood that for a little while he squatted on his heels, his arms and hands limp, his mind bleak and empty; and when at last he rose, looking very unhappy and crestfallen, he saw that the fire had burned itself out against a green forest. There was only a little smoke over there now. In looking around him he saw the piece of seasoned wood with which he had sawed across the edge of a rock; and with the wood and two stones he turned homeward. For him these tools had become more priceless than any others he had known in all his wanderings or as far as he could see.

2

In the primitive time of these people sons learned at an early age all that their fathers knew, and sometimes before puberty they left the family group and became solitary hunters. Harg thought of going away now, and he might have gone if he had not smarted under humiliation. He tried to explain to the women that he had made fire, but they manifested no interest; and again he strove to make the men understand. But Gugg threatened him, and Harg withdrew to sulk and consider.

His people numbered several hundred and roamed over an area in what is today known as France. They were not by any means the most intelligent people of their time. On the contrary, they were one of the most stupid and backward, apelike in appearance, and living almost at the level of the apes. Harg was the most intelligent member of his family and had by far the greatest knowledge of things; he had wandered farther in his hunting and had seen more. Into an adjacent region had come a strange people, and several times Harg had spied on the men. He not only had seen a man rubbing stones together; he knew also that these men were amazingly tall, that they ran with the speed of a deer, and that they had strange and deadly weapons much better than his own.

He had seen them only a few times, and then only while hiding at a safe distance; but his mind had been stimulated by what he had seen. Harg and his people hunted only small game like rabbits, rats, and birds; these tall men hunted the deer, the horse, and the mammoth. Harg resolved to make fire and to be a mightier hunter.

He knew he had made fire but he did not know how he had made it. Rubbing stones or sticks together seemed to be a part of fire making, but he did not understand that the friction threw off tiny bits of flame or produced heat in the sticks. And so, when he went off by himself again to experiment, he suffered one disappointment after another. He was so foolish that he tried to ignite grass that had already burned and was only ash, or green things that would never burn; and it was quite by chance that he squatted again where dry grass was deep around him. It was by chance, too, that he rubbed two sticks and not two stones. It was only after many days of faithful and almost frantic effort that he understood that dry grass and two sticks were necessary in fire making. He learned that two sticks became warm, that indeed they became almost too hot to touch if he sawed one across the other in haste and with all his strength. And after blind and fumbling and persistent labor he perceived, too, that flakes of dry grass burned when placed against the hot stick.

But still, after many days, he had only the dimmest notion of how he was making magic. By experimenting he learned that green sticks would not become warm under

17

rubbing; that some dry sticks seemed to be better than others; that some kinds of grass seemed to have no fire in them. When after furious rubbing he had a stick hot, and knew there was fire in it because there was heat, he would lay tiny flakes of grass on the stick and watch them curl and turn to ash. Time after time, desperately, furiously, he did this, and still the particles of grass merely burned without flame. Now and then the edge of a very dry flake would turn red with fire, and in his eagerness Harg would go down on hands and knees to stare at it and watch the red edge fade and die.

It was while he was staring one time that he blew breath, without intending to, upon some flakes curling in the heat, and at once they burst into flame. The pieces of grass burned with yellow fire upon the stick; and in his frenzied eagerness to keep this tiny fire alive and make it grow, Harg heaped grass upon it. He smothered it, and when he took the grass away he saw that the fire was dead. In such moments as this he howled with rage and jumped up and down and smote himself; or he would smite the grass that refused to burn, or seize the sticks and beat them wildly against one another. But these tantrums passed quickly. Again he would rub the sticks until they were hot and lay powdered grass on them; again he would kneel and stare and wait for a miracle; and after countless trials he perceived that there was a relationship between fire and air. He learned that a red edge glowed when he breathed on it and faded when he did not; and when he made this discovery, the miracle of fire came into the possession of his genius, and he knew that he had triumphed.

He gathered a huge armful of the choicest grass and

carried it to the squatting place of his people. The men were away hunting. The women thought only that he was going to add grass to his bed because that was a custom with all of them. They did not observe that Harg behaved very mysteriously, like a proud and vain one who housed many secrets. He took a long while to arrange the grass to suit his fancy, and when at last he turned to the women, he gestured imperiously and shouted at them. "Look!" he yelled, and pointed at the pile of grass. "Look!" he cried again, and held up his two fire sticks.

Kayah, the grandmother and boss of the group, came over to see what he was doing. Again and again Harg commanded her to look and pointed at the grass; and Kayah looked at the grass and at him and wrinkled her homely old face in disgust. The moment he saw her interest waning, Harg commanded again, shouting more loudly and dancing up and down in triumph. "Look!" he yelled; and he meant, "Just watch and see what I do!" But he delayed the fire-making because he anticipated with great joy the amazement which the women would show. As a matter of fact, he was annoyed because the other women did not come over and gawk at him. He would have been wordlessly happy if all the people in the world could have gathered round him here to watch him make fire. Kayah was a little curious, not because of the pile of grass or the two sticks in his hand but because of the triumphant emotion which she sensed in him. She placed her hands on her big hairy hips and waited.

Now Harg squatted before the grass and thrust his hands into the pile and sawed one stick across the other; but again and again he looked back to see if Kayah was watching him. He did not want her to turn away. He felt

19

intuitively that if she did not actually see him make fire, she would not believe; and so, when her attention wavered, he shouted and asked her to watch.

There was really no need to command her. Kayah had never seen anyone pile grass and thrust arms into it and make such frantic movements. Harg's behavior was so unusual that she called to the other women, and they came over; and presently all of them stood behind Harg and watched him with fascinated interest. If they had had any knowledge of lunacy they would have thought this boy was daft, because he was kneeling now and seemed to be rubbing his hands together in the grass.

Now and then Harg paused in the sawing to lay a finger on a stick and learn how hot it was; and when the larger stick, the fire one, seemed almost hot enough, he yelled at the women in wild excitement and told them to look. The women were staring with all the vision they had. Harg now thrust his head into the pile of grass the better to see what he was doing. He crumbled a few flakes of grass into powder and held this powder in the palm of his right hand with three fingers closed over it while with forefinger and thumb he grasped the stick and sawed furiously. When he felt the moment had come, he quickly laid the powdered grass on the fire stick and lowered his head to breathe on it. But he was so vainly eager to have the women stand by and admire him that he pulled his head out of the pile to see if they were watching; and when he turned again to his fire stick it was cold.

He felt then as if he had been outraged and, leaping to his feet, he yelled at the women and menaced them. They shrank away, babbling with alarm; whereupon in a tantrum Harg kicked his pile of grass and scattered it and jumped up and down and shouted. Almost at once his mood changed, and he sulked, his eyes staring balefully at the women, his mind hating them. He was so impulsive and unreasonable and vain that it seemed to him they had destroyed his fire; and not until they turned away to their children did he come to his senses. Moving on hands and knees like a grotesque beast with its lower hind legs dragging uselessly, he piled the scattered grass and resumed his fire-making.

This time he paid no heed to the women until he had fire, but the instant the grass burst into flame he sprang up and yelled like a wild man. He raced over and seized Kayah by an arm, but she had seen the fire and needed no urging. Crying with amazement, she ran to it; and like one who doubted her senses she thrust a hand into the flames and then screamed and withdrew her hand. The hair on her hand and forearm was singed. The other women came up and stared at her hand, while with a long, dirty finger Kayah swept off the ashes of the burnt hair. She smelled of the burnt hair and offered her hand to the other women to smell. They sniffed and looked at one another and gurgled with astonishment.

Harg meanwhile had been staring at the fire. It was only a yellow bed of embers now, and soon it was only ashes and a few dying petals of fire that pulsed and faded and turned gray. The women were still sniffing Kayah's arm; Harg wanted them to fix their attention on him. He wanted them to look at him with admiration and awe.

"Look!" he shouted, and pointed at the fire; and the women looked but there were only ashes to see. Realizing that his fire had mysteriously got away from him, Harg ran to gather more grass; and guessing what he had in mind the women went with him. But they gathered more than grass. They fetched green limbs, dead sticks, and even pieces of stone, piling them all together; and again Harg squatted to make fire. But now when he saw the women curiously watching him he became a very cunning young man. In his ability to make fire he sensed an advantage; it set him apart from them and gave him a very precious distinction. In his mind was the thought that he alone of all living things could make fire, that this was his secret, his special power and honor; and so he hunched forward and tried to keep from them the fact that he was rubbing sticks together. He felt angry when they moved close to him and bent forward to peer. He shouted and threatened them, and when they drew away he sawed furiously at the fire stick, and when they came close again to peer he did useless things to confuse them. He pretended to rearrange the pile or mysteriously to thrust arms into it as if searching for something or to rub together the stones which they had fetched; and all this served his cunning purpose. The more he fussed with the pile of stuff, the more he baffled them; and, sensing this, he redoubled his efforts to bewilder and overawe. When the women were not intently watching him he sawed vigorously with his stick.

This time he was so long making fire that the women lost interest in his doings, but the moment the pile came to flaming life they were as astonished as before. They stood by it, turning their naked hairy bodies in the heat and crying at one another. Like the young lord that he was, Harg stepped back and watched them; and if for a moment their fascinated interest seemed to waver he would yell at them and point at the fire and say, "Look!"

He wanted them to stare at it until they were overcome by the marvel of his greatness.

But Kayah had another notion. She wished to keep this fire alive because it warmed her and filled her with deep joy. When it burned low she went away to gather fuel; but because fire was a mystery of which she had little knowledge, she fetched many things that would not burn. She threw stones on it and a piece of staghorn. The other women did so, too, but they also fetched grass and wood; and soon they perceived that some things were food for a fire and some were not.

Harg went away and sat on his haunches to sulk. This fire, like his tools, belonged to him, but the women had possessed it. Furthermore, they completely ignored him, as if unaware that he was a fire maker. He was cheated of the glory that he had expected to have. He could not possibly have said quite what he wanted to do; he did not want affection because among the people of this time there was no love save that between a mother and her youngest children. He hungered to have them behave in a way that would enhance his feeling of importance, of uniqueness, of enviable and mysterious worth. If they had come over to gaze at him and make exclamations of admiration and awe he would have been pleased.

And because they did not he sulked. He squatted in self-pity and hated them; but presently he remembered that the men would come soon and he hoped he would be able to make them understand his power. He would make fire for them, but he would not let them see how he made it; and then they would dance up and down and point at him and know that he was a great man.

Toward evening the men came in, bringing two birds

and a litter of rabbits; and when they saw the fire and the women warming themselves by it they were too astounded even to grunt. They felt not only wordless astonishment but fear as well. Never in their lives had they seen anything like this. Fires they had seen, but broad, destroying fires that swept across prairie and forest and killed everything in their path. They had found animals burned to death and they had come to the belief that fire was a vast and uncontrollable enemy. Yet here their women and children squatted, warming themselves; and fifty yards away was Harg who, they had no doubt at all, had fled in fear.

Harg had been watching them. He had the foolish notion that these men would realize he had made the fire and would come over to look at him with admiration. He thought they might offer him the choicest rabbit. When they paid no heed to him he rose and shouted and pointed at the fire. Still pointing at the fire, he beckoned to the men to approach and look; and the men became convinced that Harg, too, was afraid of the fire and was asking them to destroy it.

The women now rose and went off to find fuel, and the men watched them go. The men watched them gather grass and sticks and fetch these to the fire, and their mouths hung open and their eyes were bright with amazement and wonder. The women paid no heed to them or to Harg; they acted as if they had used fire all their lives. For the world around them and all the strange things in it they did not feel the bewilderment or awe or terror which men felt—or in any case they felt it less oppressively and constantly. For them things were to be used in devotion to their children, and they divided the world into what could be used and what could not be used, feeling friendly toward the one and indifferent toward the other. Fire warmed them; they liked it and intended to keep it. They did not think of it, at least not chiefly, as a mysterious and a dreadful thing.

But for the three men standing fifty yards away, this was an amazing fire. It stayed in one place instead of running over the earth on invisible legs. It did not leap on great yellow wings and disappear in the sky; and when the women threw stuff on it, the fire became larger and stood up tall.

At last Yawg, the stupidest of the three men, grunted; and as if he had searched his mind for the right thing to say, he turned to his companions and said, "Look!"

The command loosened Kahha's tongue, and he pointed at the fire and said, "Look!"

"Look!" cried Yawg again, and pointed also.

But Gugg, the father of Harg, and a little more intelligent than the other two, had been thinking of the fire and trying to understand it. "Enemy," he said. The word for enemy these people used with different inflections or gestures and each had its own meaning. Sometimes the word meant, "Enemy is coming"; or again it meant, "Enemy is going away." Gugg used the word to mean simply and only, "The enemy is there."

"Enemy," said Kahha.

"Enemy," said Yawg, and pointed.

The men, led by Gugg, approached, but not close enough to feel the warmth. They expected this fire to take to its legs at any moment and run; but they observed, nevertheless, that the women seemed to be enjoying themselves. Kayah sat with a child on her lap and moved a

25

little closer or a little back as the fire rose or fell. The other women went off into the dusk and returned with grass and wood.

Gugg realized now that he was hungry. He was holding five young rabbits in his big hands. Letting four of them drop, and keeping his anxious gaze on the fire, he stripped the hide off the fifth rabbit and began to eat. He grasped the two hind legs and tore one off and fed the dripping flesh to his big mouth. He devoured the rabbit, entrails and flesh and most of the bones—indeed, almost everything except the skull and the pelt; and the other two men, each of whom had a bird, also stripped their prey and ate.

When Kayah observed the men eating she spoke sharply and spilled the child from her lap and came over to Gugg. Upon seeing the four rabbits at his feet, Kayah picked them up and returned to squat by the fire. She stripped the skin off a rabbit and with powerful hands pulled the carcass in two; and she gave a half to each of two small children. To each of the other two women she gave a rabbit, and one of them shared her meal with Kayah's daughter Memm, a girl of ten. Harg, squatting on his heels and sulking, was offered nothing. By the women he was regarded as a man able to capture his own food.

Harg's hunger was for admiration rather than food. By far the most intelligent member of this family group, he squatted out in the twilight, observing the others and thinking his thoughts. They were simple thoughts because he had so little knowledge of the world; but he was a very intuitive young man for one of his time and perceived truths for which he could never have found words. He was now aware that the men were afraid of the fire and the women were not; that the women by feeding it

26

had learned how to keep fire alive; and that during the long darkness until light came again they would probably sit by it and refuse to sleep.

He was also thinking of the fire. It was not alive as he was, but neither was it unalive like a stone. It did not eat its food as he did, but just the same it consumed all the grass and sticks which the women gave to it. The fire made sounds, too, and it could not make sounds if it were not alive. Perhaps, Harg decided, the fires which he had seen in the past and which he thought had died had not died at all but had gone away and out of sight. If he had been a little more imaginative he might have wondered if the sun was such a fire.

While he was thinking of fire and trying to understand it, a brilliant notion came to him. It came to him with such dramatic suddenness, with such warmth of certainty, that he rose to his feet, trembling with eagerness, and slipped away into the dusk. If, the thought said, the women had stolen his fire, why did he not make another? And the thought added, with that cunning intimacy of self-love which flatters all men: "You are the only one in the world who can make fire!" Yes, he was, and he would build one of his own and defend it against all thieves.

And so with eager haste he gathered grass and sticks and made a pile two hundred yards from the group and squatted on his heels. He turned his back to the others because he did not want them to suspect what he was doing; and from time to time as he sawed with his stick he glanced behind him to be sure nobody was approaching. The joy in him was intense and triumphant. A little while ago he had been a forlorn and dejected one whose property had been stolen; but now he was a man with a secret

27

that was more priceless than staghorn spears or flint knives.

When at last he had his fire burning and was proudly warming himself in its heat, the three astonished men came over to peer at him. It did not for a moment occur to them that Harg had made this fire. They thought he had found it. They stared round them in the dusk to see if there were other fires which they had overlooked. They talked to one another.

Harg wanted them to go away. "Go!" he shouted at them and pointed into the night. Instead of going away the men drew nearer and peered at the fire as if to be sure they were not deceived. Harg thought they intended to possess it; and, acting on an impulse, he did something that filled them with terror. He seized a burning stick and hurled it at them. They backed away, babbling with astonishment; and when Harg understood that he had frightened them, he grasped a long flaming fagot and chased them. The women came forward, bewildered and confused by the cries of the men and by the picture of Harg menacing them with a firebrand. When he felt secure, Harg dropped the fagot and turned back; and Kayah, seeing the stick aflame on the earth, came over to look at it. She gathered grass and wood and piled them on the burning stick, and now there were three fires in the night.

When Harg saw two fires besides his own he was dismayed. There had been only one—the one that had been stolen from him. He had not seen Kayah build a fire on the ember he had dropped; and he concluded, therefore, that one among these persons had learned how to make fire. If he had lost one of his hands or one of his legs or had been robbed of his fire sticks he could not have felt more cheated and debased. He sulked furiously and hated them; and after a few minutes he realized that there were four fires. He was convinced now that one of them had spied out his secret.

The other women had been looking at Kayah when she laid grass and sticks on the burning fagot; and Mog had thereupon taken a flaming piece of wood and had gone off at a little distance to make a fourth fire. Harg had not seen her do that, and now, for all his careful watching, he learned nothing. Each of the women had a fire and they went off into darkness to gather wood.

Though Harg had the most intelligent mind in this group, it was nevertheless a fickle mind that shifted quickly from one interest to another; and soon in the pleasure of being warmed he forgot the women. The nights were cold now. When darkness came during the period of cold weather, it was the habit of this family group, as it was of all other groups in the area around it, to leave the squatting place and seek a shelter of some kind. But now Harg was warm and happy. He learned that he could squat on his heels and slowly turn himself and so warm all parts of his body. He discovered, too, that it was pleasurable to hold his hands above the flame until his naked palms were hot and tingling. When he smelled burning hair he would move back a little to examine himself; and now and then he went away to gather fuel.

The night deepened without moon and with only a few stars. Harg could not see the men now, but he could see the women and children in firelight. There were three groups, each tending its own fire. The fires were golden rooms in the vast darkness. Harg looked above him and could see nothing, but within the circle of his fire everything was visible, and he began to feel a vague unhappiness that deepened to awe. He had never known that fire also made light, that it destroyed the darkness around it; and this was a wonder so huge and splendid that he trembled while trying to understand all its infinite meaning. The fire could warm him and it could make him see.

He was awed by fire because he saw in it both enemy and friend. In the great darkness around him he knew that beasts lurked everywhere, hungering for his flesh and blood; but fire was an enemy, too, because it would kill him if it could. When he approached too close he felt sharp pain, and in the eager flames that leapt up he saw a wish to destroy him; but if he stood back a little, and turned round and round in the heat, he felt only friendliness that ravished his senses.

After he had thrown on another armful of sticks and was soaking himself in the heat he learned another lesson. A spark flew off unseen by him and lodged in the thick hair on his belly; and a moment later he leapt into the air and yelled as if he had been stung by a huge insect. He clawed into the hair and found the ember, and it burned his fingers, and with a howl of rage he hurled it from him. After sucking his fingers he parted the hair and searched for the wound. He could still feel the sting of it. While thus engaged other sparks smote him and he stepped back, staring at the fire, convinced that it was attacking him. Parts of it were leaping at him in the way of stinging insects; and when another ember caught him off guard and burned him, he fell into a terrible rage and seized his stone axe and struck at the fire in an effort to kill it. Strangled with fury, he tried to destroy this thing which he had made and which he had loved as he loved his weapons and himself.

He was still smiting the flames when he heard a scream. It was the shriek, naked in its pain and terror, of a small child. It stiffened Harg and the other men because a cry like that was a summons to battle. They all thought that a wolf or hyena or some other dreadful beast had crept in and attacked one of the children, and they seized their weapons and ran toward the sound.

Kayah had gone off to gather fuel, and the younger of her children, a girl of two, had tottered into the fire. Kayah came back out of the night like a wild thing and plucked her child out of the embers and hugged it to her breast. It was badly burned on its hands and feet and continued to scream while Kayah strove to soothe it, and the other women cried aloud with pity. In the confusion the night darkened, the fires sank to ashes and died. The three men had come over, carrying their stone axes and flint knives; but they did not draw close to the women until they saw that the fire was dead.

Then Gugg spoke, using their word that meant sleep or rest. He wanted to seek a thicket or cave into which they could crawl and be sheltered from the wind and from their enemies. "Sleep," he said; and when the women paid no heed he spoke sharply and menaced them with his axe.

"Sleep," said Kahha.

"Sleep," said Yawg.

Gugg turned away, and the others followed him, moving anxiously through the darkness. They were all filled with that nameless dread which never wholly left them and always became more acute in nighttime. Harg came last, an unhappy young man who wanted to make fire again but was afraid to try; but together with his weapons he carried his fire sticks.

Upon coming to an overhanging ledge of stone under which they had spent a previous night, Gugg stopped and peered into the gloom. He knew that beasts might be lurking there. He looked for a sign of eyes in the darkness, and when he saw none he shouted, and the other men gathered stones and hurled them into the shelter. The only sound was that of stone striking stone. Gugg entered, very cautiously, grasping his axe and ready to strike; and when he decided that the chamber was empty he called to the others. Then they all went back under the shelf to the far wall and huddled together there to share their warmth.

The child still whimpered at its mother's breast.

3

THE race of people to whom this family belonged was not among the physical giants of its time. Gugg, who by virtue of both size and age was the male leader of his group, stood only five feet and four inches in height, and very few of the men of his race were taller than that. He weighed about two hundred pounds.

In their appearance these people were apelike. Gugg's body was short but very deep and rugged, with a broad curved back that gave him an habitual stoop. He had a huge head but almost no neck at all, and his head was set forward on his rounded shoulders. His arms were short and powerfully muscled; his hands were heavy with short fingers. His lower leg in proportion to his thigh or torso was grotesquely short; and his knees, when he stood upright, bent forward, so that his whole appearance was that of a stooped man, with head and shoulders hunched forward, and legs crooked as if he had never fully straightened them. Indeed, he never had and was unable to.

His face was extremely large and broad and strong save

for a weak chin. He had a long upper lip and a huge flat nose, wide between the nostrils and deep in its arch. His eyes were far apart and rather small for his face; they were of a pale brown color that had the metallic hardness of jewels. His brow was low and recessed, with very heavy brow ridges and deep lines across the forehead and between the brows. His mop of hair, thick and coarse and dark, hung in a dirty tangle to his shoulders. Along his jaws, but not on his cheeks or upper lip, he had a short beard that was almost black and a little curly.

There was not much intelligence in Gugg's eyes when he looked at things. They were cold and cunning eyes full of fear and utterly without any hint of compassion or kindliness. When he was enraged, the pale brown of the iris turned yellow, and the heavy coarse brows drew down in a deep scowl. His wide straight mouth was habitually open, especially when he was relaxed; and his parted lips revealed two rows of strong teeth discolored by age, though Gugg was not yet thirty.

The other men looked much like him but were smaller. Harg was the handsomest male in this family group; he had a little more thrust to his chin, stood a little straighter, and had more alert and inquiring eyes. He was more nimble on his feet. Though these men were hunters, like all their contemporaries, they did not run with swift effortless ease, as was the way with men of another race, but loped along in a gawky and ungainly trot. Their legs were bent because of their custom of squatting on their heels, and this crook in their legs, together with the forward thrust of heavy shoulders, made running difficult. They walked as if they were stooped and chastened by extreme old age.

The women were a little shorter than the men, though

34

there was not between the sexes that physical difference in size and strength common to most people today. They had the same body stoop and bent knees, and like the men they were very hairy, but in respect to hairiness they varied a great deal. Mog was the hairiest of the women. She had a heavy thicket of black hair all over her back and chest and belly; and a huge mane of hair hung from her skull to her waist. The women were all sparsely bearded and Mog had more beard than any of the men. Their faces were coarse and dull; and their eyes were lifeless except in moments of danger or when they were busy with their children. When enemies threatened they were more savage than their men and fought without any regard at all for their own safety.

These people went naked, with only their hair to clothe them in bitter weather. If they had had clothes, they would have worn them, and gladly; and sometimes the women did try to make simple garments of animal skins. But when the skins became soaked by rain they were too stiff to be used as garments and were laid on the earth with the hair side up to serve as beds.

They were an improvident and thriftless people. They lived in a time after great glaciers had moved down from the north, driving arctic beasts before them; and the winters were bitterly cold. But they had not learned to build shelters or to store food. In times past, when they felt the approach of cold weather, they had tried to drive the beasts out of a cave; but they had only clumsy stone weapons to fight with. The cave hyena they could frighten, but the cave bear stood his ground and fought desperately, and they were all afraid of him.

For food they ate raw flesh when they could get it; and

35

when they could not, they ate nuts and roots and the more succulent plants. Hunting engaged the daylight hours of the men, but they were awkward and ineffectual hunters who often had to be satisfied with eggs and mice or the putrid remains of beasts slain by the lion or the wolf. They ate frogs and snakes; and when driven to it by hunger they ate all kinds of insects. Once in a while they came upon a large beast, helpless from wounds or old age; and after stoning it to death they ate gluttonously and what they could not eat they wasted.

These people had very little sense of the future and almost no memory of the past. They had learned to dread the approach of winter but not really to expect it; and when it came they were always rather surprised and deeply saddened. During the winter they suffered terribly, and the weaker ones among them died. During the winter, too, food was more difficult to find, and often for days at a time they huddled together in their shelter and stared at the white, cold world while flesh wasted from their bones.

The coming of spring aroused in them the deepest joy they had power to feel. They did not worship the sun or think of it or even realize that it was a source of heat. They knew only that the cold and the deep snow went away and warmth came, bringing with it a greater abundance of things to feed on.

Except for the affection between mothers and their smallest children, their family life was little more than a loose association of persons who lived together for their own protection. They had no sense of shame, no notions of right and wrong. They were not monogamous and had no permanent mates, though Gugg felt that all the women belonged to him. He embraced them more frequently than Yawg or Kahha who, afraid of the lord, had to be sly and secretive in their amorous life.

But there was not much sexual striving among these people. For one thing they were undernourished and dwelt constantly on the problems of enemies and food; and for another thing the women were rarely embraced against their will. Though the men were always sexually receptive, the women were only infrequently so. They accepted no male during the period of lactation, and this period was a long one; a child had to be nursed three or four years because if weaned earlier it could not live on the kind of food they gave it. Sometimes in moments of intense excitement, and especially after a triumphant struggle against enemies, the women yielded, even though pregnant or nursing, and the men sated their lust in a sexual orgy.

Of paternity they had no knowledge. The child when very young belonged to its mother, but after it was weaned it belonged to all the mothers in the group until it reached puberty. Harg was Kayah's son, and Memm was his twin sister, but Kayah no longer recognized them as her children. For years they had belonged to the three women; but now, as they entered manhood and womanhood, they belonged to themselves. As among the beasts, the offspring passed to its own custody when it was old enough to care for itself.

Between the mother and her young child there was affection; between the men and women or between man and man or woman and woman or among the older children there was none. The men loved themselves and their possessions, such as weapons and a few ornaments, because these were extensions of their personalities; the women loved those children who were dependent on them. For a young child, suffering, a mother felt compassion because she still felt it to be a part of herself; but a man felt only that anxiety which possessed him when he sensed that the security of himself and his group was threatened.

In all of them there was awe of blood; this was one of the few traditions passed on from generation to generation. It seemed to them that living things died because the blood ran out of them, and they had come to feel, therefore, that blood was the essence of life. The mothers lost blood during their menstrual periods; and these people had the notion, much too vague to put into words, or even to formulate as one of the certainties, that the child in the mother was made of her blood. The periodic loss of blood by the women worried all of them, and particularly the men; and during this part of the female cycle the men did not like to be near the women. They felt for them both resentment and awe. Men wanted the power—or at least they wondered why they did not have the power—to make children in their own bodies; and sometimes, perplexed by the matter, they would squat on their heels and stare solemnly at a menstruating woman.

Because they felt that blood was the essence of life, it had become for them a curative. If, for instance, Gugg had a wound or sore on his body, he would bathe it with blood after he had captured a bird or beast. In trying to heal their sick or wounded children, the mothers would lacerate themselves to get the warm fluid. All during this night after burning itself Kayah's babe whimpered or screamed; and when daylight came and she could examine the hands and feet, she found a sharp stone and thrust it into her tongue. Then, with blood in her mouth, mixed with saliva, she licked the child's feet and hands. In the eyes of those who watched her there was eager approval. The other women moved close to Kayah and peered at the burns; they looked gravely at Kayah's mouth to see if she had made enough blood to salve the hurt. They had a word for blood, and Youee now spoke the word. For them the word meant not only a curative but also the precious and mysterious quality of life.

"Blood," said Youee, and with a big thick finger she gently rubbed Kayah's spittle across the soles of the babe's feet. She thought the salve was not red enough and she made motions to suggest to Kayah that she ought to cut her tongue more deeply. When Kayah did not, Youee took the stone chisel and thrust it into her own tongue; and then Youee bathed the feet while Kayah bathed the hands.

Outside, beyond the gloom of the shelter, another day had come. Taking his fire sticks with him, as well as his weapons, Harg rose and went out, and stood for a long moment looking at the frost on grass and stones.

4

During the night when he was not dozing Harg had thought about fire. Perhaps it would be more exact to say that he felt rather than thought about it, inasmuch as his attitude toward it was chiefly emotional, and he had so few concepts with which to think. Of fire he knew that it was hot, that it could run and was therefore in a strange way alive, and that for him it might be either enemy or friend. Though afraid of it, he remembered nevertheless that he had power to make it; and because the other men could not make it, and felt for it superstitious dread, they did not follow him when he went to the ashes.

During the night he had been able to formulate one conclusion, and this was to become a decisive conclusion in the management of his life. He alone in his group, he liked to think that he alone of all people in the world, knew how to make fire; and this secret he would keep. He sensed that his knowledge would give him power and prestige, would set him apart as an enviable person, would make the others dependent on him and subject to his will.

40

He would make a fire to protect him against enemies and cold, and whether he allowed the others to share it would depend on their behavior toward him.

He had in mind a plan. Procuring food was the most difficult work for him and his people. Around them in the forests or on the prairies were huge beasts of many kinds, but some were too fleet to be run down and cornered, and others were too ferocious or tough to be killed with stones. Harg had decided that he could kill them with fire.

In the previous year, when he and Gugg and the other men were hunting, they had found an old woolly mammoth that had fallen into a pit. It was trapped there, and they had tried to kill it by hurling stones; but it had almost buried itself by charging at the walls of its prison and excavating with its great tusks, and it had squealed so dreadfully that they had been frightened away. It seemed to Harg that if he could find a beast down in a hole, he could make fire and throw fire on the beast and kill it. This, at least, was the plan he had in mind as he looked at the ashes of dead fires and felt for himself new wonder and pride. This morning his enthusiasm for life was almost boundless.

But first, it occurred to him, he ought to go away by himself and experiment with this new weapon and friend and learn more about it; and so after a few minutes he disappeared, following the course of a stream until he came to the yellow splendor of cottonwood trees. He realized then that he was very hungry and, looking round him, he saw insects crawling in the grass and knelt and set a beetle on the palm of a hand. The flavor of most insects he did not like but after gazing for a moment at the beetle he thrust it into his mouth, tongued it quickly back to his throat, and swallowed it. Around him were birds, and he hurled stones at them, but his arm was awkward and his aim was poor. He saw a rabbit and pursued it, but it was fleet and he was a slow, ungainly fellow who loped along with knees bent and his head and shoulders thrust forward. The hunger pangs in his stomach became so severe that he ate a handful of the yellow cottonwood leaves while searching for mushrooms and birds' nests.

The sun stood at noon and the air was warm when he saw a rodent vanish into a hole. He had caught these creatures many times. After finding a tough dry stick that was sharp on one end, he lay on his belly by the hole and piled grass against the opening and reached through the grass with the stick. He arranged the grass so that he had a tiny hole through which he could peer; and with the stick ready to thrust he waited. When the rodent came up he swiftly impaled it. Rising, he grasped the head with one hand, the hind legs with the other, and pulled the head off. He drank the blood first and then ate the flesh and smaller bones, peeling the hide back as if he were sucking an orange. When he had only the fur and claws and skull left, he laid the skull on a stone and with another stone crushed it; and with a finger he dipped into the skull cavity and licked crushed bone and brains off his finger.

It was not much of a meal, but he felt better and now turned his thoughts to fire. Instead of going out to a prairie, where he would have been visible to enemies or his people, he piled grass here under the shelter of big trees, and he broke off dead limbs and laid these by the grass. While gathering these materials he left his fire sticks with his stone axe; and now, instead of fetching the sticks that had served him so well the day before, he took two pieces of brittle cottonwood limb and sawed with one across the other.

About the making of fire there was much that he had not learned. His methods were so fumbling and experimental, and his memory of yesterday's success was so vague and fickle, that he imagined he could make fire by rubbing any two things together—including, as it turned out presently, his own hands. When the brittle cottonwood limbs broke under the sawing, he looked round him and found stones and rubbed them; and in despair after a few minutes he tossed them away and tried everything that his capricious gaze fell on. While again rubbing two sticks he observed that they became warm; and laying them aside he rubbed his palms vigorously together and learned upon putting them against his cheeks that they were warm, too.

Not until he prowled desperately in search of other fire tools did he see the sticks lying by the axe; and as if a window had been opened on the darkness of his mind he remembered that it was with these that he had made fire. With a cry of recognition he took them up and trotted over to the pile of grass and knelt there and sawed furiously. Soon the fire stick was warm, and Harg's eagerness became audible. With renewed zest he sawed again, holding the fire stick with his left hand and rubbing across it with the stout piece of wood in his right hand. He made heat and a little smoke and some tiny bits of flame that burned on the fire stick; but he had forgotten to put powdered grass on the wood.

Squatting on his heels, he strove to think of the matter.

43

He had made fire, and with less effort and time, it seemed to him, than he was spending now. He sawed again until the fire stick was hot in his grasp; and when he saw a hint of flame he knelt and breathed on the wood. It was then that he remembered the grass. Memory of it came so over-poweringly that he moved with frantic haste, as if his life depended on his industry in the next few moments. He piled grass on the fire stick and sawed across the grass; and for a good part of the afternoon he labored faithfully here in his laboratory, learning very slowly, and more by chance than by intelligent direction of his efforts.

When he succeeded again in making fire he decided to spend the night here; and by the time morning came he was in possession of precious knowledge. During this night he did not sleep at all. He kept his fire burning by piling dead limbs on it; and eagerly, with the joy of one devoted to truth, he gave the night to experiments. He learned first that there was some kind of relationship be-tween fire and wind. When the wind blew on his fire it stood up tall and waved yellow wings and seemed frantic in its efforts to get away; but when there was no wind the fire was quiet and low. Harg thought at first that the fire was afraid of the wind, but after pondering and observing, he took an ember from the fire and knelt and blew on it and made it leap into life. He decided then that there must be invisible fire in wind.

He also experimented during the night to learn how to control fire and make it obey him. He could kill it, of course, by taking its food away; but he wanted it to live and be a friendly thing, obedient to his will. He learned that his fire would crawl away, especially if a wind blew upon it, unless he had a black circle around it; and before

44

morning came, he had his fire imprisoned within a burned margin many feet wide. Then it was helpless, no matter how much the wind made it leap and try to run. Then it died down if he did not feed it, or sprang up in glad life when he did. That is the way he wanted it to be. He could have a big fire or a small fire to suit his pleasure.

But the greatest lesson he learned during this night came from an impulsive experiment. Wondering if earth was food for fire, he threw a huge double handful on the flames. Where the earth struck, his fire died. Filled with astonishment, he threw on more earth and almost killed his fire entirely. With a long limb he stirred the embers and laid wood on them, and when the fire was large and hot he threw earth on again. He repeated this experiment until he perceived beyond all doubt that he could kill fire with earth.

This realization eased a little his natural dread of fire, and enhanced the pride he had in his power and skill; and while wondering if there were other ways to control fire, he thought of water. Water would feed fire or would kill it; and to determine which it would do, he went to the stream and returned with water in his cupped palms. He knelt and spread his palms a little and allowed the water to run on a red ember, and he heard the ember hiss and saw the life in it die. Then he seized a burning fagot and rushed to the stream and thrust it into water; and then for a long moment he curiously examined the stick in his hands. It was still warm, but after he had repeatedly doused it in water it was cold and dead.

Having discovered two ways to kill fire, he stood in the luxury of its warmth and friendliness and wondered how he could use fire as a weapon to capture food. There had gathered in him tremendous excitement and eagerness which he restrained only with difficulty. If he had yielded to the sense of power in him he might have danced and yelled like one out of his mind; because brilliant recognitions pressed upon him—that in fire he had a potent weapon to use against enemies, to slay beasts which he wished to eat, and to make himself enviable among his people. It was the last of these recognitions that flooded him with the ecstasy of self-esteem. He thought of himself as a great one whom all others would hold in awe and fear; as a destroyer of the wolf and the lion and the boar; and as a man of power and property, with plenty to eat, a fire to warm him, and a cave in which to live.

Knowing that other living things were afraid of fire —he had seen them flee before the yellow moving across prairies—he had the thought that with this new weapon he might be able to drive beasts out of a cave and possess it for his family. But what he wanted most in this moment was to be able to take fire with him when he moved against enemies or ran after his prey. How he was to do that he could not imagine; and impulsively, as an experiment, he seized a burning fagot and loped off with it; and when it blazed up in his grasp he was delighted but when it became too hot to hold he dropped it with a cry of rage. While looking down at it he perceived another truth; at least he could move fire from place to place. He piled grass and sticks on the ember and had two fires. He took burning fragments and carried them a little distance away and built a third fire. He understood now that he could make as many fires as he wished to. But after reflection he decided it would be best to have only one, lest others steal from him and make fires of their own; and so by throwing earth on them he destroyed two of the fires.

He was very hungry. During the lean seasons he had little to eat except earthworms, small snakes, and insects and their larvae. Sometimes he had eaten the carrion of a beast or bird, but flesh too putrid gave him a bellyache or made him vomit. In warmer seasons his people dug the root of carrot and turnip and manioc, but they preferred the flesh of the larger animals, and it was of these that Harg was thinking as he searched in the grass and fed bugs into his mouth. After eating a great many insects he felt need of water and salt; and so he lay on his belly by a stream and drank, and then sought a claybank favored by ruminants and knelt and licked the clay.

After returning to the fire he decided to join his group, but first he would destroy the fire so that nobody else would find and use it. Killing the fire distressed him because at once he missed its warmth, but he remembered his power to make another fire at will. He would make it secretly, allowing nobody to watch him; and he would let others share it if they gave him what he wanted—leadership and admiration, the choicest weapons and food.

Upon joining his group he behaved so strangely that they all stared at him, amazed or fascinated. He walked before them, shouting, gesticulating, trying to make them understand what a marvelous person he was. He felt pretty arrogant. No longer was he afraid of Gugg, and he did not intend to suffer any more humiliation from the hands of that tyrannical man. He kept speaking, with varying intonations, the words for fire, enemy, food, shelter, and cold, trying to communicate to them his sense of vast importance without giving them any hint of his

47

secret. He had forgotten that he had made fire for them and that they had used fire.

After a few minutes their faces became dull and impassive. They had breakfasted on insects, too, and had returned to their squatting place by the stream, waiting, with the patience of time, for nothing at all. While strutting pompously back and forth, yelling at them and making inexplicable gestures, Harg looked again and again at Memm. She was his full sister, even his twin sister, but he had no knowledge of that. He had no knowledge of any blood relationship except that between mother and child. For him, Memm was a female, a mate, and he wanted her. He wanted all the women, and he would have rejoiced in the death of all the men.

After yelling at them vainly and seeing in their heavy, dull faces none of the admiration and amazement he wished to see, Harg resolved to go away and hide and make a fire. And this he did, sawing across his fire stick in a pile of grass and putting the driest flakes on the stick. He was very sly about it; he faced in the direction of the group and watched alertly for intruders. After gathering wood and building the fire, he returned to the group.

"Come!" he cried impatiently, with a lordly gesture. Nobody paid much heed. "Fire!" he yelled, and pointed in the direction of his fire. The men squatted on their heels and ignored him; but the women, always attracted to the abler male, the stronger protector, the better hunter, were curious.

"Fire?" asked Kayah, and held her babe up to show its burnt hands and feet. "Enemy," she said.

Harg was impatient. He gathered grass and made a pile of it and threw earth on the pile, trying to explain to

48

Kayah that he was the master of fire. He went to the stream and returned with water in his palms and threw this on the grass. "Come," he said, and indicated to them by walking and pointing that they were to follow him.

The women were curious and they could now see the smoke of the fire; but they were afraid. Disgusted with them, Harg resolved to bring fire to the group, and he vanished and came back, carrying a huge blazing fagot. He came trotting toward them, triumphantly waving the firebrand, and their astonishment was as boundless as their terror. They all fled from him. If they had bowed to the earth in humble obeisance, Harg could not have felt more victorious. The knowledge that they were afraid of him and his fire was a wild song of triumph in his whole being; and he was so overwhelmed by a sense of his power that he wanted to kill them. They fled and he chased them, waving the torch and howling; but when the heat in the fagot crept close to his hand he dropped it and looked round for materials to make a fire here. He fetched grass and kindling and big hunks of wood; and after his fire blazed and stood up taller than a man he proudly warmed himself and looked contemptuously at his people who were cowering in terror fifty yards away.

To impress them with his power, Harg decided to destroy this fire. "Look!" he shouted to them and pointed at the flames. "Look!" he cried—and then in haste, while fascinated eyes were upon him, he gathered earth with his big hands and threw it on the fire. It was a big fire and it took him several minutes to kill it. When it was dead he told them to come, and they advanced a little, the women leading, but they could see smoke and they were still afraid.

"Enemy!" Kayah said, and pointed to the smoke.

"Enemy!" said Mog.

Harg gathered more earth and so buried the embers that at last there was no sign of smoke; whereupon the women, with the men trailing several yards behind, came toward him. "Dead," Harg told them; and to convince them of this he stood on the earth which covered the ashes.

Kayah came close. She looked first at the fire bed to be sure there was no deception, and then fixed her brown eyes on Harg's face. It was an astonishing face to look at; it was convulsed by the elation and pride that flooded him with warmth. His eyes shone as Kayah had seen the eyes of beasts shine in the dark; the muscles of his face twitched in little spasms of triumph; and the hair on his skull moved visibly like grass disturbed by a breeze.

And while she gazed at him, Kayah's face became strangely luminous. She was looking, not at a son whom she had forgotten, but at a man who seemed able to make fire and to force it to obey his will. For her he was what in a later time the maker of magic was to be for his people—the sorcerer, the medicine man, the curer of ills, and the conqueror of evils. She was afraid of him but she wanted to share his power or at least to be its guardian mother. She wanted him to show her how to make fire and control it, and with words and gestures she beseeched him to do so.

Harg's demeanor changed at once. He became suspicious. If she had demanded his weapons, his axe and knives and scrapers, he could not have distrusted her more. He shouted and menaced her and looked around him for something to strike her with; and if there had been a blazing ember at hand he would have chased her with it. He alone of all people knew how to make fire; this knowledge was his priceless secret, a part of his unique and enviable self.

"No!" he yelled when he understood the meaning of her words and gestures.

"Yes," said Kayah, persisting with the right of the queen mother.

Harg stared at her with distrust and hate, wondering if he should threaten her or go off alone by himself. He wanted her to understand that he and fire were the same mysterious force. It was his way and the way of all people, and especially of the males, to identify themselves with what they owned and used. Harg's weapons were an extension of his arms and his meaning; and so now was fire. Kayah wanted to rob him of a part of himself, and he hated her for that. She could have outraged him no more if she had asked to cut off one of his hands.

"No!" he roared and, seizing a stick, he threatened her.

"Yes," Kayah said.

Then, changing with the startling suddenness of the impulsive and primitive mind, Harg slowly backed away from her, a sly and cunning fellow who thought he should go off with his secret and hide it from thieves. Kayah followed him, and the others followed Kayah. All save the small children felt awe of him, convinced now that he was in possession of a strange and enviable power that was denied to them. It was the way of these people to revere their wise leader and to invest him with almost supernatural greatness. This family had begun to look upon Harg as a superior being. If he had known that, he would not have retreated before them; but he thought they were following him to spy out his secret. And so

51

for some time, unhappy and confused and resentful, he tried to steal away from them—until at last, weary of their persistence and a little frightened by the way they looked at him, he squatted on his heels, with his fire sticks and weapons in his grasp, and refused to move farther.

They gathered around him and looked at him or at one another. If he had been more observant or more intuitive, he would have seen the awe and admiration in their eyes. He would have known that they accepted him as their leader and were the servants of his will.

5

It was several days later when this realization came to him. It did not come at once, but slowly, as it must have come to one who had been knocked around by the men and made to feel unwanted. It came from the things he was allowed to do.

One evening, for instance, he embraced his sister Memm and nobody moved to stop him; and the next day he became so bold that he embraced his own mother, who, because of awe or bewilderment, made no move to resist. Harg thought of these privileges as well as he was able, and the privileges for him became rights. And when, without rebuke or chastisement, he was able to satisfy his hungers and impulses, he became more and more domineering; and presently he was the undisputed lord of the group.

He had made another fire, and this one the women jealously guarded. They were still afraid of fire but they cherished it nevertheless as the dearest value in their lives; and they warmed themselves by it night and day when not gathering wood or searching for things to eat. During the first nights they would rise from sleep and go into darkness to find fuel; but they were afraid of darkness, too, and after a few days Kayah understood that during daylight hours she could gather wood to use during the night. Thereafter she and the other women spent a part of each day gathering sticks or dragging pieces of log to the squatting place which for them was home.

Harg learned that by threatening to kill the fire he could have his way in anything. If anybody crossed his will he would howl with fury and begin to throw earth on the flames; and in wild alarm the women would try to restrain him and to make it known to him that he was master and all things were his. In Harg, or in other men, there was neither generosity nor mercy, nor even humility when he was not in danger. He became an almost insufferable tyrant. He lorded it over them, struck them when there was no provocation save his own outraged vanity, and treated all of them as if they were his slaves —as indeed they were. He did not allow the other men to approach the women. In fact, it was now a habit with the three of them to squat at some distance from the fire, apprehensive, abject, shivering with cold, and ready to flee if Harg ran toward them with a torch.

Of the three, Gugg, who had once been lord suffered by far the greatest loss in self-respect; and while squatting on his heels he thought in a dull and ineffectual way of the change in his life. He would look at the women, whom he no longer dared approach; at the fire; at Harg. He lived in dread of Harg because he believed that Harg was the master of a mysterious and destructive power; and though Gugg hated the young upstart he lived in

54

awe of him, too, and chose to flee rather than to fight.

As for the women, they were only dimly aware, if at all, of the change of station among the men. Almost their whole interest was in their children. It was the function of men in a woman's scheme of things to protect women from enemies and to fetch food. The man to whom they gave their loyalty was the man who served them best.

And as for Harg, he was too vain and curious a young man to be content with petty tyrannizing over his family. A little power begets a lust for more power; and now that Harg had a little power, he wanted to conquer the beasts and to fill his belly with the food of his choice. With fire he believed he could do that. He could not trap fleet animals like the deer, or creatures as nimble and savage as the lion or wolf; but the huge woolly mammoth was an awkward monster that sometimes fell into a hole and was unable to get out.

Daily the three men went off together to hunt food, and Harg went, too, but always alone, because he had a plan in mind. It seemed to him that he might be able to make a trap for a mammoth. If he could not find a natural pit, perhaps he could dig one and disguise it with brush and leaves so that an unwary beast would come down a path and fall into it. Once he had the beast trapped, he would kill it with fire.

Harg spent several days upon the trails of the mammoth that led to drinking places or to salt licks. With a flint scraper he tried to dig a pit where a path led through a thicket, but he soon perceived that digging a great hole with such tools as he had would take a long time. He could easily scrape off the surface, but under the topsoil the earth was hard and in it were roots and stones. Harg won-

55

dered if he could compel Gugg and the other men to dig the pit for him. It pleased him to think of himself sitting idly by while they labored; but he gave up the notion because he did not want them to learn from him or to share his triumphs. It gave him greater pleasure to imagine what their astonishment and the astonishment of the others would be, and how they would tremble in fear of him when he led them to vast piles of food which he had trapped in pits and slain with fire.

But like all the men of his time Harg was a lazy fellow. In his efforts to dig a hole he spent most of the time squatting on his heels and dreaming of himself as a great one whom all living things feared. For each minute that he labored he spent an hour in blissful reverie, and after a week of such toil he had removed only a few cubic feet of earth.

Then he gave up the project and looked round him for an easier way. He resolved now to find a pit, but all his exploring upon trails discovered none that was deep with perpendicular sides. The only thing he came to that looked as if it might serve was a depression about thirty feet long with gently sloping walls. It lay upon a path, and all the animals that followed this path went down into the basin and out of it. If he could make the side steep enough, Harg believed that this hole would do; and one morning he set to work, laboring at first with such zeal that sweat mixed with the filth on his hairy body, and fatigue ached in his muscles. The earth of the walls was soft; he found no stones or roots. Not knowing how deep the pit would have to be, he went to a hole into which a mammoth had once fallen and died, and with a stick measured its depth. It was about eight feet, but Harg thought of it in terms of his own height. It was taller than he was by about one and a half times the length of his arm. Taking the measuring rod with him, he returned to his pit.

It took him several days to make the walls perpendicular, but he often interrupted his labor to think of himself with vain joy or to forage for food; and when at last he had a hole from which he was convinced a trapped beast could never rise, he was dismayed by the task of roofing it. The width of the depression was three times his own height. None of the branches could he break off easily, and none of the dead sticks lying around was long enough to span it; and in consequence Harg was driven to further resourcefulness. With a flint knife he felled a small tree and laid it across the pit; and one by one he laid other trees side by side. Sensing the end of his task, he labored more faithfully and took pride in his labor. Over the roof made by the green trees he scattered sticks and upon these he spread leaves and earth; and when at last the job was done, the roof looked so natural and firm that he felt tempted to walk across it. He was so proud of himself now that he burst into a kind of wild guttural song. He dashed round and round the pit, stopping now and then to stare at his handiwork, and all the while making sounds that were the overflow of the song of triumph in him.

Impulsively, in one moment, he wanted to run to his family and bring them all to see what he had done; but in the next moment he felt sly and secretive, and he would have been enraged if he had seen anybody spying on him. He wanted the world to see and applaud, but even more than that he wanted to keep his knowledge and to cherish this miracle as a part of himself.

The next day he returned to add the final touches. Native cunning told him that the approach to the ambush ought to look natural and undisturbed; and so on both sides he spread leaves on the path until it looked to him like any other part where he had not labored. Even the ambush looked so natural because of all the earth and leaves he had spread on the roof that Harg had to peer sharply to tell exactly where the pit's boundaries were. Yes, he had done the job well and he was inordinately pleased with himself. Now a beast would come down the trail and fall in and he would kill it with fire and have all the food he needed. He would give a part of the food to the others, and they would know him as their leader and a great one among them.

For three weeks while making the ambush Harg had lived on insects and roots. Not once while he labored had the men from his family or any other man come within sight of him, though often Gugg and his companions had hidden to spy on Harg and wondered what he was doing. For them he was almost as strange and awful as lightning. When, toward evening of each day, Harg had rejoined the group, the men had sat back on their heels and stared at him. The women, too, had been sharply aware of him when he came in. They knew he was a fire maker, but they would have been aware of Harg without such knowledge because of his arrogant behavior. He yelled at them for no reason at all, abused them, menaced them, and assumed a kind of supervisory deityship over the fire. For the women, however, Harg was not a tyrant; he was a greater being than they and, by reason of his mysterious powers, was privileged to treat them as he pleased.

The women kept the fire burning day and night and spent a considerable part of their time gathering fuel for it. Never did it occur to them that if this fire died, Harg could make another. For them this fire was more than simply a fire; it was *the* fire, and they cherished it. They were still afraid of it, but their fears diminished as they learned how to use and control it. Kayah's child had been badly burned on its hands and feet, but the wounds had healed over, leaving deep ugly scars which had twisted the feet especially, drawing the toes back in unnatural positions and making it difficult for the child to stand or walk. Now and then Kayah would take the child to her lap and look at the scars and bathe them with saliva.

At all times the mothers kept an anxious eye on the children. When squatting by the fire they would let the children stand or sit between their knees; but the moment they smelled singed hair they would babble with alarm and move away. Fire, they had learned, was not only a friendly but also a treacherous thing. Sheets of flame would leap suddenly and lick toward them like long tongues, or small embers would fly at them and lodge in their hair and sting like insects. They had to be constantly on guard against the fire's unpredictable impulses. But after learning that they could let it burn low and it would still live, they quieted it to a bed of embers during the day and fed it generously as the chill of evening approached. During the night they slept with their backs toward it, with the small children cradled in their arms; and now and then one of them, usually Kayah, would rise to lay wood on the embers.

The three men lay so far back that they were unprotected, and so they shivered in the cold; and if, seeking warmth, they rose and came nearer, Harg would yell at them and they would go away. Little did Harg care if the men froze to death. He regarded them as enemies and would have been happy to see them slain by predatory beasts. During times past, when he had been too large to receive a mother's care but too small to pretend to be a man in his own right, he had been abused and knocked around by the men, as all big boys were by men everywhere; and such dim memories as he had of his past were not happy ones. He was too simple a person to nurse grievances or plot vengeance; his attitude toward them was that found throughout the kingdom of mammals— the attitude of the adult male toward all other males. These men were rivals for the things he wanted—for tools and weapons and females that were for him a part of the meaning of himself. If he had been more imaginative he would have enslaved them, now that he had them in his power. He would have forced them to dig snares for the mammoth, to bring food and water to him, to pick the vermin off his filthy body, and to be ready always to serve his needs or his whims. But Harg's mind did not envisage such resourceful plans for his own self-enhancement. These men were simply three males whom he would tolerate as long as they gave him no trouble.

Now when he menaced them he always used a flaming torch. If he had advanced to strike only with his hands, or with his stone axe, Gugg probably would have stood his ground and fought; and in that case he might have learned that he was still the young fellow's master. But when Harg went after him with a piece of fire, Gugg fled in terror because in his dull mind fire was a part of Harg. Harg made fire and fire obeyed him; that is the

60

way Gugg thought of it. The other two men thought of it that way, too, and day after day they lived in miserable fear like three abject vassals whose lives were wholly in another's keeping.

A dramatic happening a few days after Harg finished his trap served only to deepen their sense of helplessness. Daily, Harg went to his snare. Each time he went he fully expected to find a great mammoth imprisoned in the pit. His reasoning had been simple. He would build the trap, a beast would fall in, and he would kill and eat the beast. When, therefore, he found nothing in the hole, he was astonished and confused and imagined that enemy forces were conspiring against him. In no other way could he explain the failure. The vanity in him impelled him to believe that he had done his work superbly well. Here was a trap, there were beasts roaming the earth, they followed paths, they sometimes fell into holes; and if none tumbled into his pit, that was no fault of his own.

He felt not only astonished and confused but angry, also, and would look around him for an object on which to vent his rage. When his emotions cooled, cunning then would replace anger, and he would examine his handiwork to learn if beasts had come and spied out his designs against them. Across the roof he always found marks left by tiny animals, but upon the path leading to the trap he found no sign of big feet. Now and then, not out of humility, but out of the belief that he could master all things, he would wonder if by any miracle of labor he could improve his ambush. Perhaps with fire he somehow could drive the beasts down the path, or make here a pile of the kind of food they ate to lure them to their death.

The mammoth fed on sedge, wild thyme, and the leaves and stems of willow and juniper; and so Harg went off one day to find and bring an armful of the beast's food. During his search he was approaching the bank of a river when he heard a sound. He knew at once that a large animal was near, and, like the wary hunter he was, Harg slunk back noiselessly until he was hidden by trees. He had his axe with him but he never hurled his axe into jungles. He looked round him for objects to throw and found some stones and then crept forward as quietly as a shadow until he could peer out.

Before him was a small opening on the river bank where beasts came to drink; and a moment later he saw the animal come in sight. It was a huge boar. The boar stood still and looked from side to side up and down the stream for sign of an enemy. For perhaps a minute he stood there with all his senses wide awake. Then he gave a low grunt and advanced a few feet and stopped and looked. He grunted again, a little more loudly this time; and out of the jungle behind him came the mother and her litter of five pigs. The pigs were eager to drink, and the one in the lead came abreast of the boar and was moving to pass him when, with a sidelong blow of his head, the parent knocked the little one back to safer ground. In turn as they came abreast of him he knocked all of them back and for a few moments they squealed with pain or amazement; but after they had been repeatedly chastised they stood perfectly still and waited.

For what seemed to Harg a long while they all stood as motionless as seven stones while the parents turned their heads and looked up and down the stream, or listened for sounds in the jungle around them. Then the boar grunted again, and the mother moved down to the water, with the young ones trailing her, and they all drank while the father stood guard, shaking his big mane and turning his head swiftly to right or left. After the mother and her brood had drunk, they all turned and came back quietly and vanished into the jungle; and the boar went to the water's edge. As he drank, Harg could see water squirt along a big tusk. Then the boar also disappeared, going very softly, it seemed to Harg, for so large a beast.

While staring at them with fascinated interest Harg had breathed very gently. He wanted the small pigs to eat but he would never have dared to attack the boar, or even the mother of the brood; for him and his people these great shaggy creatures were almost as unconquerable as the lion or the bear.

While he watched, there had been in him more than the emotion of physical hunger. He recognized in these animals a family group like his own and understood that the big fellow was guarding and protecting the others. It would be too much to say that he now felt tenderness for his females and their children; but he did feel something akin to a sharper recognition of his own responsibilities as a guardian. He wondered if he ought to leave his family alone while he went away to hunt. Possibly, it seemed to him, the boar did not. Among the larger animals, he remembered now, family groups always wandered together in search of food; and for a few moments Harg squatted in the jungle and reflected as well as he was able on his duties and privileges.

Then he thought of his trap and asked himself if he could frighten these beasts over to the path and into the ambush. He knew they were still in the growth around him because now and then he heard a stick break under their feet. Coming out of hiding, he stood up and hurled a stone in the direction of the sounds; and because he was afraid he began to roar and scream in a dreadful babble that was wild with menace and fright. At once he heard a crashing in the jungle and knew the beasts were fleeing; and he hurled other stones and grasped trees and shook them or ran back and forth by the river, smiting the earth with his stone axe. He frightened birds and small ground creatures, and before him through the forest fled all living things.

Harg did not enter the jungle. He skirted it, racing back and forth, casting stones and sticks, shaking trees as if to uproot them, and howling like one gone mad. When at last he could hear no sounds he went over to the path and to his ambush, fully expecting to find seven hogs imprisoned there; and, upon seeing no sign of them, in his disappointment and bewilderment he behaved like a small child. Again and again he knelt at the edge of the pit and made a hole in the roof and peered through the hole into the gloom below. He walked round and round the ambush, exploring the earth for footprints; and when he had to admit, with sulking stubborn resentment, that his attempt to capture the hogs had failed, he turned homeward, going like a man against whom all the evils of the world plotted incessantly. It seemed to him that vines and branches strove to impede his going, and he struck at them furiously with his axe or tore them from their anchors and hurled them from him.

After he had joined his family, there was a troubled memory in him of the way the male hog had behaved. It was more in his subconscious than in his conscious mind.

He was, like all people of his time, and like people to-day, very imitative and suggestible. From watching the beasts generation after generation, his ancestors had learned many things, and this knowledge was a part of his heritage; but because it was not formulated in precepts of conduct, Harg was moved by it only in impulsive and erratic ways. In now assuming the role of arrogant guardian, he was moved not only by his observations of the boar but also by similar observations in other times and places.

For a few moments he looked around him as if to see whether everything was as it should be. The fire was burning; there was a pile of wood near it; and at a little distance from the fire the women were squatting, with the children by them. These things Harg observed and found good. He moved close to the fire to warm his hands and while he turned them over and over in the heat he continued to gaze speculatively at his family. After a few moments one of the older children walked toward the fire; and when he came abreast, Harg reached out with a huge hairy arm and swept the child back. Like the boar he had no notion of his strength and spent too much of it on small tasks. He knocked the child end over end and it set up a terrible cry, and the mother came rushing over to gather it in her arms. She looked at Harg, wondering what he had done.

"No!" Harg shouted. He pointed at the fire and said: "Enemy!"

He felt better then. While standing here, he looked behind him from time to time to see if other children were approaching. He wanted them to, so that he could sweep them back and save them from danger. All evening, until at last he lay to sleep, he dwelt with stormy pride on his job as boss and guardian, and kept an eye on the children, ready to knock them sprawling if they came within what he regarded as the zone of danger. The emotion in him was huge and vain and deeply pleasurable. After this, he decided, he would go with his family when they drank, preceding them, like the boar, and making sure there were no lurking enemies before he allowed them to advance to the stream. A man loved his duties and his tasks if they were a part of him and enhanced his self-love; and Harg was determined to do his job well.

6

THE woolly mammoth, king of all land mammals of its time, usually roamed in small herds, together with the woolly rhinoceros. It was an elephant, but in appearance it was, in several respects, unlike the elephant of today. A dreadful beast to look at, with its enormous bulk set on four thick columns, it was covered with a great mass of hair and wool that made it seem to be more monstrous than it was.

The head was high and enormous, and was crowned with a huge mop of long hair. From it descended two mighty tusks that curved down and back up until their points almost touched the hanging trunk of the snout. Behind the head was a deep depression, and just back of this was a great hairy hump of fat. From this hump the back fell sharply away to the small tail that hung from the beast like a useless duster.

Because it was used to bitter climates, this monster was warmly clothed. Its overcoat was of coarse hair which varied in color from pale to reddish brown and in length from two or three inches to ten or twelve. Under the overcoat, woolly hair, an inch or two in length and very dense, blanketed the entire body. Mixed with the shorter hair were patches of mane, especially on the cheeks, shoulders, and flanks.

Its invariable companion, the rhinoceros, also warmly clothed with hair and wool, was less awesome in bulk but more terrifying in its weapons. From its massive head hung two huge horns thrust straight out. One, short and extremely heavy, was set about halfway down the broad face; the other, growing from the bone of the nose, was slightly curved. It was about three feet in length, and its tip was as sharp as a lance.

Many times Harg had watched these monsters from a safe distance. They were ferocious when attacked but they were vegetarians and, unlike the lion, the tiger, or the wolf, they did not prowl through the night and leap upon unwary creatures. Nevertheless, Harg and his people lived in terrible fear of the mammoth and rhinoceros because against them they had no weapons. They knew their flesh was savory because once they had eaten part of an old male that had died; but until he learned to make fire, and discovered that it was a more potent weapon than his stone axe and daggers, Harg had never dared dream of felling a mammoth.

One morning when he went to look at his trap he was astounded. In it was a male mammoth. Harg had hoped to find one of these beasts in the pit; but he had always seen them from some distance and had not been aware of their prodigious size. The creature before him now seemed not only to fill the hole but to tower several feet above the ground level. And when Harg saw him there, looking like a small red hill, he began to shake with fear, and his

68

emotion was so extreme that he urinated. Trembling, he slunk away and hid in the jungle to look out.

There was no movement in the elephant. He had fallen into a hole from which he was unable to rise, and there he stood, a dull-witted monster unaware of his doom. His head was away from Harg, and after a few minutes of anxious peering Harg realized that the beast could not see him. He became a little bolder then and crept forward to the path and advanced until he was thirty yards from the beast. There for a little while he stood and trembled and stared with amazement at the great hulk.

His impulses were so contradictory and confused that he could do nothing but gawk. He thought of hurling a stone to see what the monster would do, but fear restrained that impulse. After a few minutes he wondered if he should make a fire and hurl fire on the beast. All the while there was growing in him a wish to creep around through the woods and come face to face with the creature and look at its eyes—because he had learned that in the eyes of things he could most unerringly read the purpose in the mind. But presently he thought of his family, and with this thought came the realization of what a mighty hunter he was; and so, yielding to a wish for admiration, he softly withdrew until he was beyond hearing of the mammoth and then loped homeward at full speed.

As soon as he came within sight of the fire and the persons by it he began to gesture and yell like a man gone daft. Emotionally overwhelmed by his success, his cunning, his prowess, he shouted and waved his arms and jumped up and down as if in a tantrum. The women knew he had something extraordinary to tell them; they had only to look at his bulging eyes and slobbering mouth to be sure of that. And, besides, he was shaking from head to feet. He was shaking as if from terrible cold; his teeth clicked, and the hair on his skull moved as if insects were scurrying through it. But when he pointed in the direction of the mammoth and yelled and made running motions with his arms, they had no notion at all of what he was trying to say. Kayah thought perhaps he had made another fire somewhere out of sight; Gugg wondered if he had been pursued by lions or wolves.

Suddenly, impulsively, Harg decided to warm himself. He stood in the heat and turned round and round, and the heat relaxed and soothed him. Now he was so delighted with himself as a fire maker that he almost forgot the mammoth; but a few moments later, upon remembering it, he yelled, "Food!" and pointed. The women began to babble. Food was what they wanted above all things; but if it was food, they did not understand why Harg had not fetched it home.

"Come!" he shouted, and they were eager to go with him; but after she had loped along a few yards, carrying her child, Kayah remembered the fire. If she went away it might die. Turning, she said, "Look," and pointed at the fire; and they all looked. She set her child down and ran back; and when she returned she carried a blazing fagot. They all understood that she wanted to take fire with her, and the other women went back to get torches. Harg was impatient. He tried to tell them that fire was a part of him and he could make another fire. When they did not understand, he seized the fagot in Kayah's hand and threw it away. That enraged her. She howled at him in fury and ran off to retrieve the fire; and the other two women drew away from Harg to protect their embers.

70

Harg wanted them to hasten with him and see what he had trapped, and to gaze at him with admiration and awe; but the women were resolved to take fire with them. They had learned that fire uncared-for would die.

But none of them was able to solve the problem of carrying both fire and children; and, besides, while they tarried here their embers died. Harg now threatened them. He commanded them to come with him, and his behavior was so menacing that the women took up their children and followed; but again and again Kayah stopped and gazed back at the fire she was leaving. If she started back, Harg would shout at her and advance to strike, and, deeply unhappy and anxious, she would go with him. Only in leaving their children could the women have been more outraged than in leaving this fire which they had faithfully tended for weeks.

Their anxiety over the fire was lost in astonishment when they followed Harg down the path and saw the great brown monster. A cry escaped them. The beast stirred in its prison and they were all terrified. Though Harg was frightened, too, he pretended not to be because he had a part to play. With gestures he strove to explain that he had dug a hole and trapped this creature; and when at last they understood him, their awe of him was hardly less than their awe of the beast. The three men withdrew several paces and stared in turn at Harg and the mammoth, their dull minds, wondering what sort of man Harg could be. He had made fire and now he had ambushed the hugest of all their enemies. If they had had any concept of supernatural men, they would have set Harg apart as a god.

Going back down the path so that he could talk in a low voice without being heard by the mammoth, Harg summoned his family and made it known to them that he intended to kill the beast. Then they would eat. He explained to the women that he wanted materials to make a fire. "Fire," he said, and waved his arms at the trees around him. "Food," he said, and pointed at the mammoth.

The mothers left their children in the care of Memm and hunted through the jungle for grass and sticks; and when they had gathered a pile, Harg chose an armful and went out of sight among the trees. He wanted nobody to watch him make fire. Hiding from them, he sawed with one stick across another, from time to time laying fine dry grass in the smoking depression of his fire stick. He was so eager and excited that he was clumsy in his labor and broke one stick after another; and after he had fire he rose, trembling, and looked at the miracle. Then in haste he ran to Kayah's pile to fetch more grass and wood.

While wondering how to carry the fire out to the path, he looked round him and saw the wide flat branches of a conifer. He broke one off and laid it on the earth; and upon this, using green sticks as tongs, he moved a part of the fire. Then he seized the evergreen platform by either end and carried the fire to the path. Unaware of the awe with which the others were looking at him, he laid the green bough and its fire on the path and piled wood on it; but presently he realized that he was too far from the beast and he picked up the fire and carried it down the path. Behind him came the women and the men, each with an armful of wood.

About forty yards from the mammoth Harg set the fire down and considered his problem. He was shaking with fear and excitement, but now that he had a fire by him he was less afraid. Killing so large a beast would be, it seemed to him, quite a task; he would need a larger fire and he would need to have the fire closer to the pit. So again he picked up the platform and went down the path until he was only about fifty feet from the great silent hulk. He moved noiselessly, and so did those who followed him; and they made almost no sound as they laid wood on the flames.

The mammoth could not see them because its eyes were in front of, and hidden by, its huge ears, but it felt the heat or otherwise sensed danger, because it began to stir. When he saw the monster struggling to turn, Harg ran to a conifer and broke off two green limbs and stripped them of all foliage and twigs. The women also broke branches, though they did not understand yet what Harg had in mind. They understood when, a moment later, Harg used his two limbs as tongs, thrust them into the fire to capture a part of it, and then dashed forward to hurl the fire on the mammoth's back.

Perhaps never in their lives had these people been so deeply stirred as they were to be stirred now. Understanding Harg's purpose, they all pitched in with furious effort. They began to cry aloud, making a strange and terrible sound that expressed their eagerness, their anxiety, their dread. They realized that fire would have to be heaped in abundance on the beast, and while the men assisted Harg, the women ran off in frantic search of wood.

It was not long before the mammoth sensed that he was in deadly peril. His first sound was a dreadful ear-splitting squeal that smote the air like the blast of shrill thunder and echoed for miles. The fire on his back consumed the hair and wool and settled to his hide; and when he felt the pain of it the beast began to struggle like a vast pile of convulsed flesh. His head came up, and his two great tusks plowed the bank as his head rose; and a moment later his trunk stood up and made circles in the air, seeking, like a frantic tongue, something to grasp.

The more the beast squealed and roared, the louder became the cries of those seeking to slay it. The children, sitting back in the path, began to howl and to crawl away, and Kayah slapped Memm and sent her back to watch them. The men had thrown armfuls of dry wood on the beast; and now, supported half by its rump and half by the bank behind it, the fire was burning eagerly and the air was filled with the odor of burning hair and hide. As the pain became more intense, the mammoth's whole body became convulsive; the short pillars of its legs moved up and down, smiting the earth like pile drivers; its trunk waved from side to side, vainly seeking the enemy; and the clamor of its voice rang like terrible bugles in the sky and earth. Realizing that the enemy was behind, it was struggling to turn in its prison; and its tusks plowed the bank with such prodigious strength that clods of earth were tossed high into the air and a rain of clods and dust came down.

When Harg saw that the mammoth was turning, he shouted to the women to bring more wood. Already they were laboring with superhuman strength. They found hunks of dead trees and dragged them over, and these the men threw upon the beast. The men rushed off, too, and returned with enormous boulders and threw or rolled them into the pit. They all understood that their task was to render the beast helpless before it could demolish the walls of its prison and escape. It continued to turn in the

74

hole, driving with its feet, plowing with its tusks, and hurling with its trunk any stray stone or piece of wood that it could seize. In its mighty struggle it was able to turn halfway around, and one of its inflamed eyes saw its enemies. The fire fell off its rump and burned at its feet among the chunks of log; and with desperate labor the seven persons threw in armfuls of grass and weeds and vines, pieces of tree bole, stones, and anything else they could lay hands on. Using his green tongs, Harg ran boldly to the pit's edge and hurled fire in the beast's face; and the fire fell and burning sticks lay across the tusks. These the trunk grasped and threw skyward.

Harg was not afraid now. He was too excited, too violently frenzied, to feel fear. Again and again he ran to the pit's edge to hurl embers, and stood within the waving shadow of the trunk. The fire in the bottom of the hole had become a raging inferno, feeding on the long hair and wool hanging from the legs and belly and crawling up the wall of the body as fire moves through dead grass. The sound of the creature was now such an agonized squealing and bleating and roaring that these persons would have been terrified if they had been conscious of it; but everything around them was an anarchy of sound and smoke and flame and the stench of burning flesh, and they were a part of the frenzy, working like mad people with sweat pouring from them and slobber running from their mouths. Never for an instant did they pause. Everything they could find loose, every limb they could tear from a tree, every stone they could carry or roll they brought to the pit and hurled on to the beast or into the flaming maw around it.

And when at last the mammoth was the core of a great

fire, with its hair and wool burned off, its hide smoking, and the fat in its big humps hissing as they fried, it slowly sank as if its legs were miring into the earth. The sounds of its agony ceased, but still these people labored with frantic haste. They did not pause until the deep quiet of the beast, its utter helplessness, overwhelmed their senses, and then, as one person, they came together and looked at their victim. For a long moment they were silent and shaken; but at last the women made a sound that was more of lamentation than triumph, and the men turned, with their eyes glowing like brown coals, to look at one another.

7

It was afternoon before the chunks of log burned out and they were able to enter the pit. The chief emotion in all of them as they waited for the fire to die was one of physical hunger, though they were deeply sensible, too, of the power of the conqueror among them. When they looked at Harg they thought of him not only as a fire maker but also as one who could ambush and kill a huge pile of food. For the beast that had suffered such agony when they heaped flaming death upon it they had felt no pity and they felt none now. Pity was an emotion unknown to them, save possibly in a mother for a sick child. The mammoth was food, and they were eager to cut its hide open and reach for the tender parts.

It had sunk to its belly and was now a huge, hairless mound, with its trunk and tusks obscured by the bank and by the stones that had been hurled upon them. Parts of the hide looked like gray rock. Here and there was a patch where fire had eaten through the hide and burned the flesh to black and brittle cinders. In the air was the odor of cooked meat; they sniffed the smell but did not like it. The smell of burning wool also lingered for a long while.

The men had fetched their flint knives and scrapers; but when Gugg moved to enter the pit, Harg yelled at him and Gugg slunk back. Harg felt that the triumph was all his, that all this food belonged to him. If he had reflected on the matter he might have realized that others had helped him slay the beast; but so extreme was his vanity that it seemed to him now that he had done the job alone. He was the lord of this group, and a mighty lord, too, and he expected the others to cower before him and wait on his will. He wanted to fill his belly first. He intended to take all the choicest parts for his own use.

After he entered the pit and climbed with naked feet up the greasy bulk, he squatted there, triumphant, and looked at the other men. They were so famished that they drooled, but nevertheless they stared at Harg like dogs told to stay back and await their turn. Harg gazed over the expanse under him and wondered where the heart and liver were. He was determined to have all the tender and juicy parts. But the hulk under him was so vast and round that he could not decide where to make an incision; and while thinking of the problem he wiped a finger across the greasy hide and licked his finger. Then with a flint knife he strove to cut through the heavy skin.

He became so engrossed in his labor that he was un-aware of the others who now were entering the pit, un-able longer to restrain their lusting for food. Soon all the men and all the women were gathered round the beast, cutting with stone knives. After one of them had made

78

an incision he would repeatedly thrust a finger into the hole and lick it. When they had made the holes a little larger they put mouths to them and tried to suck blood. And as soon as the holes were large enough, they thrust hands into the body and withdrew their hands to lick off the gore.

Squatting on top, and using a sharp knife, Harg made an incision a foot long and cut across at a right angle and then rolled back a triangle of hide. He had opened a reservoir of fat. Lying on his belly and sprawling like a huge insect, he chewed at the fat like a wolf, gluttonously feeding, and wholly unaware of what the others were doing. The fat was warm and soft and tender, and with strong teeth he tore it off and swallowed it by the mouthful without chewing it. His entire face was smeared; and when he lifted his head for a moment to breathe, globules of fat hung from his whiskers and brows. He devoured three or four pounds of the rich juicy stuff and then turned sick. For one who had lived in recent days on insects and plants this meal was too rich and solid.

Rising to hands and knees, a ridiculous and woebegone fellow convulsed by gluttony, he waited for the sickness to pass; but a sudden retching shook him and clouded his vision. Slowly, and much like a great ungainly bug, he slid down across the wall of a side and climbed out of the pit. On hands and knees he crawled away. Never before in his life had he felt such horrible sickness through and through him. Presently he began to vomit, and with one agonized convulsion of his whole body after another he heaved up the mess. It poured out of him with such violence that tears fell from his eyes and he began to moan as if dying. After he had emptied his stomach he still

79

retched like one whose sickness could be eased only by turning the stomach inside out.

When he felt a little better he lay on his back and gazed past tree tops at the sky. He was not thinking; his mind was almost as empty as his stomach. He was simply a sick animal fouled by his own appetite and feeling miserably unhappy about it. For several minutes he lay here without stirring and stared at the sky; and after a while he became aware of the sounds of puking. All the adults were sick. One by one, abashed and humbled, they had crawled out of the pit to empty their stomachs. Among the sounds they made were exclamations of despair; and if Harg had had even the faintest sense of humor he would have smiled at the sky. On the contrary, the sound of their distress made him hungry, and while the others crawled off to be alone with their agony, he returned to the feast.

But he had had enough of fat. He now extended the incision and rolled back a thick carpet of hide; and when this was out of his way, he cut through the fat and seized hunks of it with both hands and tore it from the body. He wanted to cut through the ribs and reach down into the chamber of the organs. Squatting on his heels, he looked like one digging a hole into a great mound—and that, literally, is what he was doing. After he had removed all the fat he hacked off pieces of flesh and tossed them aside. Upon coming to the big ribs he cut between them and shoved an arm down clear to his shoulder, sprawling out meanwhile on his stomach and trying to peer into the opening. His hand deep in the warm wet interior searched for heart or liver or kidneys; and when he could not find them he became enraged.

Withdrawing his arm he shook the blood from it; and

then, rising to his feet, he hopped up and down in a tantrum and slipped on the greasy hide and fell and rolled off the beast. Howling with fury, he climbed back up and stood on top and looked down over the wall. The mammoth was so huge that he hardly knew what to do with it. For a few moments he stood there and looked down as if he were gazing over a precipice; whereupon, descending, he explored back and forth, considering his problem. There, he told himself, was the head, and high above it was the big hole he had made near the spine; but where were the organs?

He decided to enter about halfway down the wall of a side, and he was making an incision here when the others returned to feed. Gugg came down where Harg was, and Harg shouted at him and menaced him with his knife. Gugg clambered up and over the mammoth and slid down the other side; and there he and the others labored, all of them seeking, as Harg was, the tender liver deep inside.

The hide was thick and tough, and making an incision was extremely difficult with the tools these persons had. Half an hour passed before Harg laid back another heavy flap and viewed the gray fat; and, as before, he cut this away, as well as the meat under it, until he came to the great rib slats. After cutting between two ribs, he thrust in an arm and searched. He clutched anything he could seize in the interior and strove to drag it out. Some of it he ate and some of it he threw away. Across from him other gory arms were reaching in and searching. Never before had these people explored the insides of so huge an animal; they were all baffled by the monster's size because the chamber into which they reached seemed to be limitless.

The persons laboring across from Harg had made a larger opening. While Harg still thrust into a small tunnel, they laid back a square yard of hide and cut open a big window. The men cut through two ribs high against the spine and then grasped these and bent them back and tore them out. Gugg climbed to the top and searched under the roof and found the liver. Seizing it with both hands, he wrenched a lobe from its anchor. He slid down with it, and before he was aware of their intent the women tore it from his grasp and left the pit to feed the children.

When they saw the liver the older children squealed with delight. There were three of them, ranging in age from two to four years; and the ones who had been weaned loved raw flesh. The women cut off a big piece for each of them and gave a larger chunk to Memm; and the children, squatting, with legs bent and heels together, clutched their morsels and fed like ravenous beasts. Unlike the adults, they did not have strong teeth to chew with; but the liver was tender and they tongued it and gulped it. The oldest child ate more than a pound and was still hungry. He had blood all over him; his scowling face was smeared with it, and his breast and arms and hands. He yelled and pawed the air and made it known that he wanted another hunk.

Meanwhile, Gugg and the other two men, Kahha and Yawg, had torn out the remainder of the liver and eaten it. Still hungry, they reached in and found the big kidneys and ate most of them. Then they felt nausea. Gugg, the worst glutton of the three, was the first to turn sick; and while the others ate he stood back, clutching his belly and waiting and looking very foolish. His first vomiting pain was a great belch. Turning, like a creature stricken and

82

eager to be alone, he climbed out of the pit and went among the trees; and soon there was the sound of him in violent nausea. Sensing no warning in Gugg, the other men ate until glutted and then went away to hide and vomit.

Harg was still searching for the liver, not knowing that it had been eaten. Unable to find it, or the kidneys, or the heart which was up between the shoulders and out of reach, he filled his stomach with the more tender parts which he dragged out of the maw into daylight. Then he, too, became sick and slunk away, feeling as silly as any man of this time had power to feel.

When night came they all gathered round the fire which Memm had kept on the path; but the men were still hungry. They had emptied their stomachs twice. They would have eaten again if two violent and prolonged seizures of nausea had not left them feeling sick and dejected. Now and then they turned doleful eyes toward the carcass and seemed to consider whether to eat again now or wait until morning.

All of the adults except Memm were covered with gore from head to feet. But they thought nothing of that. They never bathed or made any attempt to clean themselves; they wore the accumulated filth of years, which so completely clothed them that it was impossible to tell the color of their skins. As they became older they became more foul in appearance, and the uncleanness went with them to death. Old blood and sweat, mixed with plant seeds, leaves, earth, and a part of the offal from their own bodies, covered them with a sheath that was like a second skin imposed upon the first; and clinging to them was the strong smell of the human being that warned all other creatures of their approach. There were pockets of dirt

83

in their big ears; dirt was imbedded under their finger- and toe-nails; it matted their hair in snarls not only on their scalps but all over their bodies; and sometimes it formed a rim round their big strong mouths.

They were an unsightly group now, squatting round their fire, befouled by their gluttony, savage, dull-witted, and waiting for morning. They all realized that during the night beasts would probably come to steal their food, and they were resolved to protect it because such a pile of flesh was a wonderful thing to have. After the flesh was eaten there would be many bones from which to dig the marrow.

They were thinking of the food but they were also conscious of Harg. A fire maker, he had trapped, and shown them how to kill, the largest beast that walked the earth. If singing had been one of their ways to express joy, they would have sung tonight—because in them was deep warm happiness and a sense of new power. For Harg they felt awe that was almost touched by holiness; when he spoke to them, they came sharply to attention, and when he commanded, they obeyed.

But Harg was not in an arrogant mood tonight. Any attempt to think of himself as a great one was convulsed and engulfed by the sickness in him. A mighty conqueror, a rare genius among his people, nevertheless he squatted on his heels, feeling as if he had been gutted and might die. The warmth of the fire was a good thing; he sucked it in on his breath and turned round and round, soaking himself with heat that was like a sedative. From time to time he would arouse himself to ask the women to bring wood or to listen for the sound of night prowlers.

The huge carcass, opened to the sky, flooded the air

84

with the smell of warm flesh and broken intestines. From far and wide flesh eaters sniffed it and approached. Lions and wolves moved in. But when they drew close they saw and smelled the fire, too, and they were more afraid of fire than of anything else in the world. They saw two of their enemies, fire and man, together in the night and they were afraid; but they were hungry, too, and noiselessly they advanced through the jungle.

The people did not sense their presence until they heard a sudden angry snarl. Harg and the other men had been half-asleep but now they leapt up, as if moved by reflexes. They stiffened, and hair rose on their scalps. The other men reached for their stone axes, but Harg reached for fire.

Lying half in the fire and half out of it was a heavy green pine branch. When Harg lifted it, there was a mane of fire three feet along the limb. As he moved toward the carcass the great torch brilliantly lighted his way, but he went cautiously, shouting as he went. The other men seized torches and followed him.

The beasts had been feeding, but upon the approach of men carrying fire they slunk into the jungle and looked out. Harg stood at the edge of the pit; and when the other men joined him the four torches lighted up the mammoth and the edge of the forest. Harg saw that the animals had been feeding at the large hole which the men and women had made. He yelled again, not so much to frighten the beasts but because he himself was afraid. He knew that animals were frightened by fire but he had only a faint notion of what a terrifying weapon he bore in his hands.

Laying his torch on the earth he gestured to the men, and they laid their branches upon it. Then they turned away to search for wood but they did not go beyond the golden room of light. Within this area there was no wood; earlier they had gathered all of it for a hundred yards roundabout. Harg was nonplussed. He did not dare to go into darkness. Realizing, nevertheless, that he would have to make a fire here or the beasts would eat his food, he shouted and gestured at the men, commanding them to go for fuel. "Food!" he cried, because for him wood was a fire's food. "Food!" he howled, and pointed at the fire and then at the trees shadowed dimly by the light. The men understood what he wanted, but instead of obeying him they returned to the women.

Harg followed and again shouted to them to fetch wood. It was the women who turned to obey. They left the path, and the men could hear them out in the darkness, tearing branches off trees. When they came back, each had an armful, and all of it they threw on the fire here. Harg squatted to warm himself and doze, forgetting his food over in the pit until he was aroused again; and now, as before, he shouted furiously and went over with a blazing fagot. This time the other men did not follow him. Those by the fire could see him standing by the pit, holding the torch and looking round him; and they watched him lay the torch down and return.

A third, a fourth, a fifth time during the night Harg went over to chase the beasts away. They became bolder and did not flee in such haste. He saw a great tawny lion slinking off into the jungle as soundlessly as a snake; and while he stood and waited he saw a pair of eyes looking out at him. Then he saw many eyes and he roared out of anger and dread until the eyes went away.

The morning was pale with daylight when he was again

86

aroused and went over to the pit. This time the big savage fellows did not flee; they backed off a little, crouching, snarling, waving their tails. Harg waved his torch, but it was only a pale threat in the half-daylight. The hair on his scalp rose and he bared his teeth and howled, but the lions crouched and waved their tails and looked at him. The other men came part way over, but the women, much bolder, advanced until they stood by Harg; and when they saw the lions they set up a wild outcry. Then Kayah ran back to the fire and returned with a blazing limb; and with a daring that astonished the men she dashed toward the beasts and hurled her torch at them. Whining hideously, they withdrew, slinking out of sight into the undergrowth; but these people knew they were there in the thicket, watching and waiting.

Assisted by the other women, Kayah now built a fire at the pit's edge and went out of sight into the forest to gather wood. Then men found stones and hurled them at the jungle, where they thought the lions were hiding. And then, famished, they all descended to the carcass to eat.

8

FOR two weeks they lived by their meat, protecting it with fire through the night and spending most of the day eating as if they were trying to fatten against the coming winter. Though the weather was cold, the big fire, close by the pit, burned continuously and warmed the flesh, and the flesh began to decompose. The smell of it became such a stench that these people, used to foul odors of many kinds, were a little sickened by it. They were sickened, too, by the decaying meat. But they ate it and vomited and ate again.

It was Harg who first cooked flesh. One morning he squatted by the fire with a piece of the putrid stuff, intending to eat it, but the smell of it turned his stomach and he laid it by the fire's edge, not to cook but only to wait until he felt able to eat. Flame burned along the wood and came to the meat and fried it. When he became aware of the odor Harg sniffed it while curiously watching the flesh burn and darken. When the side next to the fire was black and crisp, with a stick he dragged the piece toward him and bent over it to smell. He could distinguish two odors, one of burnt and the other of raw flesh. Experimentally, he flaked off a burned piece and thrust it into his mouth and chewed it slowly, savoring the quality of it. He did not like it but he liked it better than raw meat that stank. He ate the burned part and returned the uncooked portion to the fire; and when it was all charred and black he drew it out and waited for it to cool and then ate it. The meat under the charred part tasted better; it was warm and soft and had a not unpleasant odor.

During this day he learned that meat which he burned in the fire did not make him sick. He did not like it. His taste, like that of his people, preferred raw flesh; but in learning that putrid meat did not make him ill after it was burned in a fire he made a great discovery. The others saw what he did and copied him. They roasted their meat thoroughly and ate the hard cinders, and none of them became sick. They were so pleased by Harg's discovery that they spent most of their time eating, each of them hacking off a chunk and laying it in the fire and sniffing it while it cooled. After a while, Kayah, more resourceful than the others, thrust a green limb through her piece of meat and held it in the flames, turning it over and over and roasting it evenly. The others, perceiving what she did, spitted theirs with green sticks. Kayah then learned that if she took a small portion the size of her thumb she could cook it without burning it to a cinder. The others also copied her in this. Each with a stone knife would cut off several pounds of shoulder or ham and bring the piece to the fire; and from this they would cut off a mouthful at a time to roast and eat.

"Good," Kayah said, using the word which for all of them meant pleasure or friendliness.

"Good," said Gugg.

"Good," said Mog.

"Good," they said in turn; and from time to time, while solemnly eating, one would announce that his morsel was good, and the others would echo him.

It was Kayah who, while they camped here, made the greatest discovery of all. After the men cut away the hide from the big mound above the shoulders, they opened a reservoir of fat; and one day Kayah cut off a piece of the fat to roast. She thrust a green stick through it and held it in the fire; and when she withdrew it to learn if it was cooking evenly, she was astonished to see that it burned with a steady flame. She was holding in her hands the first candle ever to be used by her people. She did not, of course, realize what a great discovery she had made, or, indeed, that she had made any at all. She was curious; she was baffled by the way fire clung to the fat. In experimenting with her candle she learned that fire on a stick would die if waved about or held in too strong a wind; but when she waved the piece of fat the tiny flame clung to it. She wanted to eat the morsel and she blew on the flame to kill it, but it only spread out in a flat sheet under her breath. She stood up and waved it round and round, and they all looked at it; and when she stopped waving the piece of fat, the flame was still there. Then she set it down away from the fire and watched it, and it burned for a long while.

Looking round her, Kayah found a stone with a depression in it, and in this she laid a big piece of fat. She lighted it and it burned a long while. The others were no less astonished than she was. In a group they gathered round the candle and stared at it and talked and gestured, wondering why fat burned so slowly and gave such a constant light. When they blew on the flame, they spread it but they were unable to blow it out. For a moment or two it seemed to go away but then it came back, yellow and strong. They were amazed most by the extreme slowness with which the fat was consumed. They experimented with flesh, bone, a piece of hide, but none of these would burn and give light; and again and again they turned to Kayah's candle and were always astonished when they saw it still burning.

The next day the other women found rocks and made candles of their own. They set them back from the fire, three of them together; and when the fat of a candle was consumed they fetched another piece. All day and all night they kept them burning and were deeply warmed by the sight of them; because the fire of their candles, unlike that of wood, was tame and friendly and constant. It was not enough to furnish heat but in the darkness it furnished light, a steady persistent light that bent under the wind.

At the end of two weeks the mammoth was an unsightly pile of hide and bones. They broke open the skull and ate the brain. They peeled the trunk and ate it, as well as the eyes, the ears, and everything they could roast and swallow. There was marrow in the bones, and they turned next to them.

But the huge green bones did not cut easily with their flint knives. The segments of the spine they were able to hack and tear apart, but the great thigh and shoulder bones they were able neither to cut nor crush. They spent so much energy trying to dig out a few ounces of marrow that they became ravenously hungry and were driven to chew on the tough hide or the smaller bones; and soon they returned to a diet of plants and insects and mice. They had feasted and again they starved. This was their way of life.

The women kept the fire burning day and night. They had learned to gather wood during daylight hours, and while searching for food they looked for fuel, too; when darkness came they always had enough wood to burn until morning. After three or four days in one spot they would move to another where wood was abundant. The women took burning fagots with them when they moved.

Winter was drawing near; the nights were freezing, and there was a little snow. Remembering that the snow would be deep before warmth came again, the women looked round them for a shelter. Harg was searching, too. He had in mind a cave from which, in the previous autumn, they had tried to drive the beasts. He now had fire as a weapon and thought he could drive them out with fire. In the area where they lived there were several caves, all of them in a limestone mountain which on its south face had been eroded into sheer bluffs and overhanging ledges. Harg wanted the best cave he could find, one that would have a dry floor and walls and that would be near water and wood, and daily he went away from the group and explored.

All the caves had their tenants of beast or bird, and usually both. When Harg approached one, the thing that came most vividly to his senses was the smell of wild life. The caverns, gloomy and often dank, were strong with the odors of centuries of living things; and though Harg was tolerant of foul smells, in some of the chambers the stench sickened him. It was the smell of fur and feathers, of old bones, of dung, all mixed with the odor of dank and unventilated vaults.

He never penetrated farther than the vestibule. He knew that the flesh-eating birds and the bears and hyenas were deep within, far from the light of day. In former times his family had entered far enough to hear warning growls or to see a pair of eyes shining in the cavern's deep night. He was curious to know what the deeper recesses were like—whether they would offer dry shelter with a level floor and a ceiling that would allow him to stand erect; but in regard to these matters he could only surmise while exploring the entrances. Some of the caves he rejected at once; they were high on the mountain face, and the ascent to them was steep and rough. It would not be easy to carry wood to them. And among the shelters lower down he found it difficult to choose because in their vestibules they all looked much alike.

He supposed the one with the strongest animal smell in it was most favored by beasts and would be the most likely one for him and his family; and having one day come to this conclusion, he looked more sharply at the possibilities. In the foreground, a few hundred yards away, was a forest a part of which had been swept by fire; and in the dead trees, some standing and some fallen, he saw plenty of food for the fire, and in a stream running through the forest he saw water. This cave faced to the south and the sun, and that, too, was a great advantage. The matter of food he did not consider, nor the matter of prevailing winds. Things to eat his people had always found where they could, and one area was about as likely as another; and winds for them were strange and unpredictable forces which they had never tried to understand.

He explored the entrance more thoroughly. About thirty feet above him was a great overhanging shelf of rock that formed a vaulted roof. The width of this vestibule was about twice its height, and its depth was about half its width. The floor was chiefly of stones, but most of them were loose, and Harg perceived that they could be thrown out. It was a big chamber with room for all of them and for their fire. If snow or rain blew upon them, they could withdraw beyond the entrance, though the interior, at least as far back as Harg could see, looked like a rather small tunnel. The smell of it was damp and cold.

This shelter, Harg decided, would do; and their task now was to make fire here and drive the beasts out. It never occurred to him that the animals left during the night to hunt food and that while they were out he could make a fire and keep them out. He saw his task as one for the daylight hours. The beasts occupied this home and would have to be driven from it; that is the way he saw it, and he began to formulate a simple plan.

Returning to his family, he tried to make them understand what he proposed to do. They had a word which meant house or shelter or any kind of protection against storm and cold—a term which, like most of the words they used, had many meanings.

"Shelter," he said, and pointed at the mountain, and that much they understood.

"Shelter," said Kayah, and the other women echoed her.

"Enemy," Harg said, and as he spoke the word it meant, "Enemy there."

"Enemy," said Kayah, and suspected that he had a cave in mind. She knew what terrible beasts lived in caves.

When he said "Fire," speaking the word so that it meant "Fire-the-friendly-thing," and made gestures to indicate that with fire they would drive out the beasts, the women clamored with approval. They still remembered what fire had done to a monster in a pit. At once Kayah chose a long firebrand to take with her, and the other women did likewise; and carrying both their children and fire they set off, with Harg showing the way. When their torches burned low and seemed likely to die, the women would stop and lay them on the earth and pile wood on them; whereupon, after a few minutes, they would choose fresh fagots and march again. The men carried only their weapons.

It was a mile to the cave, and on the way to it they came to the burned-over forest; and because darkness was almost upon them they stopped here and built a big fire and spent the night.

9

When morning came their first thought was of food. Leaving the children in the care of Memm, a very stupid girl who had become a kind of servant, the women and men went afield, searching for anything they could eat. Among plants they did not always know which were poisonous and which were not, and this was especially true of mushroom varieties and of berries. In former times their people had been killed by the fruit of the deadly nightshade and had been made violently sick by certain mushrooms. The season was now late, and the fruit of most poisonous plants had ripened and fallen; but they were wary in any season. The women were especially so because they gathered food for children, too.

This morning they searched for wild turnips and carrots and radishes; for unhatched eggs in bird nests; for hazel and other nuts, and for small creatures, including snakes. A snake they would eat as a person today might eat a long slender sausage, beginning at the tail and biting off segments. Frogs and toads they would cut open to suck their juices before tearing apart the flesh and bones with their strong teeth. Mice and rats they cut open, too, but earthworms, locusts, caterpillars, and all similar creatures, including spiders, they gobbled whole. They would strip the bark off trees and nibble at it after licking off the sap; and of deciduous foliage they were particularly fond of the willow's and the kinnikinic's.

If, while looking for food, one paused and seemed to be eating, the others would approach to see what he had found. But they never tried to take food from one another. A sense of property was strong in them, and even small children were allowed to keep and eat what they were able to find. If they saw a member eating, they would come to him in the hope that he had enough to share with them; or if he ate something that was not a common article in their diet, they would watch him curiously, waiting to learn if it would make him sick.

This morning Harg came to the bones of a deer. The creature had been killed by a lion or leopard or a pack of wolves, and nothing was left except the bones and hide. The bones he picked up one by one to gnaw, chewing off tiny scraps of tendon and gristle. Then he laid the larger bones across a rock and crushed them with his stone axe, and with a finger scooped out the marrow and ate it, mixed with bone dust. It was rancid, but he liked it. He even gnawed at the hide and broke apart the ankle joints and sucked and chewed at them.

While he was busy, the others came over to see what he had found. They were disappointed. They went away and searched again, wandering like cattle in a mountain pasture. The need of the women was more desperate than that of the men because they were nursing children;

they needed more food, but they were also more resourceful in finding it. Kayah, for instance, had very sharp ears and heard faint sounds which some of them would have missed. The barely audible rustle of a field mouse would bring her to breathless attention, and she would sink to hands and knees and move along as softly as a cat; and when she espied a mouse she would reach out almost as swiftly as a cat to seize it. Because, unlike the men, she did not carry a stone knife, she would not cut it open but with powerful hands would tear it apart, pulling off legs as if it were no more than a locust.

The time was late October, and in the area where they hunted there was not much food to be found. Their breakfast was chiefly one of insects and foliage and bark. The women did not go so far afield as the men but remained within sight of their children and the fire. The men ranged farther, and after an hour or two they disappeared, Harg going alone and the other men together. They all saw birds, perched in trees or flying, and they hurled stones at them; but their aim was poor, and it was rarely that they captured a bird unless they found one wounded or sick. They also flushed rabbits and other swift creatures of the earth and vainly chased them and threw rocks.

After a while Harg squatted on his heels, with the handle of the axe resting gently within his grasp, and strove to think of the matter of food and how to get it. He had made fire and trapped a mammoth, and these two brilliant achievements had stimulated his mind; and now he was like one who felt the imminence of new horizons but was unable to see them and capture their meaning. He recognized that in fire he had a new weapon, and in the pit a snare; but when he wondered if he ought to go to the pit and cover it again and try to trap another beast, he felt acute repugnance. Like all men he was lazy. He remembered with distaste akin to pain all the days he had spent there, digging the walls down until they were vertical and uprooting trees to build a roof. He labored willingly only when he was hungry for food or admiration; he was not very hungry now and he was the lord of his group. Besides, he recalled the sickness of his gluttony and unreasonably related it to the mammoth's flesh. Ambushing another of these beasts did not appeal to him today, and so, with his stomach full of bark and insects, he squatted in the luxury of idleness and looked round him at nothing much at all. High overhead was a warmth-giving sun, and he wondered vaguely if it was the kind of fire he made; and around the clearing where he squatted was the silence of a great forest. Presently he felt a need to defecate, and, without moving from where he squatted, he fulfilled the need.

The women now returned to the fire, and Memm went abroad to find something to eat. Kayah had not forgotten the cave which was to be her winter home. After the children had nursed and eaten a few caterpillars and worms, she wanted to take up fire and move toward the mountain. But she wished to have the men with her, and she called to them in a voice so strong that Harg, a half-mile away, clearly heard her. In a movement as sudden as a reflex action, he stiffened, and his right hand closed on the axe and his left hand on his flint knife. When he stood up he was trembling. A cry like that from a woman usually meant danger; and while he hastened toward the sound, loping like an ungainly man who might at any moment fall on his face, he wondered what dreadful beast had attacked. The other men came out of the woods, too, their heads forward, their knees bent, their big hands clutching their weapons. None of the four slackened his speed until he came within clear view of the fire and the women.

Then Harg yelled, "Enemy?" making a question of the cry.

Kayah, thinking of the beasts in her winter home, shouted: "Enemy!"

The men ran forward. Upon coming to the fire and seeing no sign of an enemy, they were all nonplussed, and Harg was a little angry. Being summoned when there was no danger outraged his sense of personal worth.

"Enemy?" he asked.

"Enemy," said Kayah, and pointed at the mountain.

"No!" he shouted.

But Kayah still pointed. "Enemy," she said, speaking the word so that it meant, "Enemy there."

Then Harg understood. He had forgotten the cave which he intended to wrest from its tenants; and, like the emotional child he was, he now looked forward eagerly to the task. He set off, leading his family, and the women fell in behind, carrying their children and firebrands; and behind them came the other men. Memm, who had also heard the cry, emerged from the woods and followed.

They went up and across burnt mountainside, and over scattered rocks, stopping again and again to build a fire and take fresh torches. The way women jealously carried fire, as if it were something precious to care for, Harg did not think of at all; nor did he reflect that he could make other fires if he wished to. Men were used to the chores and burdens of women. Besides a huge torch, Kayah carried her four-year-old boy and climbed with difficulty, but nobody assisted her or thought she needed assistance. When she stopped, Harg would squat on his heels, with the axe between his knees, and wait without the slightest impatience. The other men squatted, too, and none of them helped to gather wood for the fire or did more than look lazily around for something to eat.

Upon coming within sight of the cave, there was a change in the deportment of all of them. When secure from enemies they were inattentive and obtuse, with their relaxed senses communicating only dully to their minds; but in the presence of danger or the unknown, every sense became extraordinarily acute. Then their brown eyes became alert and crafty, their ears picked up the faintest sounds, and their sense of smell was almost as sharp as that of the wolf. Every muscle-controlling movement became tensely awake: fingers tightened on weapons, leg muscles were taut with readiness, cheeks twitched a little, hair rose on the scalp, and a tingling of expectancy and fear was like pricking needles in the nape of the neck and down the spine. For such a state of alertness it was not necessary to see an enemy; the recognition of his presence somewhere in the area was enough.

They knew that the cave was occupied during the daylight hours; and the sight of it, therefore, brought into painfully sharp focus the realization of what they had set out to do. The women clasped their children more tightly; and Kayah, close behind Harg, began to tremble. Physical weariness made her more vulnerable to fear; and when tremors made her shake from head to feet, she set her child down and waited for the others to come. They looked at one another with eloquent eyes that expressed doubts and asked questions.

"Enemy," said Kayah in a low voice; and the word meant for her and for all of them more than the beasts hidden in the cave. It meant all the dreadful and inexplicable forces in the world around them. It meant the horrors of darkness, the long winter nights, snow and cold, thunder and lightning and blinding rain, sickness, pain, and death. It meant everything against which they struggled to remain alive. Because life for them, from birth to death, was a desperate and haunted pilgrimage.

"Enemy," she said, and in low voices the others repeated the word.

The time had come for the lord of the group to be brave—but Harg did not feel very brave. Nevertheless, he pretended to be unafraid; he brandished his axe and made threatening gestures at the cave opening. In him, as in all men, was the instinctive behavior of ancient ancestors. He now advanced with a short furious rush and fetched up suddenly and smote his breast; and after a few moments he rushed forward again. When he looked back at his family he saw the women building a fire, and memory of fire and of what he could do with it strengthened and calmed him. Returning, he gathered wood, too, and they made a big fire fifty yards from the cave entrance. A little later Kayah went forward with a torch and built another fire; and so fire by fire they advanced until the last of the fires was only a few yards away.

It was Kayah's practical mind that perceived the need of a great pile of wood. If they were to drive the beasts out, they would need a big fire and plenty of fuel to keep it burning; and after they possessed their home they would still need fire to keep the beasts from coming in.

She tried to tell them this. "Fire," she said, using their

word for friendly thing; and "food," she said, meaning that the fire would have to eat. Leaving her child with Memm, she went down the hill and returned, dragging a piece of dead tree. Now the other women left their children with Memm and went for wood; and Harg, who had been watching them with speculative interest, decided that he ought to assist. Women did the chores, of course, but this was an adventure in which he would be the leader, using fire as a weapon. While he was considering the matter, the notion came to him that the other men, his servants, ought to gather the wood.

"Go!" he cried, pointing down at the dead timber and at the fire, and with gestures indicating they were to go and grasp wood and fetch it up the hill. And obediently they went.

Harg was delighted. He sensed again his position as leader and lord, and he bathed himself in the heat of the fire and felt invincible. Excitement usually aroused in men a sexual lusting. After he had warmed himself, thinking meanwhile of what a great one he was, he yielded to an impulse as strong as life; and grasping Memm by an arm he led her away from the fire to mate with her. Submissively she went down on hands and knees.

While Harg was embracing her, the other men came with wood and saw him. Their arms relaxed as if dying, and the wood fell to the earth. In their eyes there was terrible pain, a cold hard pain mixed with hate and rage. Gugg made a move toward Harg but checked himself and was afraid. He began to shake. His thoughts and emotions were a dark bewilderment in which the hungers of the male were confused by fear and awe. His first impulse had been to attack Harg; but a moment later he remem-

103

bered that Harg was a great and mysterious one who made fire and captured monsters. When the impulse was checked, he began to shake, caught, as he was, between two forces of equal strength.

His helplessness was relieved by Harg. Seeing Gugg staring at him with rage and hate, Harg leapt toward him, shouting a challenge; and Gugg fled, and the other men fled with him. Like mutilated males they slunk away and went back down the hill to be alone with their sense of debasement.

It was about midday when the group came to this spot. All afternoon the three women carried wood up the mountain, bringing pieces of log chiefly because they had learned that these would burn longer. Before darkness came they had enough to keep a big fire alive for many hours. But still they fetched wood as long as they were able to see. Then, tired and famished, they squatted by the fire and nursed their children. After darkness closed in, most of them were not sharply aware of the cave, and some, indeed, almost forgot it. Kayah did not. It was her instinct as a mother to hoard, and she rebuked Harg, who was too prodigal in his use of wood, and tried to make him understand that it had not been gathered merely to warm him. For Kayah a low fire to protect them during the night would be enough.

Because of the pangs of hunger they were all unhappy, and their sleep was restless. Some time in the night, the cave beasts, unknown to them, slunk out and went softly away to hunt their food; and though fire and human beings, both in plain sight, were two of their enemies, they returned before morning and entered their lair.

These persons, dozing by their fire, did not know. Their

104

simple minds did not range beyond what they could see. Under the vast darkness and a few wan stars they lay by the fire in a room of light, distressed by hunger, tormented by vermin, and haunted in their dreams by a deep anxiety that was as constant in them as the beating of their hearts.

IO

WHEN morning came they went away to hunt for break-fast, and it was noon before Kayah moved to the task before them. The night had been cold, and the day was gloomy with a threat of snow. If it had been a warm clear day, the task might have been postponed; but when Kayah felt the presence of winter in the atmosphere she took some live fagots and went to the cave entrance to build a fire there. She had the childlike notion that it would be necessary only to set a fire in the vestibule and the beasts would then come out and flee. The other women helped her carry wood, and they made a big fire, with flames leaping to the ceiling and with smoke rolling across the vaulted stone and downward in dense clouds.

They then returned to the other fire, and the adults gazed at the entrance and waited. They were all so tensely expectant that they hardly breathed. Harg was thinking that the beasts would come pouring out in terror, and he hoped that some of them would be killed by the fire. A great cave bear would be food for many days.

But they watched and waited in vain. All of them but Memm carried wood to replenish the vestibule fire; and now, instead of returning, they cowered anxiously by a stone wall. They could look across the fire and into the darkness beyond and watch for a pair of eyes that might come out of the tunnel.

"Enemy!" said Kayah, peering sharply; and then she spoke the word as a question and it meant, "Enemy-come?"

"No," said Harg.

But Gugg, also peering, thought he saw eyes back in the gloom. "Yes," he said. "Enemy"—and he pointed.

Huddled together, they all looked, but there was no beast in sight. Gugg had seen sparks from the fire floating back in the darkness.

"Sound?" asked Kayah, and they listened. Far back in the cave there seemed to be a muffled uproar. Certain that the beasts were coming out, they hastily withdrew, going to the other fire to seize torches; but they waited for several minutes and no beast came.

After adding wood to the cave fire again and again, they became bolder, and this was especially true of Harg. Conscious of himself as the leader, who did phenomenal things, he wished to astound them now; and, leaving his weapons with Memm at the lower fire, he went to the entrance and flung stones back into the corridor. He roared a challenge. He could hear the stones strike stone back in the darkness and reverberate in the walls; and his loud cries rang in the vault above him and were muffled echoes far down the tunnel.

When his efforts fetched no beast out, he thought of throwing burning fagots back into the gloom; and one after another he hurled until in the corridor's darkness a third fire burned and the walls danced in firelight. Becoming bolder still, he called for wood; and when the women fetched it, he carried wood back into the tunnel to the third fire. Soon the flames there completely filled the throat of the cave. This fire he kept burning for an hour or more, but no beasts came out of the mountain.

Baffled, he went to the lower fire and considered the problem. He thought perhaps there was another entrance to the cave by which the animals had fled, and while looking up the mountain he saw smoke. It was to the right of the entrance and two hundred yards farther up.

"Look!" he yelled, and pointed.

They all stared up the mountain. "Fire," Kayah said, and they looked at one another, their eyes bright with questions. If there were a fire up there, who had made it? Did it come from a cave occupied by other people? These were questions in Harg's mind. In the stupid minds of the other men was the thought that Harg had made a fire of the entire mountain. He alone could make fire, and so the smoke they reasoned, belonged to him.

Deciding to see what was going on up there, Harg picked up his weapons and turned to the men. "Come," he said, and set off in a comical loping gait. The other men trailed him but at a considerable distance behind. Harg for them was a strange one, and it was impossible to tell what he was going to do now.

When he came to the smoke, Harg saw that it was coming from a fissure in the stone floor. This fissure was only three or four inches wide and as far down as he could see it was no wider than that; but he knew the stuff that came

108

from it was smoke because he could smell it and feel its warmth. Baffled again, he squatted on his heels and looked at the cleft and wondered how there could be a fire so deep in the earth. It did not occur to him that this smoke came from the fire in the cave throat; a relationship so complex was beyond his grasp. He knew only that deep in the mountain here there was a mysterious fire; and when the other men came up, he told them to look at the smoke, and he stared at their faces to see what they made of it. They were afraid. They believed that Harg had made this fire, only the smoke of which they could see; and they were so overcome by dread of him that they left in haste and returned to the women.

Harg lay on his belly and tried to look deep into the fissure. He took tiny stones and dropped them into it and could hear their muffled journey downward. He sniffed the smoke again and again to be sure he was not deceived—because sometimes fog seemed to rise out of the earth. Standing up, he looked round him over the mountain for sign of other fires; and after a while he began to be afraid, too. He was troubled by the thought that far down in the earth, hidden from sight, were fire makers like himself; and he took his weapons and stole away.

All afternoon the women kept a big fire burning in the vestibule. Darkness came, and still there was no sign of the beasts; but while Kayah was tending the fire, she heard a deep, muffled growl.

"Enemy!" she screamed, and moved over against the flanking wall. Grasping their axes, the men hugged the wall, too, and peered around the stone corner. They all huddled together in a group, waiting and watching, with Harg in the most exposed position. They were expectant and fearful. The fire was against the wall next to them, and between it and the opposite wall was a wide path for the beasts. They could come out safely and flee if they would.

From time to time they heard a growl and knew that the bears were coming, but several minutes passed before Harg could see a pair of eyes. The eyes were unsteady, and he knew that the body behind them was moving; and soon he could make out the bear like a deeper shadow moving in shadow.

"Enemy!" he whispered. He was trembling. They all trembled, not knowing whether these beasts would attack or go away quietly.

The cave bear was a huge and savage creature, but it was not so formidable as the grizzly of today. It was omnivorous, living chiefly on plant and small animal life, but it did not fight unless cornered or denied its lair. These bears coming out were as terrified as the people who waited for them. There was a big fire in the entrance of their home. They could smell both fire and human beings and they were afraid of both. So they came out softly, slowly, growling as they came, with the father leading. When he felt the heat of the fire, he stopped and looked at the yellow light and beyond the light at the darkness. He was unable to see human beings, but he could smell them and he knew they were near.

Harg moved forward to peer around the stone wall. He saw the bear, and in the same instant the bear saw him; for a long moment man and beast looked at one another. Then the bear growled. Its growl was not a challenge but a warning. It wanted to come out safely with its family and go away and feed, but for several minutes it stood on great paws and looked at the fire and did not move. Harg slunk back out of sight.

The others, pressing behind him, felt terror, but they were curious, too, and wanted to look into the cavern.

"Enemy?" asked Kayah.

"Yes," Harg said.

"Look?"

"Yes."

When Kayah moved forward to look, Harg shoved her back. He gestured to them, and they all withdrew a little; they understood what he meant. If they would all get back out of sight, perhaps the enemy would come out and go away into the darkness.

After what seemed to them a long time, the enemy came out. There were four bears: the father and mother, and two cubs about half-grown. They came out in single file, the parents growling as they came. The father was first, a great rolling hulk, and close behind him was the mother, and close behind her were the cubs. When they were out of the cave and past the fire, the father either heard or smelled the people; he stopped and turned his head and looked at them.

It would have been more cunning of Harg to have remained quiet and let the beasts look and go away; but when the male turned to look at him, the emotion in Harg was more than he could restrain. He gave a dreadful roar and brandished his axe, and at once the other men took up the cry, and the women screamed. The noise they made was loud and terrifying, but for a full minute the bears did not move. The parents looked over at the people and made no sound.

The savage yelling, which never for a moment ceased, helped to quiet the fear in these people and to summon their courage. If the men had thrown stones and struck the bears, they might have attacked; but they were only menaced with axes, and by men who jumped up and down and howled. And presently the male bear moved off, going softly, soundlessly, a great bulk of fat and fur, with his family trailing him. Again Harg acted rashly and without cunning. Thinking he had frightened the creatures, he rushed forward, and the other men rushed with him; and together they made a terrible uproar. The bears stopped and turned their heads and looked back, and from the parents came low growls of warning. Harg and his companions retreated.

The beasts were troubled by the feeling that their home was being taken from them. If they had been elsewhere, far from their cave, and had heard such wild menacing cries from human beings, they would have fled; but now they went reluctantly, their dull minds disturbed by the presence of their enemies here. After the men rushed back to the women, the beasts seemed to hesitate, as if trying to decide whether to fight or go away, but in a few moments they moved off again. And again Harg dashed toward them, howling like a madman; but the bears did not pause this time, nor did they hasten their going. They went slowly down the mountain and vanished into the night.

While the people were babbling with relief and triumph, they became aware of other creatures coming out. These were the cave hyenas. They were small and swift, and they dashed out like shadows, turning their heads to snarl and to snap their teeth but never pausing in their flight. There were six or seven of them, but they all disappeared before the men could shout a challenge. A little later some owls came out, followed by bats. Confused by the brilliant light of the fire, one of the owls struck the stone ledge and fell; and it was struggling to rise when Kayah dashed upon it. She hurled stones at it, and a moment later the others closed in with her, all of them throwing rocks; and when the creature seemed to be knocked senseless, Harg leapt forward and seized it. He grasped it by the head with one hand and by the legs with the other and pulled its head off.

It was a huge owl with long curved talons. When Harg saw blood spurting over him, he dropped the bird, but almost at once he picked it up and began to tear the feathers off. The others clamored for a part of it. Grasping the two legs, Harg tore one from the body and handed it to Kayah; he tore off both wings and gave them to the other women. Laying the owl on the earth, he set a foot on the body and pulled the other leg off, and this he gave to Memm. He intended to feast on the choicest parts; and while the other men watched him and drooled with hunger, Harg squatted against a wall of the cave and began to eat.

Thrusting fingers into the torn body, he pulled out the organs and fed the liver, heart, and lungs into his mouth. Next he ate the windpipe and a part of the guts, and then he thrust his face into the bird to suck the blood. A few small portions, which he did not want, he tossed away, and these the other men picked up from the earth and ate without trying to clean off the dirt. After chewing at bones and sucking them dry, he tossed them aside, and these the men also pounced upon and crushed between strong teeth. They even picked up the feathers and sucked the tips that had been imbedded in flesh.

The women gave most of their meat to the children. When Kayah came over to see if Harg had more to offer, he growled at her like a feeding cat and motioned her away with a gory hand; and when she did not leave he looked up at her and shouted, "No!" By the time these ravenous people had finished, there was nothing left of the owl except feathers and talons and beak.

Thinking there might be other birds waiting to come out, Harg took a firebrand and entered the cavern, shouting as he went. But nothing more came out; and when he returned to the fire, they looked at one another and had in their minds the same thought. The cave was free of their enemies and now their task was to hold it when the beasts returned. They would come just before daylight, and they would not be the gentle and frightened creatures they had been on the way out.

How to defend their new home they did not know. Kayah thought it would be best to make a fire clear across the entrance, but upon considering the matter she realized that such a fire would make them prisoners within the vault. The men were not thinking so clearly of the problem. Indeed, Harg, who had eaten generously, did not think of it at all but squatted by the fire, warming himself and preparing to sleep. It was the women who went to the hoard of wood and carried it to the entrance. The fire was against one wall; against the opposite wall they piled the wood. Then Kayah perceived that the wood formed a kind of barrier; behind it and the fire they could be sheltered and protected while waiting for the bears.

After further thought, Kayah decided that they would

need more wood; and, while the men leaned against the wall and dozed, she went into darkness, and the other women followed her. They labored until midnight, and when their task was finished they had a huge pile of wood which, together with the fire, completely blocked the entrance. They climbed over the pile when they entered the golden room of their home. By the wall on the fire side they lay down with their children; and though Memm and the children slept, and the men sat in slumber with arms sprawled and chins resting on hairy chests, the mothers resolved to stay awake.

Now and then they looked at one another, their eyes full of questions; or Kayah would rise to lay wood on the fire. They gazed beyond firelight at the deep and terrible darkness where creatures of the mysterious world were hunting one another and killing and eating. There was no moon tonight; there were only a few dim stars. There was no sound except the talking of the fire and the snores of persons asleep.

Kayah looked at the men, but she felt for them no tenderness or love. She did not remember that Harg was her son, and she did not know that Gugg was the father of her children. She had no knowledge of fatherhood. For her, the men were persons who helped to protect the children and find food. That was all. Still, that was not quite all; for Harg she felt awe and fear, though more and more, as the days passed, she came to look upon herself as the guardian of fire. She would take it with her wherever she went, and never would she let it die. It was the friendliest thing in her life, and, next to the children, she loved it.

If they heard or thought they heard a sound out in the night, the women would look quickly at one another and ask questions.

"Enemy?" Mog would ask.

"Enemy?"

After listening, Kayah would say, "No."

"Look," said Mog, and pointed at the men.

Yawg, a very stupid and sluggish fellow, had sunk forward until his forehead rested on his knees; and when Mog spoke he was making aimless movements with his arms and hands, as if trying to sit up. If he were to topple over on his face, he might fall close enough to the fire to get his hair singed. That is what Mog had in mind, but she did not rise to lift his back to the wall or to drag him away from the fire.

"Look," Mog said again, still pointing.

After staring at Yawg for a few moments, Kayah rose and went over to him. With big powerful hands she grasped his head and pulled him back from the flames. Only half-aroused, Yawg nevertheless reached instinctively for his weapons, his hands searching clumsily over the floor. His hands found and closed on two stones, and he drew them to him, perhaps thinking that they were his axe and knife; but he did not open his eyes and he was only half awake.

Kayah dragged him away from the fire and propped him against a wall, holding him in an erect position until his head sank to his breast. Then she returned to the children. The danger that had threatened Yawg reminded her of the child who had been burned; and now she looked at its hands and feet. The palms were deeply scarred, and on one foot all the toes but the big one had been drawn down and under when the wounds healed. After inspecting the hands and feet, Kayah looked at the genitals, searching them for vermin.

"Listen!" cried Mog, and they all listened; but it was only the cry of an owl.

"Look!" said Kayah. Far away across the forest and on the mountains beyond was the pale gray light of morning.

II

A few moments later they were all wide awake and expectant, but the men, unlike the women, did not believe that they would have to fight to keep their home. They had a simple and childlike faith in the protective power of fire and in the barrier of wood, only a small part of which had been consumed during the night. They thought that the beasts would come and be frightened and would then go away. But Kayah had a different notion. When convinced that daylight was near she built such a great fire that the heat of it drove them back to the throat of the cavern. There they set the children behind them, deep in the gloom, and Memm squatted with them while the others stood in a group and waited. The men grasped their axes and knives. Harg stood a little in advance of the others, acting as lookout and leader; and when he thought he heard a sound out in the darkness he yelled, "Listen!" and they all listened so intently that they held their breath. But the sound he heard was only the talk of the fire. Nevertheless, he was convinced that

118

an enemy was out there, looking in, and he went to the wood barrier and climbed it to peer out. His next cry was a bellow of rage and terror. In his haste to retreat he fell and rolled off the pile; and when he rose, the hair on his scalp was standing up and every muscle in his face was twitching.

"Enemy!" he shouted, and at once they all set up a wild clamor. Harg had seen the male bear a few yards away, his head pointed and his nostrils sniffing. The men now swung their stone axes and roared, trying with menacing sound to frighten the enemy away; and the women seized rocks and hurled them across the barrier. Back in the gloom the children began to cry.

Without pause they made all the din they could— shrieking, yelling, striking weapons against stone walls, and beating the earth with sticks; and all the while they leapt up and down or raced back and forth from wall to wall as if to convince the enemy that a great multitude awaited him. The sounds they made echoed in the ledges and poured like thunder back into the vault. The children were so terrified that they began to scream; and Memm, overcome by dread, left them and grasped a hunk of wood and beat the floor. They all behaved like wild things out of their minds; the dreadful racket they made increased their excitement, and they redoubled their efforts until not one of them was in clear possession of his senses or quite knew what he was doing.

Meanwhile, beyond the barrier the great male bear sniffed the smells and looked at the fire and waited. He was alarmed but he did not intend to flee. The din aroused his anger, and he growled, and the growl was a warning; and then he advanced with head down and paws ready to strike. He decided to enter where the pile of wood lay loosely against the wall.

An upheaval in the pile and the sound of crashing wood told them that the bear was coming; and when they realized that he was bold enough to force an entrance, every adult person became a savage animal, guided by instinct alone. The men rushed over and heaved stones at the barrier. The mothers swung to their children and set them roughly by the wall on the fire side far back against the cave throat; and in the next moment Kayah seized a torch. Bolder than the males, as most mothers of all kinds are when fighting for their young, she dashed recklessly to the bear who was now coming in and thrust the fire against his face. With a roar that shook the mountain he stood up, pawing and hurling the wood aside; and on hind legs, slowly, like a hulk of darkness, he marched in. In an instant the three mothers were upon him with torches. They were trying to shove fire into his eyes and blind him; but in her wild frenzy Youee slipped and fell within reach of a paw, and a moment later she was gutted from her collar bone to her crotch. With one powerful sweeping blow the talons ripped her wide open. She rolled, bloody and dying, into the path of the beast, but nobody saw her there or knew that she was hurt.

In this dreadful scene nobody saw much of anything except the marching hulk which, with desperate courage, they now attacked. Using two tongs Kayah gathered fire and hurled it on the beast, and it blazed up in a patch of fur. The sound he made now almost ruptured eardrums. He came down on all fours; and while Kayah continued to hurl fire, and the men, from a safer distance, to throw stones, the beast headed for the tunnel. The children were in his path, and with one sweep of a forearm he hurled them aside. Upon his broad shoulders he carried a small fire that had eaten through the fur to his hide; and now the sound of his rage and pain was such thunder in the vault that pieces of stone were loosened and fell from the ceiling. Back down the corridor he went with the flame on his back lighting the way and the sound of his voice like cascading ledges.

He was still in sight, a living torch vanishing into deep gloom, when Kayah rushed to the children. Her son, the child with the burned hands and feet, was dead. His skull had been crushed. One of the other children was bleeding, and both of them were screaming like living things burning in a fire. Mog went over and knelt by Kayah; but a moment later a yell from Harg brought them to their feet.

The mother beast stood against the barrier and was looking in. If her frightened cubs had not hung back, she would have followed her mate; and while she hesitated, Kayah and Mog grasped torches and ran to the barrier. Harg dropped his axe and seized a firebrand, and he dashed back and forth, aimlessly, shouting to the other men. They, too, gathered fire, and all of them, four men and three women, threw fire in the path of the she-beast. When the bear drew back a little, Kayah clambered up the wood and hurled her torch at the bear's head. It struck her across the eyes. In a moment of wild hope, Harg thought he could kill one of the cubs for food; and he threw a rock and hit one of them, and when the mother heard her child's whimper, she opened her mouth and moved forward to attack.

But the women were ready for her. The three of them stood on top of the pile of wood with flaming brands, and the instant the beast came within reach they thrust at her. When the bear opened her mouth again, Kayah moved forward swiftly and thrust her torch into the mouth and deep against the throat. With a cry that was less a roar than a scream, the bear fell back on her haunches, and when she closed her mouth she closed it on fire. Maddened and terrified, she swung and set off in a rolling gait down the hill; and at once the men and women raced after her, the men throwing rocks and the women hurling fire. Harg, feeling bolder now, rushed ahead, trying desperately to fell one of the cubs with a stone; but in a few moments the mother and her young went down the mountain and vanished from sight.

Morning had come.

They went back into their home, and at once Kayah rushed to her dead child and hugged it to her breast. She sat on the earth with her back to the wall, clutching the child to her and rocking gently back and forth; but after a little, as if hoping it might still live, she laid it across her legs and stared at its eyes. She felt over it for wounds and found none until her exploring hand came to a part of the skull that was soft and crushed; whereupon, knowing that it was dead, yet hoping that she could bring it to life, she hugged it and made low sounds of love and grief.

The others had been gazing at the dead woman.

"Look!" Harg said. "Dead."

"Dead," said Gugg, and bent forward to peer at the corpse.

"Dead," said Yawg.

Death of their own kind always aroused in them a feeling of awe and humility. In circling the woman to look at the great open wound in the belly and chest, they moved softly, humbly, overwhelmed by a sense of the dreadful forces in the world that struck them down. Death they did not understand beyond knowing that a person ceased to breathe and move and wasted away slowly until only bones remained. And because they were unhappy and fearful in the presence of death the men wanted to take the corpse away and hide it.

"Come," Harg said, speaking to Gugg; and Harg grasped the hands, Gugg the feet, and they took the body over the pile of wood and outside. Then, supporting their burden, they stood without moving, with Gugg staring at Harg and Harg looking round him for a hiding-place; and suddenly Harg let his part of the burden fall and went away to search. He looked up and down the stone flank of the mountain, seeking a crevice into which the body could be thrust; and when he found one he returned and said, "Come," and they carried the dead woman along the base of a ledge.

"There," said Harg, indicating a crevice shoulder-high in the wall. They lifted the body and pushed and rolled it across a stone shelf until it was back several feet from the face of the ledge; and then Harg did what, in the burial of a dead one, none of his people had ever done before. He gathered stones and laid them on the shelf against the body until it seemed to be protected from beasts and birds of prey.

The two men returned to the cave. Kayah was still hugging her dead son; and now Mog went over, moved more by instinct than thought, to take the body from

Kayah's arms. But Kayah fought against her. Then Harg went over and looked at Kayah and perceived that the child in her arms was dead. He was on the point of wresting it from her when Mog came over with Youee's child.

A human mother of this time fixed her love on children and did not clearly distinguish between another's children and her own. If her child died she could be comforted if a living child were given to her in its place; and when Mog set Youee's child on Kayah's lap, Kayah embraced both children, the living and the dead. Then Harg seized the dead child by a leg and dragged it away, and though Kayah struggled and cried in protest, the living child in her arms slowly focused her attention. If she realized that the other was being taken from her, she showed no sign of it after a few moments. She now mothered Youee's child, hugging it to her and uttering low cries of joy as if she thought the dead one had come to life. Perceptions are dull when grief is deep; and in a mother the stir of young life within her arms can gather all emotion into the core of her being, until the world is shut out and senses no longer communicate its presence.

Harg took the dead child away. When he could find no burial crevice that suited him, he removed the stones from the shelf where Youee lay and pushed the child back against her. Then he replaced the stones. Instead of returning to the fire at once, he stood here and gazed across the valley, a man who felt desolate and afraid. There was in him no affection for these dead ones, but he did feel a sense of loss. For survival in a terrifying and unfriendly world there was need of numbers, and two of his family were gone.

In his emotion there was more than that. Death always

124

brought into sharper realization the hazards of living, the perils, the uncertainties and mysteries; but as he stood here, gazing across the valley and the morning, there was no thought, no recognition, in his mind. His mind and his body were one deep and wordless emotion—of anxiety and awe, of fear, of loneliness, all overcast by the humility which he felt in this hour. He was not now the lordly conquering one; he was a humbled one in a strange world who had buried two of his kind. If he had been a more civilized man he might have knelt in prayer—because prayer is the confession of one who feels that insurmountable obstacles lie athwart his egoistic strivings. Or he might have tried to propitiate the dreadful forces around him. But Harg was only a simple man who was unable to formulate definitions of powers stronger than himself. He had little sense of his own meaning and even less of the world's meaning; and so for several minutes he stood here, abject and fearful and terribly lonely, and looked at the gray autumn light upon forests and hills.

12

WHEN Harg returned to the fire, he picked up his axe and went away to hunt food; and a little later the others went, too, except Kayah and Youee's child. Kayah still sat by the wall and hugged the child, as if the presence of death had given her an insane devotion to life. Deep in her confused pain was an unconscious wish to be impregnated and to give birth at once to another son. That was a mother's meaning and destiny. If all the children had been slain, the women would have been moved to present themselves sexually to the men, driven by the instinctive blind struggle to survive that is like the beating heart of life under the surface of all things. Indeed, Mog had offered herself and had been embraced by Gugg; and Memm, though pregnant, had not resisted when Gugg approached her. When death struck, aroused emotions reached out then, as in time of war and peril they reach out still, to preserve life in new birth.

It was noon, and the others were still prowling for food, when Kayah became aware that the fire was dying.

Next to children, she was devoted to this friendliness that gave protection and warmth; and so she aroused herself to lay wood on the embers. Upon looking round the cavern and seeing that she was alone, she came wide awake, with all the cunning of the hunted and the hunter. Remembering that the male bear was back in the cave, she went over and peered into the dark corridor; and then, carrying the child, she turned down the hill to find her people.

Soon she saw Mog and Memm coming toward her; Mog carried her child, and Memm carried two rabbits. They had eaten and they gave the rabbits to Kayah. Grasping the hind legs of the rabbit with one hand, with the other she peeled off the hide. Then with long sharp fingernails she made an incision in the belly, thrust in two fingers, and disemboweled the creature. The heart and liver and lungs she gave to her child and for herself she tore off a leg. The other women squatted and watched Kayah eat. Though each of them had eaten a rabbit, they felt hungry; and Mog skinned the other rabbit and gave the hind quarters to Memm.

"Enemy?" asked Mog, looking up the mountain.

"No," Kayah said.

"Friend?" asked Mog, meaning fire.

Kayah nodded. When they had finished eating they wrapped the bones in a rabbit pelt and took these with them up the hill.

The men returned a little later and squatted against the wall. Their weapons lay within reach. The women squatted, too, and hugged their children, feeling for them more than usual tenderness. Though they had all eaten well, they were dispirited and apprehensive, knowing

127

they were not yet in undisputed possession of their home. The she-beast might return during the night, and even if she did not, the father bear was still back in the cave.

If they had moved the fire to one side and made an unobstructed path for the bear, perhaps he would have come out quietly and gone away; but while resting on his haunches during the afternoon, Harg thought of bold things to do. He wanted the bear for food and tried to plan an attack. He thought first of taking the men with him and crawling into the mountain to corner the beast; but after a while he remembered how he had trapped the mammoth. He had fire here. He had a kind of trap here, closed by stone walls on two sides and almost closed on a third. If the bear came out and was imprisoned by walls and fire, then, it seemed to Harg, the men might leap upon him with axes and crush his skull.

This plan he kept in mind, and again and again he looked round the big room, wondering how he could close both the corridor throat and the open side. Across the open side he could build a fire; but if the bear came out and saw fire blocking his path he might then vanish back into the gloom. It would be necessary to get him out of the cave and to close the cave behind him. How to do so Harg was unable to see, and to this problem he gave a great deal of thought.

Wondering if he could enter the cave and hide there and get behind the beast to drive him out, he took a torch and entered the cavern. The others cried with astonishment; they thought he was going into the mountain to attack the bear. The men seized their axes and followed Harg to the cave throat but there they stopped, afraid, and watched Harg enter the darkness. With the torch lighting his way, he explored the wall on either side, looking for a shelf on which he could lie and wait. After penetrating fifty feet or so, he learned that the corridor narrowed and the ceiling arched downward. Here he was barely able to stand erect and he could reach out with his arms and span the distance from wall to wall; but thirty feet beyond, the chamber was of greater size, and one wall was terraced in shelves. His torch went out, but he had a live ember and, using this as a light, he climbed to a shelf and reached up to the next shelf and felt over it to learn if he could lie there. He sniffed the odors strong with dampness and the smell of wild things. He wanted to explore farther, but his ember died, and he returned to the entrance, guided by firelight.

Using a few words but chiefly gestures, he tried to explain his plan to the men. He would go back when darkness came and lie on the shelf until the bear came out; and then he would leap down and drive the creature ahead of him, shutting off its retreat. With their axes they would kill it. None of them had a clear grasp of the plan, though they understood that the bear was to be killed; but they thought Harg intended to go into the dungeon and drive the bear out. Such boldness as that they had never known in man or beast, and they looked at him with wonder like a light in their eyes. Excitedly they babbled and gestured, explaining to one another what Harg proposed to do; and when they were all convinced that Harg did indeed plan to enter the cave and face the beast alone, they stared at him with wordless admiration and awe.

After darkness came, Harg spread fire across the entrance, and they understood that he was making a barrier. The women pitched in to help him. The men stood back, clutching their axes and looking at this man whose boldness astounded them. None of the three could have said whether he would be brave enough to attack the monster; but they realized that Harg expected to drive the bear out and they were afraid. They were not too dull-witted to perceive that they would be trapped, too, with a wall of fire shutting off escape; and this dreadful suspicion became a certainty when Harg explained to the women that they were to keep fire alive clear across the entrance. They found no comfort in the fact that Harg's part of the task was more dangerous than their own. After all, he was a mysterious one who made fire and trapped enemies; he had strange power over the forces and terrors of the world, and this power they did not have. Gugg and Yawg looked at one another, and in the eyes of both there was all the bright fear that for countless generations had lived in the eyes of men.

When the night was deep and black, Harg took his axe and knife and a torch and entered the cave. He went swiftly to the shelf and thrust his torch against stone; and when the light died, those watching from the entrance thought only that he had vanished far back into the gloom. He crawled up to the second ledge and stretched himself out on his belly, the handle of his axe grasped by his right hand and the knife by his left. He was about nine feet above the corridor floor. He could see nothing. He was so high that the downward sweep of the ceiling between him and the entrance shut out even the faintest glow of firelight. But though he was unable to see, his other senses were wide awake; it was his ears and nose that would detect the beast's coming and tell him what to do.

The only sound he could hear now was the pounding

of his heart. He was lying face downward with his hairy chest pressed to the stone, and his heart was so heavy in its labor that it lifted him a little with each beat. It was so loud in his ears that he wondered if the bear would be able to hear him when it came alongside. He felt safe but he was terribly afraid; he trembled all over as if freezing, and his teeth clicked when he did not press them together. There were burning sensations along his spine, and his scalp felt as if a horde of insects were feeding there. He was probably one of the most fearless men of his time, but again and again, nevertheless, he felt an impulse to leap down and flee; and this impulse he was able to control only by changing his position a little, as if by moving his muscles he confused and thwarted them. Laying his knife aside, he reached out with a finger to test the blade of his axe. It was sharp. It was a good axe and it was heavy, and he believed that he could split open any skull in the world.

An hour passed before he heard the bear coming. The tenseness in him rose like a flood to his throat and was strangled there in a sob. His big right hand closed like a vise on the axe handle; and all through him his great muscles stiffened like bands of steel. The hair rose on his scalp, and down his spine went flashes of heat, as if a fire with legs were walking there. His heavy lips were parted, but his teeth were clenched. Breathing slowly and deeply he waited and listened; he could hear the padded feet walking in the darkness.

Harg realized now that he was facing the wrong way to see the eyes and he did not dare turn his head. He did not dare to move even a finger. When he could no longer hear the muffled tread he knew the bear had stopped, but whether the animal was only cautiously exploring the way or whether it had smelled the enemy on the stone ledge, Harg did not know. Then after a few moments he could hear the beast coming, and with his acute sense of hearing he could almost measure the distance, step by step. The bear came slowly without pause; and Harg, with his face turned so that he could look down, saw the great hulk below him. His fingers tightened on the axe, and during the next few moments he hardly breathed at all.

The beast did not stop when he came abreast. The shadow passed across Harg's vision like a deeper darkness moving through darkness; and then Harg knew that the bear had passed him. He rose noiselessly to hands and knees, and slowly, softly, without making a sound, he descended. He straightened for a moment to relieve the aches in his body. Then he moved swiftly ahead until he saw the bear in the narrow part of the corridor; and with a cry that rang like a wild scream in the walls he leapt forward to attack. The knife fell from his left hand, and in the same instant both hands grasped his axe and swung it above him; but the bear moved quickly when it heard the cry, and when it moved, Harg saw firelight ahead.

The next few moments were wild confusion. The bear rushed forward out of the tunnel, with Harg racing behind him and shouting, with three women screaming and rushing upon him with fire, and with three men leaping in with their stone axes. In the instant when he emerged, the bear saw that he was cornered and at once he rose to his hind legs, with his huge mouth wide open. One blow of a paw struck Kahha and hurled him against a stone wall, and the second blow reached out and caught Yawg at the nape of his neck and plowed furrows down his back to his rump. Gugg ran toward the fire, and the women toward the children.

The bear came down on all fours and moved toward the wall of fire, seeking an escape through it; and Harg thought this was his moment to strike. Gugg had turned from the fire with a huge blazing torch, and at once the women joined him and seized firebrands; recklessly they all dashed toward the beast to head him off. It was in this instant that Harg attacked. Swiftly he dashed forward until he stood close by a shoulder, poised for a moment while swinging his axe high, and then drove the blade downward and into the skull. He struck with such power that he followed through on the blow and tumbled head over heels, and in one continuous movement fell and rolled in a frantic effort to get beyond the front paws. He rolled clear beyond the bear and against the fire and leapt up, screaming, and dashed back into the cave, wildly looking for his weapon.

But all danger was past. The blow had split the skull, and the axe now stood upright, deeply imbedded; and like a great soft pile of fur the bear sank to its belly and shuddered. Not knowing that he had slain the beast and unable to see his axe, Harg seized stones and hurled them, screaming all the while like a man mortally wounded. The women, too, were screaming and attacking; they were heaping fire on the beast and, even after a patch of fur was blazing, they raced back and forth, dragging burning chunks with them and using sticks as tongs to pile them on their enemy. Gugg was throwing stones. Under the feet of these people, as they worked, was a dying man, and they trampled him as they ran from fire to beast or searched in frenzied blindness for rocks; but they did not see him or feel him with their feet or realize that he was there.

After hurling a few stones, Harg paused for a moment and saw his axe, and he dashed over and grasped the handle and wrenched the blade from the skull; but he was too wildly excited to realize that his enemy was dead. If the bear had been alive and fighting, Harg could not have attacked with more deadly earnestness. He raised the axe again and again and smote the skull until he had completely crushed it; and only then did he pause and step back and look at his foe. Only then did he dare to admit the thought that the beast was dead.

And now, overcome by his superhuman efforts, shaking all over, exhausted and sick, he went over and sat by a wall and began to vomit. The women were exclaiming over one man who was dead and another who was dying.

13

THE struggle cost the lives of four of them, but the survivors now had a home for the winter. They had a pile of flesh and fat and if they had been provident, if they had known how to dry and store meat, they would have had food for many weeks. But of foresight they had little more than the lion or the wolf. Again they gave their time to gluttonous eating, engorging and vomiting, and wasting a large portion of what they had.

Of the future they had only a very dim notion. They knew, to be sure, that cold and snow were ahead of them, but the wolf and the jackal knew that much. The wolf and the jackal at the fresh kill also ate until they were sick and wasted what they could not eat. With respect to food, Harg and his people lived at the level of the flesh-eating beasts: they first devoured the more tender parts; they turned away, bloated and sick, to be alone with their misery; and after a while they returned to eat again.

After all the organs were eaten, and the brain and tongue, and such marrow and juices as they could easily get at, they attacked the hams and shoulders, cutting off large pieces and going off to be alone while devouring them. They had not forgotten that they had burned pieces of the mammoth; but bear flesh was tender and they liked it raw. When the meat became tainted and the offensive smell of the open carcass filled their home, they still spent most of their daylight hours eating, even though the putrid flesh made them sick; and sometimes during the night, when awaking to tend the fire or to look out for sign of enemies, they would eat again.

Snow had come, and the world beyond their home was white. Two weeks after the bear was slain, snow fell for three days and nights without pause, and during this time nobody left the shelter. For water they ate snow; and when the wood was almost gone, the women kept only a very small fire burning. Remembering that fat made a steady light, Kayah cut off a large piece and laid it away on a stone shelf. Obscurely in her mind was a wish to hoard it and use it later for candles; but after the flesh was all eaten or had become too putrid to eat, Harg took the hunk of fat from the shelf and pawed it over, searching it for scraps of meat. When he finished with it, Kayah returned it to the ledge.

Though the soles on the feet of all the adults was as thick and tough as leather, none of them liked to wade in deep snow; and so when there was neither flesh nor fat to eat, rather than leave their shelter to hunt for food they turned to the bones. They would squat by the fire, each with a bone, and they would gnaw at their bones and bite off tiny bits of gristle or turn them over and over to search when there was only bone left. The bones came to look as if they had been gnawed by an army of mice.

136

Next they tried to cut open the bones or to crush them to get at the marrow; or they spread out the great pelt and crawled over it, nibbling at the flesh side. When not chewing at the pelt, they turned it hair side up and squatted on it by the fire.

The time came when hunger forced them to stir. Daily the women went for fuel, wading in snow to their rumps; but they did not go for food. That was a task for the two men. Kayah asked Gugg to go and find things to eat, but she did not ask Harg to do so because, like the others, she lived in awe of him. Not only had he made fire and trapped a mammoth; they all believed that he had gone into the mountain to find the bear and drive him out. Too, he had slain the beast, and that alone was enough to set him apart as a great one.

Harg sensed the awe and admiration and was deeply pleased. He became an arrogant boss. In extreme hunger he got the notion that the others should go out and find food for him; and when, one day, Kayah asked Gugg to go for food, Harg swung to the man and roared at him.

"Food!" he shouted and, pointing at the white world, he said, "Go!"

Gugg went with such haste that he forgot his weapons. He left the shelter and stood in snow to his crotch, a naked and abject fellow, shivering and uncertain; and when Harg again commanded him to go, Gugg pointed back to the room and tried to make them understand that his weapons were there. Kayah took the axe and knife to him.

"Go!" Harg roared. He was beside himself with joy. Nothing so gratified a person, and especially a male, as to have others yield to his will. Like a boy in a tantrum Harg kept yelling at Gugg, commanding him to go and find food; and when Gugg obediently went down the hill, Harg redoubled his outcry. He dashed outside, still gesturing and shouting, feeling all the while like a great conqueror; and when he returned to the women, he was so egoistically aglow that he roared at them. He forced them off the bear pelt, and the children with them, and then stretched out on it like any lord at his ease. But almost at once he leapt up, resolved that the women should go with Gugg to find food; and, with yells that could have been heard a mile away, he ordered them out into the winter. They went, taking the children with them, but when they returned they brought wood.

Gugg did not find much, and what he found he ate. When he came back, carrying only his weapons, he did not enter at once, but stood beyond the fire, looking in, as if to inquire whether he was welcome.

"Food?" Kayah asked.

"No," he said.

"Food!" Harg shouted.

In defense of himself, Gugg turned and pointed at the world. "Enemy," he said, meaning the cold and the snow.

"Enemy?" Harg said. Harg and the women looked at one another with comical solemnity. They seemed to ask, "Is there no food left in the world? Has it all died?" Then Harg made gestures of eating to Gugg.

"Food?"

Gugg pointed at the empty world. He did not shrug—such a gesture was too subtle for him—but he did droop forlornly like a man half frozen and denied entrance to his home.

Hunger moved Harg to the bones, and when he picked

up one and began to gnaw at it, Gugg softly entered. The women also chose ribs and gnawed at them, and to the children, sitting by a wall within the glow of the fire, they offered smaller bones; and like the adults the children turned their bones over and over, chewing and slobbering, or now and then looking up hopefully for something better to eat.

It was not concern for his family but his own hunger pains that drove Harg to the hunt. A shelter from storm and wind and a warm fire had made him slothful; and, besides these, there was the deep fur to lie on. Life for him had become luxurious. In former winters his family had spent the nights huddled together under a tree or an overhanging shelf of rock; and because, during hours of darkness, they ached and nearly froze, when daylight came they were always glad to hunt for food. Moving around helped to warm and relax them. But now, with a ceiling above and fire to warm the room, a man had to drive himself, or be driven, into the cold, bleak world.

Harg's legs, like the legs of the others, were covered with a heavy growth of hair; but when one morning, with axe and knife, he entered the snow, he stopped and shivered. He looked back at the dry, warm room. Perhaps he might have gone back and starved, or tried to force the others out, if he had not observed the excitement in the women's faces. Harg, the mighty one, the slayer of great beasts, was going forth to hunt; and though Harg did not fully interpret what he saw in the faces, he did perceive admiration and eagerness and expectancy, and he remembered that he was a great one. He was one who did superhuman things. Between his vanity and his wish to return and squat by the fire there was a struggle. His vanity won.

139

He had a vision of himself killing an animal and eating fresh, tender meat. His fingers tightened on his weapons, and he turned away.

He was a short man; the snow, deeper than his bowed legs, came to his waist. But for many winters as a boy he had waded in snow and was used to it. The stone weapons were cold in his grasp, even for palms as thick as his; the warmth of his body melted the snow clinging to the hair on his belly, and because he was thirsty he paused now and then to touch the drops and lick them off his fingers. Or from time to time he would squat, crushing the snow under him, and, with only his head above the white level, he would look round him for sign of living things.

He saw small birds and large ones; he saw the trails of rabbits and squirrels and weasels, and of deer and wolf; and by a stream he saw where beasts had come to drink. He looked at every tree for bird nests; and when he saw one he would bend the tree over if it was small or climb it if it was large. Sometimes in a nest there was an unhatched egg. When he found one Harg would peel off the shell and eat the contents, no matter whether it was foul juices or a dead embryo. He also searched trees and bushes for insects and ate everything that he found.

He wanted the fresh meat of an animal; but the larger ones were too fleet, and even when he spied one it was soon out of sight. Smaller ones, especially rabbits, he pursued, hurling his axe at a creature and then hunting in the snow for his axe. He was awkward, his aim was poor, and with such weapons as he had he was not an able hunter. His senses were keen and he was cunning, but it was impossible to get within striking distance of his prey. The best way to do, as Harg had learned as a boy, was to hide in ambush where animals came to drink or to lick clay banks; and today, after appeasing his hunger with a couple of stale eggs and a few bugs, he explored along a river, seeking a drinking place close by which he could hide. When he found one that seemed promising, he crept under bushes laden with snow and crouched, with his axe clasped by both hands, ready to hurl. He waited here an hour, shivering and unhappy, but no beast came to drink. Impatient, he went to another spot and waited, and to a third; and a little later, while wandering aimlessly, he came to the pit in which he had trapped the mammoth.

He thought he could roof it with brush and snow and capture another of the huge creatures, and eagerly he laid his tools aside and looked round him for covering. But there was none. During the time while his family camped here, the forest for two hundred yards roundabout had been denuded, and Harg was not a man who would labor very hard, even for fresh meat. He realized that he could find brush if he went far enough, but he was cold and wretched, and he picked up his weapons and explored again, hoping to get by luck what he was unwilling to get by toil. His simple philosophy was one of hope and chance. In the forest ahead of him he expected a miracle; and when none came there, he moved eagerly to another. And so he spent most of the day guided by nothing more intelligent than unreasonable hope; and when at last he went home, hungry and dejected, he felt that the mysterious forces of life had conspired against him.

It was not unusual, particularly in winter, for Harg's people to go for three or four days or even a week without eating; and now that Harg and his family had the luxury of a warm home, it took more than ordinary pangs of hunger to drive them out. Daily the children sucked at the empty breasts of their mothers. Daily all members of the group lost flesh and became weaker and more ill-tempered. The women went for wood because they would have given their lives rather than let the fire die; and while out gathering it they ate such vegetation and bugs as they could find. But neither of the men left the shelter for several days.

After his fruitless hunt through snow and cold, Harg drowsed by the fire day and night, demanding most of the pelt for his use. An easy and secure way of life has always been an enemy of men; it has been perils and problems, the need to fight and strive, that have stimulated their minds and developed their resourcefulness. If Harg and Gugg had had no fire, they would have gone hunting daily, not only to find food but also to keep warm; but now they were protected from wind and snow, the women kept the fire alive, and the men were content to sit in drowsy stupor and look out at the unfriendly world.

That was so until their hunger became intense suffering. Then Harg wanted Gugg to go for food, but, when commanded to do so, Gugg would withdraw into the cave throat and sulk there until he felt it was safe to come out. Harg also commanded the women to find things to eat; they would go out into the winter, but they always returned with wood. Usually they took the children with them and fed the children a few insects.

And so a week passed.

Then hunger forced Harg to leave the shelter, and Gugg, after hesitating, picked up his weapons and trailed him. New snow had fallen, and the path which Harg had made a week ago was drifted full. Though these men had phenomenal strength, they had been weakened by fasting, and in the deep snow Harg went slowly and with difficulty, pausing often to look round him like one who despaired, or to gaze back at the warm room. When he came to a forest of conifers, he ate a handful of the bitter foliage; and again he searched for bird nests, insects, and mice.

Gugg called to him and shouted, "Look!" and when Harg turned to look, Gugg pointed at the sky. Some flesh-eating birds were wheeling round and round in flight.

"There!" said Harg, and pointed beyond the woods.

"Yes," Gugg said.

The men knew that these creatures of the sky were probably circling above a wounded beast.

"Come!" said Harg, and waited until Gugg came abreast. The men looked at one another, their eyes asking a question. What kind of wounded creature was it?—a mammoth in a pit, an old and feeble lion attacked by hyenas, or a hamstrung stag? Would the two of them be able to attack and kill it? They proceeded until they could look beyond the forest and again turned to one another.

"There," said Harg, pointing to a grove of birch and alder along a stream.

"There," Gugg said.

For several minutes they considered the matter, looking up at the flying birds or over at the thicket in which, they had no doubt, there was a wounded beast. If it was a lion or tiger or wolf, Harg did not know if he would dare attack. That would depend on whether the beast was helpless. Once, two years ago, his people had found a lion that seemed to be helpless, but when they had moved to attack, the creature had leapt up with astonishing speed and power, and they had fled. He decided to go warily now

143

until he could peer into the bush and learn what was there.

He wanted Gugg to go ahead. "Go!" he commanded, but Gugg drew back. Then Harg remembered that he was the mighty one who had slain a bear and, feeling a sense of power that was supported chiefly by vanity, he went ahead, treading softly in the snow. After proceeding a few yards he heard a sudden snarl in the thicket. He turned to Gugg.

"Enemy," he said.

"Enemy," said Gugg.

Harg knew the sound had been made by a hyena or a wolf. There in the thicket was an animal, surrounded by enemies, and above it were other enemies, circling round and round.

Harg handed his knife to Gugg; and then, grasping his axe with both hands, he advanced. When he turned to look back, he saw that Gugg had not moved.

"Come!" Harg cried angrily, and reluctantly Gugg advanced. They could now hear snarling and hissing in the brush. Harg took his knife and Gugg's knife and laid them on the snow, and with gestures he told Gugg to grasp his axe and be ready. He did not intend to allow Gugg to trail behind like a scared and trembling fellow ready to flee. He took Gugg's arm and pulled the man forward. Gugg knew what Harg wanted him to do, but he was not so bold a man as his son; and, besides, he was shaking so with cold and fright that his axe slipped from his grasp.

"No!" Harg yelled. He picked up the axe and thrust it at Gugg. "Come," he said.

They advanced slowly, walking abreast, their arms almost touching. They could have moved no more quietly if they had walked on an earth deep with feathers. Upon coming to the grove they were unable to see anything except the white wall before them because every tree and bush was laden with snow. But they could hear the angry snarling; it was just beyond the wall. Harg kicked and pawed in the snow, looking for a stick or a stone, and when he found one he hurled it over the trees. In the same moment he gave a thunderous challenge, and Gugg echoed him. The two men roared like wild beasts; and moved by excitement and fear and the lust to kill, Harg seized a birch tree and shook it, and its burden of snow fell upon him.

"Listen!" cried Gugg. They listened, but there was no sound.

Deciding that the grove here was too much of a jungle to enter safely, Harg circled, with Gugg at his heels, and presently came to a path. The path entered a clearing and led to the stream, and the men followed it, hunched forward, grasping their axes, ready to flee or strike. After going a few yards they fetched up in amazement.

Back on its haunches was a stag of the fallow deer. A beast larger than the American elk, almost as large as a moose, it had enormous antlers with a spread of ten feet from tip to tip. Each of them was a broad flat wing of bone from which thrust eight curved horns turning upward to the sky. The head was small, but the neck, which supported the antlers, was a great bulge of muscle set against powerful shoulders.

In one swift moment of fright and astonishment the men saw the stag; and in the next, they saw beyond it a dozen jackals, crouching and whining. These creatures, powerfully muscled under their heavy fur, were like

145

small, rugged wolves, though they did not have the wolf's courage. They now slunk back, drooling and snarling and showing their sharp teeth. They had hamstrung the deer and dropped it on its haunches, but they had not been able to get past the gleaming fortress of the antlers. Around the stag was a beaten path where the jackals had run; but the stag had kept turning, as if on a pivot, with the huge bulk of its antlers, neck, and shoulders supported by its front legs. Its eyes, now fixed on the men, were bloodshot with rage.

Harg turned to Gugg and their gaze met, eloquent with questions. Because the stag did not rise to its hind legs they knew it was unable to, but they realized that it had full and dangerous control of its horns. As for the jackals, Harg was not afraid of them; he knew they were craven beasts that would never fight unless cornered. Now, when he yelled and menaced them with his axe, the slinking creatures crawled backward, snapping their teeth. Harg spoke to Gugg and made a gesture of throwing; and while he kept his eye on the jackals, Gugg found a piece of dead wood. This Harg took and hurled at the creatures, and whining and snarling they withdrew a little farther. They were still in plain sight, resting on their bellies in the snow, snapping their teeth, and looking in turn from the deer to the men.

How to kill the stag, Harg did not know. When he took a step or two toward it, the beast snorted with fury and lowered its antlers; and when Harg moved to the right or left, the stag swung on its haunches to face him. Remembering fire, Harg looked round him for wood, but saw nothing that would burn. The trees here were green and wet.

146

"Kill?" he said to Gugg, but Gugg shook his head. This was no task for him. He had been waiting expectantly, believing that Harg would leap on the stag and kill it as he had killed the bear.

When Harg was quiet the jackals made no sound, though the upper lip was drawn back and exposed canine daggers. When Harg moved, the jackals stood up and snapped at him.

Harg was baffled, but he was resolute. For half an hour he did no more than to advance a little and retreat, or to move from side to side, feeling out his problem. The more nonplussed he felt, the more his senses were darkened by anger; and after a while he began to shout and threaten with his axe and to advance a little nearer. When convinced that the stag was unable to move his haunches, Harg became bolder. He stepped in close, and the great antlers came down in a sudden powerful sweep that missed him only by inches. Harg leapt back. Then for a long moment he looked at the enraged eyes of the beast and wondered what to do. He felt an impulse to hurl his axe at the skull, but he knew his weapon would drop beyond his reach and he would then be unarmed. He wanted to attack from the rear, but when he approached from that side, the head moved like an owl's and the terrible antlers faced him.

While considering the matter, and drooling like the jackals at the thought of fresh meat, there came to him the brilliant notion he could use Gugg and that the two of them could work as a team. While Gugg feinted from the front, Harg believed he could slip in from the rear. To explain to Gugg what he had in mind he shouted and gestured; he assumed the position which he wished

Gugg to take; he grasped Gugg's arm and led him forward, all the while dramatizing the matter so that Gugg would understand.

When Gugg at last got the plan in his thick head, he faced the stag and yelled and swung his axe; and Harg slipped into the woods and came in from behind. The stag was unable to see him because his eyes were beyond the wings of his ears and the flat bone of his antlers. Harg came up until he could almost touch the beast; and then he gestured at Gugg, making signs for him to wave his axe wildly and jump up and down and engage the stag's full attention. All this Gugg did, yelling, feinting to right or left and threatening with his weapon; and Harg moved swiftly in, with his axe raised, and struck a powerful blow at the base of the skull, just behind the antlers. In the next moment he wrenched the axe free and sprang back, ready to strike again; but there was no need to. The beast sank, with its head on its front legs and the antlers spread on the snow.

The excitement of battle always scattered a man's fears and made him recklessly bold. Seeing that he had killed the stag, Harg swung to the jackals and rushed at them, howling and waving his axe. The creatures fled, and for a hundred yards he pursued them. If they had stood their ground, he would have attacked with headlong desperation, because again he was the mighty one who had killed a mammoth and a bear; and in his wild triumph he felt there was no enemy in the world that could stand against him. When he returned, he dashed to the stag and smote it again and again—not because he felt it was still dangerous, but to relieve the battle lust that had overwhelmed him. He faced the beast and fetched the axe down with all

148

the power he had and split the skull open clear to the chin. Then he turned, his axe raised, his body taut and poised, his eyes inflamed, and looked round him for something to attack.

"Dead!" cried Gugg, who had not lost control of himself. Gugg backed away, afraid that this killer would rush at him. "Dead!" he shouted, and pointed at the stag.

Harg looked at the stag; slowly his axe came down and hung from a trembling arm. For a long moment he was like one recovering from loss of consciousness. Then he drew himself to his fullest height and stood like a lordly one and pointed to himself. He meant to indicate that he, the great one, had slain the beast, single-handed and alone. He looked at Gugg, and Gugg nodded assent.

14

WHILE the men were hunting, Kayah was learning a new art, and Mog and Memm were learning with her. It was a day of bitter cold; and when she saw her adopted child shivering, Kayah took the stiff bear pelt and tried to wrap the child in it. The pelt was much too large, and to the mother's mind came the simple thought that perhaps she could cut off a piece. Spreading the pelt on the floor, with the skin side up, she took a flint knife and scraped and hacked until she cut off a piece; and then it occurred to her to cut another blanket for the other child. Mog and Memm understood what she had in mind and they assisted her, the three women kneeling together on the floor.

But they cut both pieces too small, and when Kayah took one to wrap around her child, turning the fur side in, she was dismayed. In all possible ways she tried to make the covering reach. She put it over the back and shoulders and drew the edges toward the front; or over the chest and belly and drew the edges toward the back;

or on either side, under the arm, behaving all the while as though she expected to find the child's circumference less if she put the blanket in the right place. But it was too small to reach around and meet; and when Kayah became convinced of this she looked at the other women. They, too, had found the other piece too small for Mog's child. Baffled, the women gazed at one another.

After a few moments, Kayah took the two pieces and perceived that when put together, edge to edge, they would cover her child; and instead of turning to the pelt and cutting off a larger garment, she wondered how she could make the two pieces one. Neither she nor any of her people had ever sewed, or even used thongs to fasten two things together. After watching Kayah, Mog chattered at her and moved over to help; and again and again they put the two pieces around the child, one to the front and one to the back, but were unable to make either stay in place. While Kayah held one and Mog the other, the women understood that if the pieces were fastened together across each shoulder they would then hang without falling. Each woman used a finger and thumb as a clothespin, Mog clasping the two garments across one shoulder and Kayah across the other; and while their eyes met and questioned, the child, scowling and patient, looked up at them.

Kayah searched the cave for something to use as a fastener, having in mind a thumb-and-finger tool, and she found what she wanted in a cleft stick. She pushed the two edges of the pelt into the cleft, and they were caught and held; and with another such clothespin she fastened the other side. Then, with admiration and wonder, the women looked at the child.

They were so excited and pleased by their ingenuity that Kayah took the garment off the child and pinned it on Mog. One piece hung down her front, hiding the sagging breasts, and the other fell to the middle of her back. Mog walked back and forth, admiring herself, and Kayah and Memm stared at her and exclaimed with wonder. Mog rubbed a big brown hand over the flesh side of the skin or reached under to the fur or around to the piece hanging down her shoulders, trying with a sense of touch to bring into fuller realization the miracle of her first garment. The other women so envied her that they seized knives and cut the remainder of the pelt into pieces; and an hour or two later they both wore a garment like Mog's. All three of them walked around, admiring themselves or one another. Kayah had been impelled at first to try to warm her child, but now the emotion in her grew out of a simple and childlike love of adornment. She felt, they all felt, more important, more distinguished and set apart, by these primitive garments hanging from their shoulders.

Love of adornment was in Harg's people, but they had never made more than impulsively casual use of it. The men sometimes had fixed bright things in their hair, but they had nothing which they kept for this purpose alone. These women now had mantles, and they were so engrossed by them that they forgot the children. They did not remember that they had cut up the pelt to make garments to keep children warm. They were so enraptured by their dress that they neglected the fire until it burned low and the cave was bitter cold.

When Kayah and Mog went for wood, leaving Memm with the children, they wore their robes; and as they walked down the paths they had made in deep snow they gawked at one another like little girls in bright new dresses and exclaimed over their garments and touched them softly with big calloused fingers. On either shoulder of the two was a forked stick, serving as a clothespin. Kayah's pins were about a foot long and stood up past her ears. These she also regarded as a part of her adornment.

When they were returning with wood, Mog's mantle fell off, and she stopped, crying with consternation. She picked up the pieces and shook snow off them and searched for the pins; but she was unable to dress herself alone. She could reach back across her shoulder easily enough but she was unable to draw both pieces of pelt into the cleft; and after watching her fumble and grow angry and bewildered, Kayah assisted. While Kayah fixed the pins, Mog stood very quietly, her large face softened by strange gentleness, her eyes tender and warm.

The men, meanwhile, after eating until they were sickened, were bringing the meat home. They had cut the beast into four parts. They would carry two of them a hundred yards and return for the other two. They did not dare leave any of it beyond sight because the jackals were on their trail. Both men were covered with blood. They did not carry a quarter upon their shoulders but clutched it with powerful arms and hugged it to their chest; and while they staggered with it through deep snow, they pressed their faces against meat and chewed flesh off and ate while they marched. When they had all of the deer in one pile, they would rest a few moments and eat while they rested. Some of the jackals were fighting over the head and intestines, but the weaker ones had been driven away and these followed the men.

It was nearly a mile to the cave, and the men spent the whole afternoon carrying the meat home. The burdens were light enough for men so strong, but they were both sick from overeating, and often they had to pause to bend over and ease the cramps in their bellies. After vomiting, they would eat again. All four quarters had holes gnawed in them where the men had pressed their strong teeth and torn off flesh and gulped it while they walked. Never before had they eaten tender fresh venison. Never, indeed, had they eaten meat of such delicious flavor; and they both acted as if they intended to devour all of it on their way home.

If the women had not been lost in vain admiration of themselves, they would have seen the men coming and would have gone to meet them. As it was, Harg staggered in and dropped a quarter of the deer on the cave floor, and a few moments later Gugg did likewise; and without speaking the men went back for the other quarters. The women were so astonished and pleased that at once they forgot their bear capes. Crying with delight, Kayah grasped a knife to cut off morsels for the children. The smell of the meat flooded her senses, and she began to drool, the slobber falling upon the quarter by which she knelt; and she was so overcome by hunger that the first piece she cut off she stuffed into her own mouth. The children now crawled over, sniffing the flesh; the other women also went down on hands and knees; and presently, like jackals, all five of them were feeding at the carcass. Finding the flesh very tender, Kayah laid her knife aside and used only her teeth. The children had no strong teeth to tear with, and so used their fingernails to dig at the meat. All three women, kneeling, with dirty hands clutching the carcass, buried their faces in the meat, lifting their heads now and then only to swallow. The sound of their ravenous eating murmured in the cave walls.

When the men came in with the other quarters, Harg shouted at the women; and they drew away, abashed, and looked at him, with blood and scraps of meat covering their faces from their hair to their chins. Harg was angered because the sight of them feeding made him hungry and he wanted to take the choicest parts for himself. He dropped his quarter, flesh side down, in the dirt, but after looking at it a moment, he rolled it over and tried to brush off the filth. Gugg also let his fall, making no effort to turn the hair side down.

The women and children began to feed again; and after vainly shouting at them Harg grasped the quarter he had just brought in and dragged it to a far wall, intending to possess it alone, in peace. He was sick from eating all afternoon, but the sound of the others made him imagine that he was hungry, and he began to eat. Observing what Harg did, Gugg took his quarter to the wall across from Harg and squatted by it. He wanted to eat, too, but he was full of nausea. His eyes looked stricken. His big mouth was open, with his chin resting in the hair on his breast. He gazed in turn from Harg and the women to the flesh by him, but he was fighting an urge to vomit and felt very unhappy. In his squatting position, his bloated belly was a great hairy bulge between his thighs. The matted hair on his skull, his chest, his arms and hands, was sticky with blood and offal. He was a greedy but also a

155

pathetic man who was afraid he would not get his share of the best food he had ever seen. Staring at the meat beside him, he moved toward it, but any change in his position aggravated his nausea, and so he sat very quietly like one awaiting disaster.

Meanwhile, the women and children, down on all fours like beasts, were trying to fill the void of weeks. Pressing their faces against the flesh, the women would sink strong teeth and then lift their heads a little to tear and bite off a mouthful. They chewed the meat only enough to swallow it. As soon as they had swallowed, chokingly, with strangled eyes, they would bury their faces again. The children tore off small morsels with their fingernails. After a while one of them moved over to its mother and clasped a long dug that hung like a brown pouch. While the mother ate, the child sucked her breasts dry and then returned to the meat.

Harg was slothful and sleepy and wanted to stretch out by the fire. When he perceived that the bear pelt had been cut into small pieces, he made such a dreadful uproar that the women rose to their feet, the children whimpered and crawled away, and Gugg slunk back into the darkness of the cavern. In turn Harg picked up one piece of bearskin after another and stared at them; and, still howling, but more with astonishment than rage now, he fell to his knees and laid the pieces out, side by side. If Kayah had not moved to possess her cape, Harg might have been content to lay the pieces together and make a bed of them. But Kayah snatched up two of them and was looking round her for the clothespins when Harg sprang up and struck a terrible blow. With the heel of a hand he smote her just below an ear and sent her reeling. She stumbled and sank to her haunches, almost knocked out; and with the fury of a crazed man, Harg leapt on her and struck her again and again in her face and on her ears and skull. He might have killed her if Mog had not screamed and loped round the cave, looking for the mantle she had worn.

Her screaming distracted Harg, and he turned to menace her; and when he saw her holding a piece of the bearskin, he wrested it from her grasp and at once dropped to his knees to lay all the pieces together and make his bed. Gugg slunk out of hiding to his quarter of meat and dragged it back into the darkness. Kayah squatted on her heels with her head bowed to her arms and rocked gently back and forth and moaned.

15

And so for this family the deep cold months of another winter passed. Most of the time they starved, but it was nevertheless the happiest winter they had ever known. The women fetched in the wood and the water, using a piece of deerskin as a vessel; and once in a while the men went out to hunt. When not busy with the few chores, they stirred little; they were content to warm themselves by the fire and sleep and wait for spring.

They had no form of art and no industry to keep them busy during daylight hours. If they had been more imaginative, the men might have sharpened or polished their weapons, and the women might have learned to sew and make garments of the pelts. They did not try again to adorn themselves with capes because Harg used the bear pelt to lie on. The fire was a precious thing, which they cherished, but it enhanced their natural laziness; and sometimes they would squat for hours, motionless in their cave, like creatures patiently waiting.

They were waiting. They were waiting for the snow

to go away, for the earth to become warm, for vegetation to grow again. They waited for the coming of night, though it was not quite the terrible thing it had been formerly. It was still dreadful, and they were afraid of it, but in their room the fire made daylight of darkness; and for them that was a wonderful thing. They were hunters but they were the hunted, too; fire repelled the enemies from which in all previous winters they had had to hide or flee. They felt more secure now; they relaxed and drowsed and looked out at the world.

Sometimes, when merely squatting and waiting, the gaze of two of them would meet. Perhaps Kayah and Harg looked at one another. They did not think of nor even feel a common fellowship and security, nor any emotion akin to affection. In Kayah's eyes was a question, and it asked why Harg did not go out and find food; and in Harg's eyes was a question, and it inquired if she was willing to be embraced. A woman always recognized and feared that look in a man's eyes. When Kayah saw that question in Harg's eyes, she would cry at him sharply, and Harg would then sulk and feel neglected. He might continue to squat and look in turn at the women or he might lie on his pieces of bearskin and sleep and dream terrible dreams. In most of his dreams he was the hunted, not the hunter; he was the one who fled for his life. When in a dream he was almost overtaken by a lion or a pack of wolves, he would utter a choked scream and sit up, instinctively reaching for his weapons. The dreams of all of them were haunted. Sometimes they would moan as if suffering agony in the grasp of a beast, but usually they would awake and sit up and tremble with anxiety before trying to sleep again. To none of Harg's people had come

159

the notion that they had a soul which wandered abroad while the body slept.

The two mothers devoted a part of the time to their children; and Memm, the stupidest adult of them all, and now far advanced in pregnancy, would watch them with dull eyes. Kayah and Mog would search their children for vermin or try to clean from their hairy little bodies the filth of their excrement. When they ate gluttonously, all these people suffered from diarrhea; and from the beginning they had used a corner of their room as a privy. Like cats they went to a spot accepted by all of them, but, unlike cats, they did not try to bury their offal. The smell of it was not offensive to them because they were used to the strong, unclean odors of their bodies.

Gugg was unhappy during this winter. Harg resented his presence as all men resented the presence of other males. He drove Gugg back from the fire and the women, and Gugg lived in the gloom of the corridor. There hour after hour the lonely fellow sat, looking out, his eyes desolate. When he emerged to go down the hill to drink or to find food, Harg would shout and threaten him; and then Gugg would slink past the fire and lope out to the snow. Upon returning, Gugg would stand outside and look in, and Harg would roar at him and tell him with gestures to go away. After Gugg had hastened back to the gloom but not beyond sight, Harg sometimes would squat on his heels and stare at the man and wonder whether he ought to attack him and drive him out. He suffered Gugg to remain only because he had been used to the man all his life.

Ordinarily, the strongest man in the family group drove the other men away, and the boys, too, as soon as they were old enough to mate; but if several boys of about the same age grew up together, hunted together, and became accustomed to one another's presence, then they might live in the same group a long time without fighting. Gugg, and the two men slain by the bear, had been such a group of brothers; but Harg, the son of Gugg, was younger and had not lived with brothers, and the time would come when he would drive his father out or kill him. He might have done so this winter if Gugg had not been content to live alone back in the gloom.

None of them had forgotten that Harg was a fire maker and monster killer, and they all lived in awe of him. No woman allowed a man to abuse her children or to embrace her when she was unreceptive; but aside from these two rights on which Kayah and Mog stood, Harg was the lord of the group and the home. He seized the best of the food. He used the pieces of bearskin as a bed and shared his bed with no one. He took his choice of positions by the fire or elsewhere in the room; and when Kayah came with a deerskin holding water, he always drank first. He was an arrogant and tyrannical man, but he was also a great genius and one who might have been destined among a more intelligent people to be honored in folklore as a patriarch or a god.

It cannot be said that this family was consciously waiting for spring; they had too little sense of the future for that. They had not learned that cold times and warm times came in regular cycles. If they had learned that much, they might have made preparations against the coming of winter. But they had learned to expect change and they expected the change always to be for the better. This was the beginning in them of that hope—too seldom supported by a reasonable expectancy—which is one of the most constant emotions in human beings. If the weather was too cold, they expected warmth; if it was too hot, they expected coolness. It cannot be said that Harg's people hoped for these things, because hope looks into the future; they merely expected them as they expected darkness after light or light after dark.

If they had had only a week or two of cold and snow, and then a warm, bare earth, they would not have been surprised; nor would they have been surprised if they had sat in their cave two or three years waiting for spring. Having almost no sense of time, they waited with the sort of patience that the timeless always have. When the storm broke away and the sky cleared and delightful warmth filled the air, they would rush outside, thinking the change had come; and when the sky darkened and snow fell again, they would return to their room and squat and look out.

And when spring came at last, they were deeply happy in the way of children. They loved the spring as they loved themselves or the fire, but they felt no worship for it. There was no impulse to celebrate its coming or to frolic with delight in the full image of the sun. This change meant that the snow would disappear and again they could walk on bare earth. It meant that food would be more abundant. That was all. They did not set stakes to measure the vanishing of the snow or look at trees to see if they were budding; and when they saw more birds around them, their presence was not a sign of spring but only the return of food. They were eager but not impatient. Life for them, as for all things which they observed, was a constant and patient struggle at the lowly level of hiding from enemies and getting enough to eat.

Life had never been kind enough to them to allow the luxury of impatience to develop; and so they squatted, day after day, and waited for the snow to melt. When again they could walk on bare earth, their robust frames had lost many pounds and their faces were sunken.

As soon as the earth was bare in patches, Harg took his weapons and went forth, determined to fill his stomach with good things. He followed a south slope, and when he came to a ridge and looked across a north slope, he saw deep snow there; and so he turned back to the sunny side and descended to a stream. Along water routes the earth was bare, and he could hunt for mice and other small creatures; or he might surprise a muskrat or a snake or a wading bird. In his eagerness, impelled by hunger and the joy of the chase over bare ground, he went farther down the stream than he had ever gone before; and when he sensed that the area around him was unfamiliar, he became frightened. He left the stream and climbed to a hill to look round him. On the hill was a patch of snow, and in the snow were human footprints.

Harg could not have been more apprehensive if he had seen the tracks of a lion. These prints had been made by a man running, and they were far apart—so far, indeed, that Harg had to take three steps between any two of them. Curious and amazed, he knelt to examine a track. It had been made by a huge foot. He wondered what kind of man could take such strides; because, to cover the distance between two of them, he would have had to run at full speed and leap. When he stepped in a track or made a print beside it he was amazed by the difference in size. Some man had crossed here only a little while ago who had feet which were enormous in comparison with

163

Harg's, and who took strides in running that made his own look like those of a child.

Harg was afraid. He felt an impulse to flee homeward but he was curious; he followed the tracks across snow, across wet earth, and down the hill. At the foot of the hill he entered a grove of trees and felt safer; but he still moved with extreme caution, ready at a moment's warning to strike or to drop his weapons and climb a tree. The man had gone through the woods. Harg followed the tracks until he came to the edge of the grove, and then, hiding behind a tree, he looked out.

What he saw in the clearing ahead was so astounding that it confused and darkened his senses. He saw first a deer that seemed to be wounded; it was running, but not with its usual speed, and in its flank something stuck and traveled with it that Harg thought was a stick. In the next moment he saw the strange man. He looked like a prodigious giant and he was running much faster than Harg had ever seen a human being run. He was running to head off the deer from another grove of trees; and while Harg watched, with his eyes bulging, the man outstripped the deer and raced ahead of it. Then the deer swung and turned back toward Harg, and the man suddenly dropped to his knees and did something with a strange thing in his hands. From his hands a stick leapt, and in the next instant Harg saw the deer stumble and fall. The man rose and bore down upon the deer with amazing speed. He seized the deer's head and wrenched it backward, and the deer lay quietly on the ground. Beside it stood a man who seemed almost as tall as the trees.

With the sweat of terror on him Harg slunk back into the woods. He crawled into a thicket to hide and, squatting there, and shaking all over, he strove to think of the matter. This strange man had outrun a deer, and that in itself was an unbelievable thing. He had somehow killed it by hurling a stick from a considerable distance, and that was more incredible still. And he was an enormous man who stood erect with his head set back on his shoulders and his legs as straight as trees.

Harg's terror had made him sick, and while squatting he emptied his bowels. Then, as noiseless as a snake, he crawled out of his hiding place and slunk away through the densest timber he could find. He wanted to creep to the edge of the thicket and spy on the man and learn what he was doing now; and for a moment he paused and considered it but he was afraid. He took the opposite direction and headed for home. When he was safely beyond the man's hearing he began to run, and a few minutes later, covered with sweat and babbling with astonishment and terror, he entered the cave.

PART TWO

I

THE tall stranger from whom Harg fled belonged to a magnificent race whose people were the Greeks of their time. In height the average of the men stood above six feet, and the one whom Harg saw was almost six inches taller than the average. Their legs were long and lithe and straight because for centuries they had been a hunting people; their backs were straight, too, and their heads were erect on their spines.

In their faces as well as their bodies they were extraordinarily handsome. The most distinctive feature of their faces was its breadth in comparison with its height, but the unusual breadth gave it an aspect of strength because of the full brow, the straight nose, and the strong jaws and chin. Their eyes were large and intelligent. Their cheekbones were broad and high.

In comparison with Harg's people or with any other people of their time they had a remarkably large brain. Indeed, the brain of the average woman was larger than that of the average man of today. They were intelligent, but—because they had so little knowledge—they were also very primitive, though in their industries and social life they had advanced far beyond all other races.

For many generations they had used fire. Before learning to make fire, they had been, like all other peoples, the prey of large flesh-eating beasts, more hunted than hunter; but use of fire had given them security and boldness and a livelier interest in the world around them. Living within its protection, and no longer forced at any hour of the day or night to fight or flee, they had been able to turn their minds to many things—to the improvement of their weapons, their homes, and their personal appearance. Long ago they had, like Harg's people, used only stone axes and knives; later they had sharpened these to make them more deadly; and later still they had polished them. They had invented the lance and the spear; by accident they had discovered the boomerang; and both by accident and simple persistent thinking they had put together the green branch, the thong, and the lance to make the bow and arrow.

The women, too, had been ingenious. They had learned to sew. At first they had used a sharp splinter of stone or wood to make holes in a pelt and had run a slender vine through the holes to lace two pelts together. When one of them was making a hole and accidentally pulled the vine through it because the vine was caught by the rough head of the stone splinter, she discovered the needle. The women also learned to cut laces from a skin to use as thread, to use skins as vessels for the carrying of water, to keep a fire alive by banking it with ashes, to gather nuts and vegetables and store them, to strip flesh from bones and dry it, and to make crude garments to wear during the severe winters.

The men loved colors, and especially the strong bright ones. Both the men and women, but especially the men, loved personal adornment. They not only polished and carved and sometimes painted their weapons; they also adorned their bodies with dyes and flowers and shining trinkets, because in every one of them was a wish to attract admiring attention. With natural dyes they smeared their faces and sometimes parts of their bodies; they wore necklaces of stones and sticks and shells; they made ornaments, often carved, of staghorn or ivory to wear in their long hair; and some, with livelier fancy, who despaired of colors that wore off easily or were washed off by rain, tried, by puncturing their skin with a stone needle, to saturate a part of their body with red and green dyes. They had not yet learned tattooing but eventually would, because the wish in them to be different, to be set apart in enviable beauty or distinction, was one of their strongest desires.

In their language they were far in advance of Harg's people. When communicating with one another they still depended largely on gesture and exclamation; but of the words they used, some contained two or more concepts. To say, "An enemy goes there," Harg would have said "enemy" and pointed; but these people expressed the noun, verb, and adverb all in one word. This word said, "Enemy-goes-there." And so it was with all their more complex ideas. Enemy was one word when used singly; but "Enemy-goes-there" was also one word without any division between the syllables. They had words for many,

171

but by no means all, of the things which interested them, including objects and modes of action; but they had no purely abstract terms. They were touched emotionally by certain aspects of their world which were not concrete and visible, but these aspects they had not formulated in concepts.

The men, for instance, had no word for soul, though their dreams had led them to believe that a part of them sometimes left their bed at night to go abroad and hunt. This was, of course, a very mysterious thing for them; and though they thought about it and tried to understand it, they were completely baffled. Upon awaking suddenly from a dream, they would sit up quickly and peer into the night and listen in an effort to see or hear the part of them that had been wandering during the hours of sleep.

They had a word which meant bright or shining, translated here as "gode." It was their word for fire and the sun; but also, for the women who lived with him, it was the name of the tall man whom Harg had seen kill a deer. Long after the first member of their race had learned to make fire, these people had evolved a word for fire and associated the word with the fire makers. The two, in a way, became the same symbol. Fire was a shining thing, but in such folklore as they had the fire maker was a shining thing also. In his group he was the shining one, the gode. The man whom Harg spied on was not the keeper of fire but he was the one who made fire when, by any misfortune, it was allowed to die. Gode's people did not understand paternity or the relationship between father and son; and much less, at this time, did they trace the origin of a shining one back to the first shining symbol. The word for them did not mean god at all except in the sense of a natural leader whom they had endowed with a shining quality.

There was a tendency in them, as there was not in Harg's people, or at least only weakly, to identify objects with themselves, and especially objects which they admired. Obscurely in the emotional attitude of his women toward him, Gode was identified with fire and the sun because he had the power of these things. If, among these people, a man had been a remarkably bold and savage fighter, they might have called him by their word for lion; or if they had held him in contempt because of his craven behavior, they might have called him by their word for jackal. In Gode's family group, the grandmother—the boss of the other women and all the children, and of such industries as making garments, storing food, and keeping the fire—was called Marigg. For them this word meant the ruler of the family group, the queen, the female guardian and tutor.

Only a very few in any group were identified by names —only the ablest and most important, only those invested with some special quality or function. One of Gode's women, Agger, and his favorite, Memmee, were nameless for those who lived with them; and so were the children. If Memmee had been a genius in discovering and mixing dyes, she might have been known by their word for color. A person took his name from things around him for which he seemed to have a natural affinity; and if he were only mediocre in his talents he went nameless. Marigg was also their word for the she-beast, the wolf bitch or the lioness, who guarded the young.

Between the family relationships of these people and Harg's there were considerable differences. Gode's people were more intelligent and therefore much more vain—or at least their vanity was more definitely expressed in sentiments and attitudes. Harg allowed other men to live with his women; Gode did not. Gode's family, like his weapons and articles of adornment, was his property and belonged solely to him. If another adult male had tried to move in, he would have killed him. When a son came to manhood, the father drove him out, or the son drove the father out, depending on which was stronger. Harg was jealous, but he did not have the watchful and tyrannical jealousy of a Gode. Kayah was a kind of queen in her group but not the domineering tyrant that Marigg was. Among Gode's people the offices and duties in family life were more fixed; there was more moral law, and, because of it, there was more repression of the rights of the weaker members. Marigg, for instance, was the keeper of the fire, and she allowed no interference with this duty and privilege.

These people identified themselves not only with certain objects in the world around them but also with duties and rights. These became an extension of their meaning and their self-esteem. A woman was willing to labor like a slave if she became thereby a person of distinction and envy; and a man, hunting with other men, was willing sometimes to take the most foolhardy risks to arouse the admiration of his companions. In their eagerness to be envied and admired, life for all of them was savagely competitive. And life was much more serious for them, too, than it was for Harg's people, because seriousness comes from accumulated foresight. Life was more dreadful because they had a stronger sense of the unknown, and the power of an idea depends not on its validity but on its vividness. And they had, of course, more conscience, though not because of a sense of sin, of which they had none. Conscience originated not as self-reproach but as fear.

Though each man lived alone with his women and their children, the men sometimes hunted together; they had learned that by going in packs, like the wolves, they were more successful. During the many generations while they had been migrating from the far south to northern lands, these people had killed and eaten chiefly the wild horse, a creature whose only defense was its speed. They had snared it in pits, trapped it in blind canyons, and stampeded it over ledges. But they had eaten deer, too, or the mammoth and rhinoceros, the bear and wolf, as well as many kinds of fish and birds. They mixed their flesh diet with fruits, vegetables, and nuts, all of which the women gathered and stored for the winter. Unlike Harg's people they seldom went hungry; they did not starve for days or weeks and then feed so gluttonously that they became sick. For centuries they had eaten a well-rounded diet and because of it had grown tall and strong; and each generation had added a little to their knowledge and intelligence.

They had no religion, but some of their emotions were almost religious. They were awed by many things, and toward some things, like their home fire or the warmth-giving sun, their attitude was touched by reverence. The sun, moon, and stars baffled them because without support they seemed to float in space; but they had come to no notion of supernatural beings or of a life after death. Their dead they hid away in mountain clefts, not because they thought their malevolent spirits would rise to haunt and plague them, but only to hide the corpses from man-eating beasts. Because of their strong sense of property rights, they often buried with the dead the tools and ornaments and garments which they had made and used in life.

These people had become superstitious of blood, and their superstition was growing. More than anything else it was a symbol of life, because when a creature was wounded the blood ran out of it and it died. They had decided that a baby came from the menstrual blood of its mother. No woman gave birth until after her menstrual periods had begun, and she did not lose blood after the child in her had begun to grow. They did not know that sexual mating was necessary to birth or that the male served any function at all. They thought birth was the mysterious privilege and power of women; and toward women, therefore, the men had strong feelings of reverence and awe. In the women, too, there was the beginning of a strange attitude toward the menstrual discharge. Believing that babies were formed by it, they came inevitably to feel that a discharge was a waste of life; and there had developed a tendency, in both sexes, to shun any woman who spent her precious substance in one menstrual cycle after another and never gave birth. Toward these barren women they felt resentful and unfriendly. Even one who had become a mother was sometimes ostracized during her menses and forced to move back from the family and live by herself until she was well again. They had not come to the notion that waste of the life fluid was a sin in women; they thought only that it was sickness of some kind and they distrusted her because the production of life was for them, as it was for all the beasts around them, the chief meaning of their existence.

Formerly men had drunk blood because they liked it; Gode and the men of his race now also drank it because they thought it was the substance of life. When they drank it as it gushed warm and red from a beast they believed that they enriched and added to their own well-being. They had also pondered other qualities in life. The horse was a fleet animal, and by eating so much of it they thought they became swifter in the chase. They felt the same way about the deer. Beasts that were savage they also eagerly devoured, hoping to add to themselves the enviable qualities of the thing eaten. For the sluggish and the dull-witted, on the other hand, they had begun to develop distaste. They would eat the lithe and cunning snake but not the stupid owl, the fleet hare but not the awkward porcupine. Many generations ago they had eaten anything they could kill, but prolonged reflection on the qualities which they admired and coveted had led them to a discriminating choice of food.

This was true of the men but not of the women. The women did not strive for fleetness and ferocity and courage. They gave themselves to the home and the children, and they never joined the hunt except in lean seasons when driven to it. They did not share the man's childlike and avid love of red. As the cradles and guardians of life they would have preferred green, because it was the color of most growing things and of the seasons when life was most secure; or they might have chosen blue because it was the sky-hearth of the sun and the sun was the most constant of all fires. But the men loved strong colors, and when they painted their faces they chose bright red and used other colors chiefly for contrast.

In eating the enviable qualities of the beasts they killed, Gode and the men of his race believed that they became more unconquerable, and because of this belief they became bolder. There were animals which they stood in fear of—the lion, the tiger, the boar, and wolves when these traveled in packs—but they did not live in constant stealth and terror like the men of Harg's people. Though they sometimes hunted together, they more frequently went alone, ranging for miles and using as weapons the bow and arrow and the lance. With both they had great skill. A man like Gode, standing six and a half feet in height and weighing two hundred and fifty pounds, could, at twenty yards, hurl a lance almost through the body of a deer. His bow of yew had a spread of six feet; its string was a horsehide thong softened by urine, and the arrows were of ash fitted with sharp flintheads. At fifty yards he could drive an arrow into a beast, clear to the hilt. And in moments when weapons failed him he could run with amazing speed or climb a tree with the agility of a cat.

But he seldom had to flee from an enemy, because he never attacked unless convinced that he could kill. The lion and the boar he did not hunt when alone because of their ferocity; nor the mammoth and rhinoceros, because of the thickness of their hides; nor the wolves, because of their number and their cunning. Of all beasts he was most afraid of the wolf because it had a courage that only fire could daunt. Of them all, this was the killer he most admired.

2

ON THE day when Harg spied on him and saw him kill the deer, Gode was hunting alone. He had taken with him both his bow and his lance, but when he jumped the beast he had leaned his lance against a tree and had set off in pursuit. After breaking the deer's neck and drawing the two arrows out and drinking blood from the wounds, he tossed the carcass across his right shoulder and headed for home. He had not forgotten his lance. While carrying his burden he looked for it, but he had chased the deer a half-mile or more and was now confused. Hanging the carcass across the limb of a tree, he found his tracks and followed them to the lance; and upon returning to his meat, he heard the snarl of a beast. Suspecting that some animal was stalking his game, he went softly on bare feet, with bow and arrows in one hand, the lance in the other. He entered a juniper thicket, where he had hung the deer, and advanced warily from tree to tree.

The beast was a she-wolf with a pup about a third grown. The bitch had yanked the carcass from the tree, and the pup was feeding, but the mother was waiting for the return of a man whose scent was all around her. When Gode peered through a clump of juniper, the wolf saw him and crouched and bared her fangs.

For several moments Gode considered the matter. The brush between him and the wolf was too dense to shoot an arrow through, and so he moved slowly to one side, maneuvering for position. But before he could reach a clearing and fit an arrow to his bow, the wolf charged. She came with such a swift and determined rush that Gode dropped his bow and arrows and grasped his lance with both hands; and he barely had time to brace himself, with his right foot back from his left, his right hand on the heel of the shaft, and his left poising the lance and ready to guide it. In the next instant the wolf was almost on him. Calmly, without a tremor of fear in his big frame, Gode struck at her open mouth with the lance point, and at the same moment his right hand swung down with all the power of his great shoulders behind it. He drove the lance down her throat, through her stomach, through her guts, and impaled her to the earth. In the instant after driving the lance home, he leapt back from her claws and then leaned forward with only his right hand grasping the lance. Her bared talons raked the staff, but she was helpless. Realizing that his lance had gone through her body and impaled her, Gode kept his body and legs back from her claws, his right hand holding the heel of the spear, and waited for her to die. The pup had stopped eating and was watching him. Gode looked round him, thinking that other wolves might be near; and he marked the spot where his bow and arrows lay, and the distance to them.

When the wolf was dead he drew the lance out and knelt to drink blood. Then he took the staff in both hands and moved it back and forth across his mouth, licking off the blood, his gaze fixed on the pup meanwhile and his ears alert. He decided to take the wolf home and eat her flesh and add to himself her boldness and courage; but he could not carry both the wolf and the deer. This matter he considered while licking the blood off the lance.

He decided to carry the deer part way home and return for the wolf, and when he approached the deer he poised his lance to strike if the pup should attack. But the pup ran away and turned and looked at him. It did not bare its teeth or show any will to fight, but seemed, on the contrary, to be curious and afraid and a little friendly. Gode thought of shooting it or of trying to run it down with the lance, but when he went toward it, the pup ran away and again turned to look at him. Gode threw the carcass of the deer across his back and turned toward home.

The cave where his family lived was a considerable distance away and high in the south wall of a mountain. He carried the deer several hundred yards and laid it across two branches at the height of his head; and when he returned for the wolf he ran with enormous strides, lithe and graceful, like one born to the chase. He found the pup with its dead mother, but it ran when he approached and turned to squat on its belly. The wolf was heavier than the deer; it weighed about a hundred and sixty pounds. But it was no burden for this man. Easily he slung it across his broad back, took his weapons in one hand, grasped a hind leg with the other, and set off.

Not until he came to the deer did he realize that the

pup had followed him. When he dropped the wolf and turned to look back, he saw the pup a hundred yards away; and now, as before, it sank to its belly and watched him. Gode hardly knew what to make of that because never before had he killed a bitch with a pup. While he stared at it thoughtfully, wondering whether to kill it or drive it away, he felt a little disturbed. His emotion was not one of affectionate interest, because in men of this time there was no love—no love for anything save themselves and their property that was a part of them. It was not pity, because they never felt pity. Perhaps it was only a momentary friendliness; or perhaps obscurely in his dark mind Gode realized that the pup wanted and needed its mother as the human child needed its mother. Whatever it was, Gode felt no wish to kill the creature. He looked at it for several minutes, wondering why it followed; and then he picked up the deer and his weapons and covered another lap on his journey home. When he returned to the wolf he brought with him only the lance.

The pup followed him again and was following on the third lap when Gode met a man whom he knew and with whom he had hunted.

"Enemy-look!" cried the man, and pointed at the pup. He was fitting an arrow to his bow when Gode stopped him.

"No," he said. "No-kill."

"No-kill?" asked the astonished man. "Kill-enemy. Food."

"No." There were things Gode wanted to say for which he had no words. He wanted to say that the pup was following its mother and thought she was still alive; that it was still young and needed its mother; that it had shown no will to fight. But such thoughts were too complex for the words these men used and understood. Pointing at the dead wolf, Gode said, "Mother." The word his people used for mother meant much more than the physical relationship; it meant also guardian, the one who nursed and cared for them, as well as the one who had mysterious power over birth.

"Dead," said the man.

"Mother," said Gode, and turned the bitch over to show the dugs on her belly.

"Food," said the man, indicating the pup.

"No-kill," said Gode.

Between men there was fear or admiration or envy but never affection or friendship. This man was now angered; Gode had food and he had none, but back there was a wolf pup, lying on its belly and looking at him, and he wanted to kill it. He was angry, but like all men in the presence of Gode he was afraid. "Hungry," he said, and pointed at his mouth. "Kill-food."

There came to Gode a notion that was not quite like any that had come to him before. Certain things were his, things like his weapons, his ornaments, his women; but never had he thought of claiming a wild beast that was alive. He thought of it now.

"Mine," he said. "Enemy-mine." He pointed at the pup.

For the man this was an astonishing thing to say. The live beasts, like any other food, belonged to the man who first possessed them. Gode did not possess the pup; it was back there, alive, able to run away, and it was the property of the man who could kill and seize it.

"No," he said, stubbornly, angrily, and moved to fit an arrow to his bow.

183

Gode raised his lance to menace him. "No-kill!" he roared, and his voice was so threatening that the man withdrew, abashed. "Look," said Gode, and with gestures, and words, and drawings made on the earth with his feet, he explained to the man that he was to follow at a discreet distance and observe what happened. Then Gode tossed the wolf across his back, turned to the pup and cried, "Come!" and set off for home.

When the man saw the pup follow, as if answering the call, he was too amazed to shoot, even if he had been bold enough to risk Gode's anger. Never had he seen, never had any other man seen, a wolf pup following a hunter home. He understood now that the creature actually did belong to Gode but he had no notion of the mysterious power by which Gode was able to make a wild thing follow him. He was so overcome by amazement and awe that he began to sweat. Gode, he had known, was a great one and a mighty hunter, a fearless one of more than human prowess, but he had never seen in him the magic that drew humble wolves to his trail. Overwhelmed by awe and fear he slunk away, and Gode never saw him again.

The home of Gode's family, like that of Harg's, was a big chamber in the face of a mountain, overhung by a sheltering ledge. Into it Gode marched and threw down the deer. The women came forward, not to kneel and eat gluttonously, as Harg's women would have done, but only to see what their man had brought. When they saw a young, fat deer, their guttural murmuring was of happiness and approval. Agger and Memmee stood back, humble and self-effacing, while Marigg, the tyrannical grandmother, grasped the carcass with big powerful hands and turned it over. When she saw the hole which the wolf had chewed in the belly, she exclaimed with displeasure; she thought Gode had found a dead beast and she did not like putrid meat. She sniffed at the open belly and looked up at him.

"Enemy-eat," said Gode. "Enemy-there." He pointed down the mountain. Marigg's grunt was the equivalent of an "Oh." Gode set his bow and arrows by a rock wall and, taking his lance, went back for the wolf. When he was coming up the hill with it, the women saw the pup trailing and ran out to meet him, screaming and pointing. They thought he was unaware of the pup. Gode dropped the wolf carcass and looked back down the hill; and the women came up, still screaming and pointing.

"Kill-enemy!" Marigg cried.

Gode's response was almost a shrug. "No," he said.

"Enemy!" said Marigg.

"No," said Gode.

The pup, as before, lay on its belly, chin on its paws, ears pointed forward, and looked at them. When the women saw that Gode had a bitch wolf, they knew that the pup was the wolf's child but they felt no friendliness for it. It was an enemy that might slay their own children, and they wanted it killed.

Though Marigg was queen of the women, Memmee was Gode's favorite. She was his sister, but he knew nothing of such relationships and thought of her only as his woman. Almost six feet tall, and stronger than some men of her race, she was a handsome person, with long straight legs, a strong and almost hairless face, and intelligent eyes. In turn she now looked at her man and the pup and asked:

"No-kill?"

"No-kill," said Gode.

"Friend?" asked Memmee.

Gode had not thought of the creature as a friend, but now, while looking down at the pup and reflecting, it seemed to him that it was friendly. With a toe he thrust at the wolf carcass and said: "Enemy-mother."

The women realized that the dead creature was the pup's mother, but they hardly knew what to make of Gode's statement. Gode tried to explain that the young one needed its mother, but that hardly made sense either, inasmuch as the mother was dead. Nor did it make much sense for Gode. The emotion in him was so confused and strange that he could not have told why he had allowed the pup to follow him home. Possibly it was because of his loneliness. Affection a man did not feel and could not have understood and therefore did not seek, but he did want attention. He felt himself to be the center of the world and the most meaningful thing in it; and the attention of others, especially if humble and devoted, enhanced his sense of well-being. Though Gode knew that the pup was following its mother, he liked to feel that it was also following him—that it recognized in him a superior one and wished to be near him. Such a notion flattered and pleased him. Besides, the wolf was afraid of him, and that pleased him, too.

That was a part but not all of his attitude. During his many hours at home he had observed that the children gave all their attention to the women or to one another. Jealousy is a feeling of neglect, and Gode had felt jealous and neglected. He had wanted the children to feel need of him, to recognize their protector in him, to be conscious of him as a great one who made fire and brought food to them and drove enemies away. He felt—his vanity

186

found it easy to believe—that the pup perceived in him such qualities. For two miles the creature had slunk along, humble and fearful, with its gaze constantly upon him. It was looking at him now. He was pleased and he did not intend to kill it.

Slinging the carcass across his back he went up the hill, with the women at his side, and laid the wolf on the cave floor by the deer. At once the women became excited and alarmed. When the pup could no longer see its mother, it came close to the cave and looked in, though at once it ran away and squatted about thirty yards distant and looked at the people and the fire. For several minutes, with the lance resting between his feet and both hands clasping the staff, Gode stood motionless and gazed at the pup. When at last he moved toward it, the pup ran away and out of sight, but it soon returned. For the women it was an enemy, and they wanted Gode to kill it; but the more persistent they were in demanding its death, the more determined Gode was to protect it and claim it. Again and again he went out, hoping to get near the pup, but it always ran into hiding and came in sight only after Gode had entered the cave.

After a while the women forgot about it. Marigg had meat to take care of and children to feed, and after skinning the deer with a stone knife, she cut open the belly and gave pieces of the tender organs to the young ones. Memmee and Agger would have helped, but Marigg wanted no help. A woman's sense of her worth was found in the work she did and in the dependence on her of others. For the queen of a family it was a jealously guarded right to labor while others stood idly by.

After she had fed the children, Marigg gave portions of

187

flesh to the women and to Gode. They ate what she gave them, and none would have dared to ask for more or for choicer pieces; but neither did Marigg take the choicest parts for herself. She gave the best to the children and she shared the remainder impartially.

Gode refused his venison. Dragging the wolf to one side of the cave, he skinned it, opened the belly, and thrust in an arm to pull out the heart. This he ate with great relish, believing that he was adding to himself the boldness of the wolf. Marigg had never eaten wolf meat. She came over and cut off a small piece of thigh and slowly ate it, her old eyes blinking solemnly. If it was good food she intended to use it, and if it was not she would throw it out. Her man was such an able hunter that she had become almost fastidious in her taste for food and refused to accept anything that seemed to her inferior. This flesh, she decided, was all right, and to Gode she said:

"Food-good."

"Food-good," he said, and tore the lungs from their moorings.

Marigg knelt to examine the wolf pelt and was pleased with it; the fur was deep and thick and would make warm garments. When Gode tore the liver out and began to eat it, she cried angrily and took it from his grasp. She carried it over and laid it inside the body of the deer. In her home the children always ate the livers. Gode sat by the wolf carcass and looked like an offended man but he was not offended. Certain traditions had been established among his people, and these had the force of ancient and unalterable law. He pulled out the kidneys and took them over to Marigg and then cut off a piece of thigh and stood up to eat it and, while eating, he looked out and saw the pup. He had forgotten it. When his gaze fell on it again, he was so deeply moved that he went outside and sat on a stone; and for a long while he sat there and looked at the pup, and the pup looked at him.

3

THE big chamber in which they lived was the mouth of a
cave from which in the previous autumn they had driven
its wild tenants. It was larger than the one occupied by
Harg's family and more comfortable. On the wall deep
within, the limestone was terraced in shelves on which
Marigg stored provisions. On one she had spread nuts to
dry and ripen; on the next one below were the water vessels—a natural stone urn, which she had found in their
wanderings, and two pouches made of horsehide. The
pouches had been taken from the legs. Instead of cutting
the hide down the leg she had skinned round the leg and
had drawn out the flesh and bone. The lower and smaller
part of the skin, she had doubled back and up; and using a
green vine as a rim, she had sewed the skin around the
vine and so had vessels that were watertight and easy to
handle. The horsehide she had softened with urine.

On a third shelf, recessed deep in a corner, she stored
their meat; and she always stacked the larger bones against
a wall, because these they broke open for the marrow

190

of which they were fond. There was a fourth shelf on which the other women laid their needles and thongs and unfinished garments.

Their clothes, very simply fashioned, they wore only in coldest weather. They made capes by sewing pieces of hide together, with a hole through which the head was thrust, allowing one piece, with the hair side in, to fall down the front and the other to hang down the back. They also made garments which were suspended from girdles at the waist, and aprons which the women usually wore during their menses.

There was in them no sense of shame or modesty or coyness. They had devised clothes chiefly to protect them from cold, though they had learned that their tough garments also protected them against thorns and briars when they moved through wooded areas. At this time they made little use of clothes as adornment. At least the women did not do so; Gode had a huge bearskin cape which he wore sometimes because it made him feel more kingly. But he never wore it while hunting; it was a nuisance then that impeded his movements and made him feel slow and awkward.

For the more intelligent and sensitive families the wearing of the menstrual apron had become a custom. They resented a woman in her menses because they felt she was unnatural; that, for mysterious reasons, she wasted the precious blood that made young life; that she was a threat to their survival, which, for them, as for all other creatures, was assured by the birth of young ones. The apron was devised to hide all evidence of the woman's squandering of life. The offending one wore it during her menses and then laid it aside. Though for several generations the apron had served this purpose and had been invented for no other reason, their superstition in the matter had not impelled them to establish taboos. She was not driven out of sight to be alone during this time; they had no notion that she was sinful and guilty. Their attitude toward her was one of distress and bewilderment; and like people today they strove to hide from sight and to put out of mind all the inexplicable things that seemed to threaten their survival.

The wall to the left, facing in, was a great perpendicular slab almost as smooth as polished stone. Gode had used it during the past winter as a canvas for his art. He had drawn there, sometimes with charcoal, sometimes with dyes, the likeness of the horse, the mammoth, the rhinoceros, and the wolf; and in black manganese he had the image of a boar, and in red ochre a fine drawing of the antlers of a stag. Now and then with sharp flint he carved the outlines before using paints, but for the most part he used freehand drawing. When an image did not please him, he erased it, using a torch to burn the paint and then rubbing over the surface with a handful of earth.

In men, much more than in women, there was a deep and inherited urge to alter their environment and make it conform more nearly to their sense of their own meaning. There was also a constant wish to find extensions of themselves and their power. These two urges impelled them to the lowly beginnings of art. When Gode drew a likeness that seemed to him unusually good he would dance with excitement and demand the attention of the women. "Look!" he would shout at them; and if they stared as though fascinated he would be deeply pleased, but if they ignored his work he would fall into a rage.

He drew those animals he most admired and envied. As in drinking their blood and eating their hearts he thought he partook of their qualities, so in setting their likeness on stone he was trying to master and assimilate them. He was extending himself into the world and enveloping, by becoming intimate with them, the qualities he wished to have in great measure. He was altering his environment by bringing the beasts, obedient and subject to his will, into his home. In fancy he was enlarging his view, exploring his hidden powers, and identifying himself in a kind of fellowship with all the things he held in esteem.

He did not, of course, think of it that way. He was a child in his devotion to art; and like any child he was trying to explore and enlarge and enrich the world around him. He not only painted on the wall; he also carved the likeness of animals on his weapons. He had a staghorn lance and a bone knife, and these he had covered with the images of a lion and a wolf. His weapons were a part of him; they were merely extensions of his arms and his strength. In carving on them the likenesses of his more unconquerable enemies, he felt that he was gaining some power over them. It was simple magic that had not yet been fixed in ritual.

The women had little interest in his art. Their way of life was more egoistically ingrown because they delivered a part of themselves into children. They found their extension in their own flesh and blood. They projected themselves into things that came from their bodies and nursed at their breasts; but a man, without any knowledge that he participated in birth, turned to his weapons and his art. A woman's art was her children, and for her that was enough. She had the burden of motherhood, and her mental horizon was drawn in to the circumference of her home. A man, freed from such duties, and lacking the deep egoistic joy of giving birth, turned to the world around him and sought there the larger meaning with which the woman was already endowed. Home was the woman's lodestar; a man's lodestar was the world.

And so it came to be that the man was more lonely and alone. All day and all night, month after month and year after year, the women and children were together in a small world that was theirs, and that was filled with its duties and meanings and industry. The man was the hunter who went alone to find food. For the women, he was useful, but not—so far as they could have told—wholly necessary in any respect. So far as they knew, he had nothing to do with the miracle of birth; on the contrary, he was a hungry pest who often wished to mate with them when they had no desire to mate. It was inevitable, therefore, that the more intelligent and sensitive man should have come to feel rather neglected and shut out; and because he felt something akin to misgivings in regard to his function in life, he turned to art and adornment. In a way his art was an attempt to give birth to something; but because he had no natural urge to give birth to children, and could not have had any wish to, he turned to abstract qualities. And in wearing necklaces of bright stones and shells and staghorn, and in painting his face, he was trying to make of himself a person whom life could not ignore. He was trying not so much to be attractive to the females as to be attractive to life, to be an object of worth and meaning.

It was in homes where there was a queen like Marigg,

a grandmother who ordered the routine of living, crushing the unessential and giving life and light to duties and chores—it was in such homes that the men were driven to self-development. In homes without a strong-willed woman, where the mode of living was haphazard and undirected, there was no art on the walls, no delicate carvings on staghorn. Without being aware of it, then, Gode was a fortunate man. He was driven out of his natural laziness to build for himself, if he could, such a world as would enhance his own meaning. His mind was forced to catch light from his own unhappiness and to look round him for ways by which he could alter his environment and make it flower with his needs.

But tonight he did not feel that way at all. After storing the meat and covering it with skins, after gathering wood and building up the fire, and after laying the children on pelts to sleep, the women turned to other labors. The wolfskin they liked because of its deep fur, and they intended to make a garment of it. First they had to soften it, and in turn they urinated in the big stone vessel and then with strong hands worked the urine into the skin.

For a little while Gode sat back and watched them. There were interests to which he might have turned, but he was unhappy and restless. He was erotically hungry but he had learned not to interrupt women while they were busy with a task. It had been different a few years ago. Then, as a young giant entering manhood, he had driven his father out and taken over the family. Because his sisters, Agger and Memmee, were not old enough to embrace, his mother had become his woman. He had been the boss, and for a while they had been afraid of him. But as Marigg became older, and barren, she also became set in her ways, and little by little she took over the management of things and her will became law.

Gode was not looking back and remembering all that. He was thinking only of the present and of his unhappiness; and soon he rose and went to the shelf where he kept his paints and ornaments. He had a handsome necklace of horsehide lace on which he had threaded bright stones, bits of amber, shells, pieces of staghorn, and large seeds. Some of the pieces, including the seeds, he had painted, but most of them wore their natural colors. He now hung the necklace round his neck. He had no mirror here. In former times while wearing his ornaments he had admired himself when gazing into clear still water or at a slab of shining stone. Round his waist he fastened another horsehide string from which hung an engraved staghorn dagger, an engraved stone knife, and several large pieces of coral. A third ornament, made of shells and teeth, all perforated and threaded on a string, he set on his head. It encircled his dark heavy hair and his brow just above his eyes.

With his regalia on, he wished to attract the women but he had too much dignity to ask for their attention. He merely walked back and forth, hoping they would look up and admire him; but they were very busy and wholly unaware of him. Returning to the shelf, he laid his ornaments aside, but in removing the belt his interest was captured by the engraving on the dagger. It was of a rhinoceros, and he observed, almost with dismay, that the creature had only two legs. This piece of art he had done three or four years ago; he was a better artist now. Taking his engraving tools—small sharp pieces of flint—he sat near the women in firelight and was soon absorbed by his efforts to make the beast look more natural.

In front of the rear leg he made two incisions, curving downward; and then he made smaller lines in the bend and at the toe, striving for a shadowed effect that would give an impression of solid substance. He carved another leg behind the lone one in front. When the legs were finished, he tried to cover the image with hair and wool by making lines along the belly and back and down the shoulders, flanks, and legs. This labor was interrupted when he paused to look at the two horns on the snout. It seemed to him that both of them were too short and straight; and for several minutes he gazed at the fire and strove to remember what the rhinoceros looked like.

Turning to Marigg he said, "Look," and held the engraving in firelight where she could see it. Marigg looked, but she was not interested. Engravings on staghorn did not feed or clothe children or in any other way promote their welfare.

He moved over to Memmee and showed the image to her, pointing at the horns and indicating with a flint tool that he thought they should be more curved. Memmee was receptive. She was a young woman without Marigg's inflexible patterns of behavior.

"Up?" she asked, tracing with a finger.

"Up," he said.

She bent toward him, still tracing on the horn; and when she touched him and he smelled the femaleness of her, Gode moved to embrace her. She cried aloud, not with anger, but with surprise and protest, and moved away. Gode sighed and looked at his engraving. He was in no mood to make art when a great hunger filled him

197

with tenseness and expectancy. He turned to Agger, wondering if she would be receptive; but Agger was bent low over two pieces of skin which she was slowly and laboriously sewing together.

Gode looked round him. Because of the pitch darkness outside and the yellow color in the upper walls and ceiling, the room in which they sat was bright and golden. It was warm and cheerful, too, and for the women the most homelike place they had ever had. The floor was carpeted with old leaves that had been blown in from the forests below; and, unlike some other caves they had occupied, no wind blew through their chamber and into a cavern behind. For the fire bed, they had laid stones about two feet high and in a circle six feet in diameter; and these stones, pulsing with heat, gave more warmth than the fire itself.

Gode's people had used fire for generations, and they loved it, next to themselves. The women had learned to bank it or to carry it with them when moving to a new home; and when by misfortune it died, the fire maker became feverishly busy with his fire sticks, which, among Gode's people, were mulberry, laurel, or ivy. An assortment of these sticks was a part of every family's property.

Their love for fire was so deep, their attitude toward it so reverent, that they felt for it a kind of worship. It was the friendliest of all things in a vast and unfriendly world. It scattered the horrors of darkness, comforted them in storm and cold, and during the long winter nights it gave them light for their work. It was by firelight that Gode had made most of his engravings and paintings, that the women had made most of the simple things which served them. And it was fire that had made them triumphant over all their enemies except disease and old age.

Long ago, before they made fire, human beings had been among the most relentlessly hunted of the earth's creatures. Without the bulk of the mammoth, the strength of the lion, or the fleetness of the deer, they had survived only because they had been more intelligent. They had lived in constant fear of attack and had been eaten almost as often as they ate. The discovery of fire had changed all that. It had become not only their comfort but also their principal protection; with flaming torches they could drive away any beast in the world, including wolves maddened by hunger; and during nights like this one, they could sit relaxed and secure, knowing that their enemies would not dare attack. The security which fire had given them had been a powerful stimulus to the development of their minds and interests. Their remote ancestors had first been lifted above the level of beasts when they rose to their hind legs and released their front legs for uses besides walking. For countless centuries the release of their hands had been their greatest impulse toward progress; the making of fire had exalted them to a still higher level and made their survival certain.

These were not among their recognitions. They did not know how much fire had done for them, but they did know that without it life would have been more uncomfortable and perilous. They loved and revered it because it was the only friendliness that was constant. Their word for it meant shining, and it also meant friend. When by chance their fire died and was made to live again, they would point at it and exclaim, "Gode-there!" The sun was a gode, too, because they had decided that it was a fire that mysteriously floated above them. They knew that it gave warmth and light, because the earth always turned cold and dark after the gode passed out of sight or became warm and bright again when in the morning the gode reappeared. Why it came and went, or was high above them in one season and low in the next, they did not know; but they were very ignorant of nearly all things, and nearly all things were mysterious.

Their reverence for fire was the humble beginnings of religion in them. They had no symbols or rituals; they had only awe and gratitude. It was their natural way to be vain and arrogant, but if their gode died on its hearth they became chastened and fearful until it lived again.

There was more reverence in the men than in the women. The women, as the cradles and guardians of life, with functions and duties which the men did not have, looked round them, naturally, for things that would serve their purpose. A man, with no duty except the hunt, had time for speculation and dreaming, for the vagaries of art, for the adornment of his person, for the indulgence of his fancies and whims. He thought more about the world because he had more time to think and because of the loneliness which nourishes thought. He was more impelled to awe and reverence and the creation of abstract concepts because emotionally he was more empty and felt greater need.

Tonight, while they sat in their big golden room, the women were not conscious of the fire because they were too busy. They were always busy when not asleep. During the daylight hours they carried wood and water, nursed and cared for their children, split bones open for marrow, dried nuts and vegetables, sewed garments, and experimented in an effort to find tools and ways that would lighten their labors. But sometimes the man would fetch enough meat to last for several days; and then, with time on his hands, he turned to art and his dreams of himself. After darkness came, the women were always busy until they lay down to sleep. The man after darkness had nothing essential to do.

Tonight Gode sat in thought and looked at the fire. He was thinking of the deep, dark night where his enemies prowled in search of him; of plans for the next hunt, when, with boldness and skill, he hoped to stampede a herd of horses over a precipice and so have food for a long while, and of the mysterious forces and powers and unfriendliness in the world beyond the fire.

No person of this time had become self-conscious. If one of much greater knowledge had asked Gode if he did not feel himself to be the center, the core, of all things, he might have been driven inward to an acute consciousness of himself; but neither thought nor emotion had ever detached and isolated him from the objects in his environment. In his thinking of himself, such as it was, he never left the pattern. Never did his mind shut out the things perceived by his senses and fix him in sudden and naked and complete aloneness. Loneliness was not one of his concepts.

Sitting now, for instance, he was, for himself, a part of a familiar pattern. The women, the fire, the great room, his weapons—all these were a part of him and he was a part of them. In his own feeling for the scene, he was the most important part, to be sure, but in no way a detached part. If he had been self-conscious while sitting there, he would have been a very different man, an abler and more imaginative man, goaded by ambition, driven by

loneliness, and impelled by a feeling of spiritual naked-
ness to clothe himself with ideas and philosophy and art.
He had the mind to reach for these things but not the
emotional awakening. That was still to come.

And so he sat, a great, broad-shouldered, hairy fellow,
relaxed and well-fed and idle, looking now at the women,
the fire, the pitch-black mystery of the night. He loved
the warmth and peace of his home. Indeed, fire had done
much to tame the erotically restless and wandering male
and make him feel more dependent. After a while he
stretched out on a skin to sleep. He and the children snored
and dreamed, but the women bent over their work, making holes in a wolfskin and drawing their needles through
it.

4

DURING the evening and night Gode forgot the pup. When morning came he rose and left the cave and was surprised to see it leap up and run. Only fifty feet away it had spent the night awake and waiting. Now it ran, but instead of hiding it turned and sat on its haunches and looked at Gode. It seemed to be both friendly and frightened. Gode wanted to get close to it, not to harm the creature and not to caress it, but to learn, if he could, what its intentions were. When he moved toward it, the pup ran farther away and turned and squatted; and while looking at it, Gode wondered if the beast was hungry. He entered the cave and cut off a piece of wolf meat. The pup ran when he approached, but he left the meat where it had been sitting and returned to the cave; and after a few minutes, it came warily to the meat and sniffed. Almost at once it began to eat.

Marigg had seen him take the meat and feed the wolf and she now came out and stood by him. She pointed at the wolf and said: "Kill-enemy."

"No," he said.

"Enemy," said Marigg.

"No."

For Marigg he was a very unreasonable man. She picked up a stone, intending to hurl it at the pup, but with a cry Gode moved swiftly and struck the stone from her hand.

"No!" he shouted.

Baffled and annoyed, Marigg turned to the other women. "Come-see," she said, and when they came out she pointed at the wolf. "Enemy." They all agreed that it was an enemy, but when Memmee asked Gode to kill it he said no, speaking angrily; and in disgust the women returned to their home.

Gode had, of course, no understanding at all of the emotion in him. He did not know that he was lonely, that he felt cheated and left out of the miracle of birth-giving. He would have been astonished and unbelieving if he had been told that he wanted to establish a relationship of friendliness with this wolf. To be sure, he admired the creature; of all the enemies that stalked and tried to kill him, none was bolder or more intelligent than the wolf.

Three days passed during which he did not hunt, and he gave much time to the pup. He fed it. He made friendly gestures toward it. In his deep voice he talked to it, try-ing to lure it closer to his home. But it was still a wild thing that ran when he approached and sometimes it hid, though each night it lay faithfully in darkness not far from the fire.

On the fourth morning Marigg said he ought to go hunting because hearty appetites in healthy persons had devoured all the deer and wolf. Gode turned to his weapons and prepared to leave. He had no quiver for his arrows and so tied them with a string which he hung around his waist. This morning he painted his face with red ochre, smearing his cheeks and forehead, nose and chin. The blood-color made him feel more vital and unconquerable. He was a dreadful-looking savage when he turned to go, but the women paid no heed to him; they were used to his warlike appearance.

The pup ran and disappeared, and Gode soon forgot it, because when a man took his weapons and went out to kill, all his senses became sharply alert to signs of his enemies. He depended on three senses in the hunt, and they were all remarkably sensitive. When his keen eyes saw that a leaf or a stick or piece of earth had been disturbed, he would drop to his knees; and his sense of smell was so acute that by sniffing he could tell whether the foot of a beast had touched the object. Sometimes he could tell what kind of animal had passed. His sense of hearing was so sharp that he could detect faint sounds that today would be inaudible to most human ears. Perhaps in a thicket it was the rustling of a branch or leaves whispering along moving hair or the soft movement of padded feet.

Toward every sound he turned quickly; and while he walked, his eyes searched the country roundabout and his nose puckered a little as he sniffed the air. To gain time, he usually ran across open spaces, but when he went through woods he moved with graceful stealth, his left hand grasping the bow, his right the bowstring and an arrow and the lance. The arrow and lance he held in such a way that he was prepared to drop either instantly. If set upon suddenly by a beast at close range, he would stiffen; and his left hand would drop the bow, and in the same moment the arrow would fall from his right; and the left would swing over to seize the lance for attack. But if it was an animal that would run rather than fight, or if it showed itself among trees at a distance, then it was the lance that fell in the moment when his right hand drew the bowstring back, with the arrow set.

Today he was crossing a wide open space when he thought he heard the sound of feet. Motionless, breathless, he stood and listened. Dropping the lance, but holding bow and arrow ready to shoot, he sank quietly to his knees and put an ear to the ground. In the earth he heard the gentle pulses of running feet. When he was sure of their direction he rose and looked away at a patch of timber through which he had come; and for perhaps a minute he watched and waited. When nothing came in sight he picked up the lance and moved toward the woods, going softly, with bow and arrow ready. Soon the beast appeared and stood at the edge of the timber and looked at him; and Gode was on the point of shooting when he realized that this creature was the wolf pup.

He felt the shock of a strange emotion; and almost without his knowing it the lance fell from his hand and the bow sank. The pup was about sixty yards away; and now, as in former times, it sat on its haunches and looked at him, revealing in its posture only fear and friendliness. Since leaving his home, Gode had covered two or three miles; he had crossed streams and gone through forests; and there the creature was, following him, and humbly waiting. Again feeling an impulse akin to friendliness, Gode approached, but the wolf vanished into the timber. Gode retraced his steps, and the pup came out and rested its chin on its paws and looked at him.

"Come!" Gode said. He did not whistle. He did not pat his thighs in an effort to lure the creature to him. He merely commanded the wolf to come; and when it did not move, he again advanced, and the pup vanished.

Gode resumed his hunting, resolved to keep an eye open for the wolf; and he learned that during the whole day's journey it followed him. By hiding and waiting he tried to deceive it into coming closer, but it, too, had a keen nose and always trailed about a hundred yards behind. It was clear to Gode that the wolf was afraid of him and would never attack; and why it followed was, therefore, a complete mystery. Did it hunger for food? Was it seeking its mother? Both of these notions he rejected. It could not be foolish enough to search for a mother that it had already helped to eat—to search when there was neither smell nor sight of her anywhere; and it had been well fed only this morning. Gode was baffled but he was deeply pleased; and during the day, while hunting, he remembered again and again that he was not alone, that behind him, usually out of sight but never far away, was a young wolf hunting with him. This realization that he was not alone, that with him was a creature that seemed to be both friendly and faithful, gave him a kind of joy he had never known before. He felt a little stronger, a little bolder; the world today was not quite so unfriendly or so huge.

Because he felt bolder he went far from home and, without knowing it, invaded the land of Harg's people. Indeed, he had never seen any of these people and did not know that they existed. Toward evening of this day he saw one, and he was so amazed that he stood in his tracks like a man turned to stone.

He had been going through a patch of alder and birch along a stream, and upon reaching the far edge he had peered out. About two hundred yards away, in open ground, was a man of Harg's race. He was walking and in one hand he carried a big stone axe. The man was so short, his legs were so bent, his body was so stooped and hunched forward, and his whole appearance was so hairy and shaggy and unhuman, that Gode did not recognize him as a creature of his own kind. He was astounded, because never in his life had he seen an animal like that. He did perceive, of course, a resemblance between this creature and himself; but this man had no neck and his head was thrust forward and he walked like a thing bent by age and unable to straighten. For a man like Gode, tall and straight and fleet, there could be no recognition of close kinship with this ungainly and awkward and shambling beast.

He felt an impulse to kill the thing and he did raise his bow; but the bow slowly sank as he continued to stare with unbelieving eyes. The creature was now walking away from him, and Gode was looking at a hairy back that was bent over and at the short bowed legs; and while he wondered what kind of animal this could be, the man went over a hill and out of sight. For a long moment Gode thought of the stranger and then he went forward quietly to look at the tracks. He realized at once that they were human footprints, but he did not accept them as human even after he had knelt and sniffed the unmistakable human odor. Gently, with a finger, he touched the impression left by the toes. He examined several tracks and stood up and looked round him, expecting to see another of these strange animals; but what he saw was the wolf pup back at the edge of the thicket.

This day's experiences had been more than enough to confuse and bewilder any man. Since morning he had been followed by a wolf; and now he was looking at the footprints of a kind of creature which he had never seen before in all his years of hunting. After pondering the matter, he decided to trail this humanlike animal and learn what it did and where it went to; and so he set out, guided by his eyes and his nose. Dusk was coming, but when he was unable to see any sign of the tracks he would drop to his knees and crawl to right or left and sniff until he had picked up the scent. After going a few hundred yards he saw the creature ahead of him, still moving slowly like something very old or tired, with the big axe hanging from the end of a long arm. Keeping well behind, and most of the time out of sight, Gode followed. The creature came to a mountain and plodded up it; and presently Gode saw a light far up against a stone ledge. He knew it was a fire. He thought this fire belonged to a family among his own people.

The man he was trailing was not going toward the fire, and for a few moments Gode could not decide whether to follow him or to climb to the fire to learn who was there. He chose to investigate the fire, and when he came within clear sight of it his astonishment was boundless. Squatting by the fire were several creatures like the one he had seen—because Gode was, of course, spying on Harg and his family. For half an hour he watched them but he could not see any meaning in what they did save when one laid wood on the flames. They were all stooped and awkward and short of stature and very hairy.

Disturbed by the feeling that in spite of differences these were living things much like himself, Gode turned away to seek his home. It was a moonless night, but his eyes were accustomed to darkness, and he moved in a long graceful trot, with all his senses doubly alert. Now and then he would stop and hold his breath and listen. Avoiding all patches of timber, he kept to open ground, each stride spanning five feet. Seldom had he been caught far from home on a dark night; and though he was afraid, like all men on dark nights, he felt a little bolder than usual because his ears had told him that the wolf pup was following. He did not think that the wolf would leap to his defense if a beast should attack, but nevertheless it was good to feel that a friendly thing was with him. He would have felt a little less afraid if his companion had been no more than a small bird, riding on his shoulder.

When he reached home he was agog with excitement. He had few words to describe what he had seen but he had gestures and wordless sounds full of meaning; and soon the women understood that their man had seen a strange creature which none of them had ever seen. They understood that this amazing thing resembled themselves but was much shorter and bent over and very awkward and hairy.

"Enemy?" asked Marigg.

Gode did not know whether or not it was an enemy; he had not challenged it to battle. He looked blank and made a gesture that was like a shrug. "Fire," he said, using their word for light; and he made them understand that some of these creatures were squatting in a cave by a fire. He squatted to show them the position and bent forward with his arms hanging.

The women looked at one another, their eyes bright with wonder.

"Weapons?" asked Marigg.

"Yes," he said, and pointed at a stone axe which he rarely used.

The women looked at the axe. "Weapons?" asked Marigg, and indicated the bow and lance.

"No."

"Children?" she asked, using their word to mean any young one.

"Yes."

"There?" She pointed to the children asleep on a fur mattress.

Gode wanted to give an answer that meant both yes and no. He tried to explain that their young ones resembled these children but were unlike them, too.

"Up?" asked Memmee, and held a hand to suggest height.

"Here," said Gode, and indicated little stunted creatures.

"Ahhh!" said Memmee.

"Food?" asked Marigg, wondering what they ate.

Gode had seen no food. "No," he said.

"No!" cried Marigg. What kind of creature were they if they did not eat?

"Far?" asked Memmee.

"Far," said Gode, and nodded.

"Ahhh!" said Marigg, and the sound she made was one of relief. If they were far away she saw no reason to feel alarm. For her all things in the world were friendly or unfriendly, and in comparison with this quality nothing else mattered a great deal. She lost all interest in these strange beings; but while eating his supper, chiefly of dried fruits and nuts, Gode continued to think of them. He was disturbed by the fact that they used fire and yet were not like himself; and while he sat in the glow of fire-light and ate his supper, unhappily remembering these dwarfed and bent-over animals that walked on two legs and used stone axes, he thought of the pup.

In the next moment he rose to his feet with an exclamation of surprise and joy. In his hand he had a small piece of flesh which Marigg had given him, and with this he went into the darkness to see if the pup had come home. He called to it. In his voice there was a strange quality, which no woman had ever heard in the voice of a man. Marigg was so upset that she followed him into the night, thinking he was calling to the creatures about whom he had told her. She came up and stood by him.

"Enemy?" she asked.

"No. Friend."

"Where?"

He pointed into the darkness, but she could see nothing. Gode had seen the pup move. He now left Marigg and went down the hill; and when the pup ran away Gode could hear its feet. On hands and knees he crawled in the darkness, seeking the warm spot of earth on which the pup had been lying. When he found it, he laid the meat there and stood up. "Come!" he said. He wanted to call it by a name and he thought of the word they used to mean friend. "Friend-come!" he called, and stood in the darkness and listened. He waited several minutes, and when the wolf did not come, he turned softly back to his home, his face touched by a strange gentleness.

5

DURING the next few days Gode hunted, but his interest was absorbed by the wolf. The creature faithfully trailed him and became steadily more friendly and more unafraid. At night it slept close by the cave, though it would run away if it heard sounds within; and during the day it followed Gode, sometimes only a few yards behind. He wanted to touch it, but the wolf never came close enough for that. It would wag its tail and look at him expectantly, but when he went toward it the pup would run away. Gode fed it night and morning, and the wolf now depended on him for its food.

Word went among Gode's people that he had a wolf that followed him and slept close by his home. The men were astonished. They were envious, too, and during the hunt, when Gode met one of them, he would stare at the wolf and ask questions about it, eager to learn how Gode persuaded it to follow him. Gode's name for it was his word for friend, and it seemed to him that the wolf recognized its name. If he called it by name and made friendly gestures, the pup would wag its tail and show a wish to come to him; but it was still a wild thing as confused by the new relationship as its master.

After he explained to men that he had killed the mother and that the young one then had followed him home, they wished to own a wolf that would follow them and they spent a part of their time hunting for bitches with pups. Upon learning that other men envied him, Gode cherished his possession all the more; he fed the wolf night and morning and kept an eye on it, fearing that someone would steal it. Sometimes during the night he would rise from his bed and go out to see if the creature was in its accustomed place; and after a while he wondered if the wolf would like a bed, too. He took a deerskin out and laid it with the hair side up and tried to explain to his friend that this was to be its bed. When a few nights later Gode saw the pup lying on the skin, he was deeply pleased.

A month passed, and one day Gode came by the notion that the wolf was trying to assist him in the hunt. He had crippled a stag with arrows, and while he was chasing the beast, trying to overtake it and fell it with his lance, he saw that the wolf was chasing it, too. Gode stopped, amazed; and a moment later, seeing that he no longer ran after the deer, the pup stopped, also. It looked at Gode and Gode made sounds of encouragement, urging his dog to run forward and attack the beast; but his voice abashed the wolf and it slunk away as if rebuked. But in later hunts Gode clearly perceived that it was the wish of his dog to help him, and nothing in his life had so deeply gratified him as this recognition.

He told the women about it, but they were incredulous.

214

This relationship between a wolf and a man had baffled and disturbed them; they had watched it grow day after day and had felt a deepening concern. For them the wolf was an enemy and nothing else. They did not like to have it lie close by the fire at night or to follow their man during the day; nor could they understand Gode's pleasure in the creature's company. They realized more sharply than he did that the pup would grow until it was a big wolf—and, for them, the grown wolf was their most deadly enemy. Gode was aware that the pup was growing in size, but he also knew, as the women did not, that it was growing in friendliness. For him the animal had become as precious as his weapons because, like them, it was an extension of his meaning.

The women, and especially Marigg and Memmee, became a little jealous of the wolf. Jealousy is an emotional attitude toward something that threatens the moral anchors of a person and his insecure sense of his personal worth. For the women, the wolf was doing that. They had no love for their man, but he was a part of their meaning; he fetched food and protected them from enemies and gave strength to their home life. The more Gode devoted himself to the wolf, the less he devoted himself to the women and the welfare of the children. That is the way they intuitively felt about it; and the more friendly Gode and the wolf became, the more the women resented the relationship. They would not have been jealous at all if they had seen him embrace another woman. They cared nothing about that. But as the ones who gave birth and cherished and cared for children, it was natural for them to resent invasions of their security. The wolf was such an invasion because Gode gave food to it, a bed to it, and spent a part of his time talking to it in a way that seemed to them utterly senseless.

It was the grandmother who was most angrily resentful. As the days passed, she learned to hate the wolf and she wanted to kill it; and one morning, when she was the first to rise, she looked out and saw it lying on the deerskin, only a few feet from the fire. Yielding to an impulse of anger and fear, she seized a stone and hurled it. Her aim was good. She hit the wolf, and it leapt up with a dreadful yelp and ran away. In the next moment Gode was on his feet. He had seen her hurl the rock and he knew she had thrown it at his friend; and when he faced Marigg he was a violently angry man. He made a move to strike her down, but in the next instant another emotion blocked his first impulse and he ran out to learn if his dog was hurt. He called to it, but it did not come. He went down the hill, calling, searching, and trembling with outrage. During these minutes his anger cooled, and it is well that it did so or he might have slain the queen mother of his family.

When at last he entered the cave he was sullen, and the women were frightened. This was a terrible disaster in their lives, this strange and unnatural and disgusting relationship between a man and a wolf. The very thought of it infuriated and sickened them. They hoped that the wolf had gone away and would never come back.

Without eating any breakfast, Gode took his weapons and left. He was angry and morose. Neither he nor any other person of his time had formulated any notions of right and wrong; but he felt intuitively that anything was right that pleased him and promoted his own delights and interests. All the sense he had of his own dignity and meaning had been outraged, and he hated Marigg for it. His feeling for her was similar to what her own would have been if he had struck one of the children.

While going down the mountain, he called again and again to his dog. It did not come, but after an hour or two, with an exclamation of joy, he discovered that it was following him. In a voice vibrant with emotion, he called to it and made every friendly gesture he could think of; but the wolf had been struck and it was suspicious and afraid. It remained at a considerable distance and, when called to, it did not wag its tail or sink to its belly and make a slight movement of creeping toward him. If Gode had been more reflective, it might have occurred to him that the wolf thought he was the one who had struck it. He might have known that it did not have his power to distinguish between friendly and unfriendly things. He knew nothing of all that; and all that he knew and did was not enough to quiet the suspicions in his friend or draw it a single step toward him. It followed him all day, but at a greater distance than usual, and it always ran when he turned. It followed him home, but when after darkness Gode went out, he saw no sign of it, and the deerskin was cold under his hands.

The next morning, standing in the cave entrance, and pointing at his dog fifty yards down the hill, he said with deep angry emphasis: "Friend! Friend-there!"

Marigg's wise old face wrinkled with disgust. If she had known anything about lunacy, she would have said that her man was out of his mind. He was indeed strange, and what he asked her to believe was stranger still.

"Enemy!" she cried sharply.

"No!"

"Kill-enemy!"

"No!" he roared.

"Kill-enemy," said Marigg stubbornly.

Gode swung toward her with a menacing gesture. Agger and Memmee drew back to a wall; but Marigg had fought many a battle for children, and there was nothing in the world, man or beast, that could make her give ground in defense of her young. She was not afraid of Gode, and he knew she was not afraid.

"Enemy," she said, and shrugged like one weary of arguing with fools.

"Friend," said Gode, but his voice was not so positive. He did not intend to let the women drive his dog away; but on the other hand he did not have the stamina to face this old woman's will. Feeling that further explanation would serve no purpose, he resolved to watch his friend and see that it came to no harm.

Ever since the wolf had first followed him home his hunting had been more casual; and after Marigg hurled the stone he did not seem to care if his family starved to death. There was a sharper cleavage between the points of view and interests of the two sexes. They resented one another more and became more suspicious and unreasonable. Not even Memmee, his favorite, was friendly toward him now; and when at home, he sulked and scowled at the women. They seemed to ignore him and to ignore the dog.

One evening, when erotic hunger was a consuming fever in him, he strove to lure Memmee to an embrace; but she rebuked him with sharp cries and angry gestures, and he withdrew to a wall on which certain frustrated longings had been represented in art. With charcoal he

218

now intended to draw an image of his wolf friend, but his subconscious mind guided his hand; and he was surprised to learn that he was drawing a female horse. He became excited and tried to add all the more obvious female features. He rounded her belly, hung dugs under her flank, and made marks to indicate her genitals; and when he had a likeness that pleased him, he next tried to draw a stallion mounting the mare.

He had often seen beasts, and especially horses, in the act of copulation. He now drew a male standing on its hind legs, with front legs hanging, and with the organ unsheathed. Even so crude an image of two mating beasts excited him deeply; and while he added finishing touches here and there, he shouted with delight. The women were disturbed by his cries, and Memmee rose and came over to see what he was doing.

She perceived at once what his drawing meant, and she, too, was excited by it. When Gode reached to take her, she did not resist; and while he embraced her, with the violence of his heart shaking him and his breathing sounding as if he were strangling, the other women turned from their work to look. Agger's face filled with gentleness; but Marigg, like any old woman whose youthful hungers are dead, made a face of disgust and turned back to her sewing.

A little later Gode was again busy with his art. He thought his drawings were superb—and, for a man of his time, they were. From time to time he exclaimed over them, or stepped back to see them in better perspective, or hastily added new lines to suggest contours or hair. With red ochre he drew his wolf friend, trying to represent it in a squatting position, with chin on its paws and ears cocked. He called to the women to come look at it, but they were busy and had little interest in the strange vagaries of a man's fancy. They would grunt or turn to look at him a moment, while he waited, eager and expectant; and when they refused to come he would stare more critically at his work, trying to see flaws in what seemed to him to be flawless.

The next morning, while preparing for the hunt, his attention was attracted to his drawings and he spent a considerable while admiring them; but when late in the afternoon he returned, bringing several rabbits, his drawings were gone. Marigg had taken a handful of earth and tried to erase them. Where the two beasts had stood in embrace there was only a charcoal smear, and the image of his wolf friend was a blotch of red paint.

6

BECAUSE absorption by fresh interests had made a poor provider of Gode, Marigg nagged and tormented him. Repeatedly she told him there was not enough food, and to press the shortage on his attention she gave him very small portions to eat. "Food!" she would cry, and gesture at the bare shelves. And after he had eaten his bite of breakfast she would bring his weapons to suggest that he was not a lord of idleness, luxuriously warming himself or lying on deep rugs, but a man who had many mouths to feed. Gode understood what she meant. It was the way of a man to be lazy, and it was the way of women to drive their men to work. In former seasons of warmth Gode had fetched not only meat but vegetables also—carrots, turnips, radishes, as well as such mushrooms as they had learned were not poisonous. Sometimes he had brought such delicacies as frogs and eels and eggs. But since taking up his strange relationship with the wolf he had fetched only flesh, and by no means enough of that. Marigg had been patient with him for many days, but the time came when she had to remind him sharply of his duties.

Gode remembered then that he had planned a big hunt; and one morning, after Marigg had angrily rebuked him and almost pushed him out of the cave, he set off down the mountain, trailed by his dog, to find some men with whom he had hunted. Usually the men hunted singly, but they were more successful when they hunted in packs like the wolves. Together, they could stampede animals over precipices or drive them into pits or ambush them in blind canyons. It was a herd of horses that Gode now had in mind.

They fed about three miles away on an open prairie along one side of which ran a ledge with a sheer drop of a hundred feet. On another side, and at a right angle to the precipice, was a deep river. His plan was to build a kind of fence along a third side parallel with the river and stampede the beasts over the cliff. To do that would need several men, and this morning Gode set out to find them.

The women, meanwhile, were busy. They were usually busy, though they accomplished very little when it was all added up, chiefly because they were so slow or did the same simple tasks over and over. A large part of their time was spent with the children.

In this family there were three children. Memmee had a husky son who was five, and Agger had two girls, one four years old and the other an infant.

Among the people of her time Agger was a moron, a stupid and sluggish and dirty woman who seemed always to be in the way. Marigg and Memmee had a few habits of personal cleanliness. They never bathed, of course, or entirely freed themselves of vermin; but sometimes they tried to remove the filth from their finger- and toenails, and the excrement from their bodies they dropped many yards from their home and covered with earth or leaves. Agger was such a dolt that she had to be watched. As likely as not she would drop her offal in the cave if Marigg did not go screaming toward her and drive her out. She took no care of her body at all except to pick off the larger insects, and she took little care of her children.

The other women tried to teach the children not to foul themselves. The girl was more tractable than the boy; she had been taught to leave the cave, but Memmee's boy would go to a wall and squat there if unobserved. All of them, both children and adults, had a strong unclean smell; but this they were used to and did not mind.

Nobody was kind to Agger. Disgusted by her stupid ways, the other women resented her, and sometimes Marigg would shout at the poor creature and drive her outside. Agger had heavy dark hair over her body and a short thick beard on her face; her dugs were ugly brown pouches that hung almost to her navel; and she had broken off several of her front teeth when gnawing bones. When angry she drew back her thick lips and looked ferocious. Not even by her older child was she liked. In fact, this girl had been so faithfully cared for by the other women that she no longer recognized Agger as her mother.

The children were a constant problem except when they slept. Strong, healthy, vain, greedy, and eager for mischief, they fought one another and screamed and made a dreadful clamor all day long. The boy pilfered Marigg's hoard of food from the stone shelves; put on Gode's orna-

ments and strutted to show himself off; impudently urinated on the fire when the women were not watching
him; or tried to indulge in erotic play with his sister.
When caught in mischief he was severely slapped. Then
he would go away, howling with outrage, and for a few
minutes he would sulk and stare at the women and wonder how he could avenge himself. Marigg and Memmee
had to keep an eye on him at all times. When angry he
would have slain his sisters and he would have been happy
to see them dead. In another year or two he would be
old enough to go hunting with Gode, and Marigg looked
forward to the time when he would be out of sight and
off her hands for a little while.

When wood was to be gathered, Marigg usually stayed
with the children and sent the other women down the
hill. If there was a pile of wood at hand, and water in
the skin vessels and food on the shelves, the women would
sit on animal hides and laboriously make simple garments.
They might spend a whole day trying to soften a deerskin or horsehide lace to use as thread, or to make an eye
in a big-stick needle, or to shape a hunk of clay into a
crude pot that would hold water. They made a kind of
cape without arms for the older children, but in warm
weather the children refused to wear them. They preferred to be naked. Indeed, in warm weather there was
no reason to wear clothes, because in none of them, young
or old, was there any sense of modesty or shame.

Garments which women fashioned for themselves they
sometimes tried to make more attractive by adorning with
pieces of stone or shell. But the wish to be attractive, or
distinguished and admired, was not in them the strong

hunger, the almost consuming passion, that it was in men. It was men who first adorned themselves; the women only copied a part of what their men did. They were not hunters and they felt no sexual rivalry; and therefore there was no pressing need in them to feel enviable and apart.

In the morning when Gode set out to find the men, Agger seemed to be at the beginning of a menstrual period. Marigg, at least, decided that she was; and she rose, grunting angrily, and went for an apron. Angrily she called to Agger, "Come!" and obediently, abjectly, Agger came. Marigg hung the apron over the woman's pelvic area and tied the strings round her waist; and then she said, "Go!" and pointed to the most inner part of the cave. Sullenly, Agger went over and sat by the wall and stared at the other women. She did not understand why she was sent away. Marigg felt that the woman was unclean, that she was squandering the precious substance of life. She would not have said that Agger was sinful, because she had no notion of sin and guilt; but there was nevertheless in her emotional attitude the obscure beginning of such a notion. Agger would have to sit by herself for three or four days and Marigg would take the baby over now and then to let it nurse. Then Agger could take the apron off.

When Memmee entered this cycle she needed no prompting; she put on an apron and withdrew. Marigg had done so when younger. Most of the other menstruating women among her people did so. This practice was becoming a taboo, and though its meaning and purpose were vague for all of them, the custom had become fixed as a part of their lives.

225

The children were always puzzled when a woman went away to sit by herself. The boy now stared at Agger, curious, solemn, and full of wonder; and after a few moments he beckoned to her and said, "Come." Marigg heard him and turned with a cry. She drove him outside, and he went beyond the fire and lay on his belly, with his chin cupped in his hands, and looked at Marigg.

Marigg and Memmee had intelligent minds but very little knowledge, and their thinking, in consequence, was hardly more than troubled wonderings. They took it for granted that babies were made of the blood in a woman's body—because when a woman stopped shedding blood she no longer had the power of birth. It had been that way with Marigg. Among her people it had been observed that it was that way with all women. Why during the menstrual period the blood was wasted they did not know, but they believed that the fault in some mysterious way and for some inexplicable reason was the woman's. In such thinking they had come close to a concept of sin.

But they did not spend much time dwelling on such matters. When they became aware that a woman was in her menses they thought about her because children were the meaning of their lives. They wanted many children. Any woman would have been delighted to have a hundred or a thousand. For the barren woman they felt disgust and something akin to pity; and for the woman with many children they felt envy. That a woman should have to waste any of her babies was for all of them the darkest riddle in life.

After Agger was sent to the rear of the cave, Marigg and Memmee turned to their work, though they had little to do. There was wood and water, they had no meat to dry and store, and they had made bedding and garments of all the skins. In their generations of wandering northward their people had brought with them the seed of barley and wheat; and when they had stayed long enough in one spot they had experimented a little with agriculture. Marigg now remembered her handful of grain which she had hidden away in a skin pouch. She decided to plant it. She went to the shelves and climbed to the highest one and reached for the pouch. After pouring a few grains into a palm and looking at them, she turned to Memmee.

"Grow-food," she said, and went outside, followed by Memmee and the two older children.

The area of her dooryard fell sharply away and was broken by outcroppings of stone. Nevertheless, Marigg intended to plant the seed here, and after finding a stick to use as a spade she looked round her for a suitable spot. She entrusted a little of the seed to Memmee but none to the children, who clamored for it. With the stick she would make a hole in the earth, drop a grain of barley or wheat, and then cover the seed with soil and step on the cover. By each tiny seedbed she set a stake. When she and Memmee had planted a handful, Marigg took the remainder of the seed into the cave and hid it.

She returned with skin pouches in which to carry water, because her people had learned that seed would not grow in dry places. It was three hundred yards from their plantings to the stream; and all afternoon, assisted by the children, the two women carried water. They realized, of course, that they could have lightened their task by planting their grain close by the stream, but they wanted it near their home so they could watch it and keep birds and beasts away. Never in any past year had they harvested more than a quart or two.

After the seedbeds were watered they were tired and hungry, but there was no food in their home. Their lazy man had spent too much time recently with his wolf. The children were famished, too, because they had plodded with the women in their many journeys up and down the mountain. Memmee's boy had been weaned but, when he saw his mother sit down, he went to her and grasped a long pendulous dug. Quietly, Memmee folded her big arms across her breasts, hiding the nipples; and to her son she said, "No."

"Food," he said.

Marigg had been standing at the cave entrance, looking down the mountain for sign of their man. She was grunting, as if talking to herself out of disgust and scorn. When she heard Memmee's boy speak, she said:

"Food-no."

Memmee rose and stood by Marigg, and the two women shaded their eyes against the setting sun and looked at the country below them. Marigg's gestures spoke of disgust. Her old wrinkled face was a picture of what she thought of a man who played with a wolf while his family starved. She wondered if she ought to go down the hill and find something to eat. Gode had been an able hunter and for years he had brought plenty of food, though Memmee and Agger had gone now and then to gather vegetables and nuts and fruits. Marigg had always stayed home with the children and the fire. It made her feel important to be in charge of these things.

Now the women stood together and watched the sun

228

sink and dusk envelop the earth. Marigg wondered if Gode was hunting or if he had gone beyond sight of them to play with his dreadful wolf. Memmee thought she saw him coming.

"Look!" she cried, and pointed.

Marigg stared with rheumy old eyes but she could see nothing. "Where?" she asked.

"There," said Memmee, still pointing.

They watched and waited, but out of the darkness nothing came. Memmee entered her home and went to the shelves to see if they were barren. Against a wall stood the thighbones of a deer that had not been split open for their marrow; and one of these Memmee gave to her boy. He knelt and laid it across a rock and tried to crush it with Gode's stone axe. Marigg stood out in the darkness, waiting and hoping; but presently she came in, sullen and angry, and laid wood on the fire. She sat on the wolf rug with her back to the wall and closed her tired eyes. She was an old woman—she was almost forty —and she was very weary tonight. There had been little for breakfast, and all day she had labored without eating.

Memmee's boy crushed the thighbone and licked bone and marrow from his fingers. The marrow was rancid, but he was too hungry to mind that. His sister approached to share his supper, but he yelled at her and struck her and aroused his grandmother. She was so startled and angered by the sudden outcry that she moved swiftly forward on her knees and smote the lad's skull. He leapt up, wild with rage, and menaced her with a long splinter of bone. Grunting with wrath and weariness, Marigg rose to her feet and grasped him by his ears and shook him. With a dreadful howl the lad gathered the bones and the axe and went back into the gloom of the cave, where Agger was sitting.

After peering into the darkness and listening, Marigg laid wood on the fire and then spread pelts for a bed and lay on them to sleep. Memmee sat in the cave entrance and waited.

7

GODE had been delayed by more than the wolf. It was
the first really warm day of the year, and life everywhere
presented itself vividly and abruptly to his senses. In running through a grove of juniper he almost collided with
a deer; and before he could set an arrow to his bow and
shoot, his dog astonished him by pursuing the creature
out of sight. For half a mile the wolf chased the deer and
Gode tried to keep up; and while he was racing across
an open field his attention was caught by an unusual sight.

A mammoth was surrounded by a pack of hyenas. It
was an old bull with wasted flabby muscles and dim vision,
and around it were about twenty hyenas, snapping and
barking or leaping in to attack. Gode observed that the
mammoth did not turn, even when the creatures attacked
its hams and belly; and upon going to higher ground for
a better look he perceived that the beast had sunk to its
belly in a swamp. It was helpless. Its trunk explored like
a huge antenna, and its great head and shoulders swayed
from side to side. Next, he saw that the hyenas had eaten

through the wall of one side. When they saw Gode, they slunk back and crouched, with teeth bared, and waited. Gode had seen this sort of thing before; and inasmuch as he did not want hyena flesh or old bull mammoth, he would have continued his hunt, indifferent to the scene, if there had not been in him a strange new emotion.

He watched the beasts and waited for the return of his dog; and when he saw the wolf coming he almost shouted with joy. He was not afraid but nevertheless he now felt more secure. He felt less alone and lonely in a world where, when away from home, he seldom saw anything except the killers and the killed. Perhaps he felt a little pity for the helpless bull; or perhaps he felt only disgust because hyenas were cowardly things that preyed on the helpless and the old.

When the wolf approached, it saw the mammoth and its foes; and at once it arched its back, with long hair parted loosely in bunches, and slowly advanced. The hyena was afraid of wolves—but not when there was only one wolf and so many of them. Gode's dog bared its teeth and arched its back and dropped its tail low; and step by cautious step it moved toward the pack. Gode became afraid for it. "No!" he shouted. "Friend-come!" He advanced until he was about forty yards from the hyenas. The wolf, much nearer, paid no attention to him. It had stopped. Tense, its hair quivering, it stood as if ready to spring. The hyenas did not retreat. They squatted a little closer to the earth, their teeth snapping and moisture drooling from their lips.

Gode hardly knew what to do. He thought that if he retreated, perhaps his dog would come with him; and so he withdrew and called to it. "Friend-come!" he cried again and again. But the wolf stood as if it had taken a position for life. It was only a half-grown pup that had never fought; and though it had sense enough to know that too many enemies were present, it behaved like one who did not intend to give ground.

Gode picked up several stones and, carrying these as well as his weapons, he advanced. He went forward until he was only a few feet from the wolf; and faced now by two enemies instead of one the hyenas slunk back a little. Gode hurled a stone at the pack, and there was sudden hissing and snapping, but the beasts did not retreat. He hurled all his stones, but the animals only cowered and snarled among themselves, too hungry to leave their prey with its open belly, too cowardly to attack.

Setting his lance in the earth, Gode fixed an arrow to his bow and pulled the string back. He aimed at the largest hyena he could see clearly and released the arrow. It struck the beast behind its shoulder, went between two ribs, and buried itself in the lung cavity. With a howl, the creature leapt into the air and then turned round and round and rolled as if fighting itself. Its mates stirred with frenzy; but when they understood that one of their number was wounded, they pounced on it and literally tore it limb from limb. They set up such a wild clamor of biting and eating that the wolf made a strange deep sound, as if in pain.

The moment Gode fired, he dropped the bow and seized the lance, ready, if the pack should rush him, to impale them right and left. He was trembling a little and he was sweating. Battle lust was strong in a man, and in the excitement of attack, hot emotions flooded and drenched him and almost obscured his mind. Emotion poured in tingling waves down his spine, became audible in his breath, and struck like the tiny feet of lightning over his skull. The hands grasping his lance looked bloodless. From the hair on his body drops of sweat hung like gray beads.

To face twenty ravenous hyenas, even with a wolf at his side, took more boldness than most men had. But after a man made his first strike, most of the fear left him and he became a killer. With his spear poised and ready, Gode now advanced, going not swiftly but softly, his body poised like his lance. Snarling, the pack withdrew, crawling backward with their bellies touching earth. Glancing to the right, Gode saw that the wolf was coming with him, back arched, teeth bared; and Gode was so overjoyed that impulsively he reached out to touch it. But it was a wild wolf after all and it leapt away and turned to face him, with lips drawn back from its teeth. The suddenness of the move startled Gode, and instinctively he raised his lance to strike. But he did not strike. Man and wolf faced one another, and in both there was the same primitive battle-lust that confused loyalties and made all things look like foes.

During the long moment while he faced the wolf with lance poised, something happened to Gode. Perhaps it was the first vague intimation of shame or tenderness—or perhaps it was only that in the moment of waiting an alert and intelligent mind was restored to its function. Whatever it was, he slowly lowered the lance and stepped back; and while making a downward, stroking movement with his hand he said, "Friend-come!"

There was a change in the wolf, too. Its eyes, intently fixed on Gode's eyes, were suspicious and untamed; but the upper lip sank over the bared teeth and the body relaxed in its fighting posture. Two ancient enemies looked at one another; and while making a gentle stroking movement, Gode said again and again, softly, persuasively, "Friend-come. Friend-come." The wolf did not come but neither did it retreat, though it was only ten feet away. It continued to look at Gode's eyes, and the suspicion in its own gave way to questioning. Its body relaxed and sank to its haunches. And so, resting on its rump and its forelegs, it looked at Gode, never for a moment taking its gaze off his eyes; and as the suspicion and fear in it died, its ears came forward and cocked to listen. "Friend-come," Gode said, speaking like a mother to her child.

When he knew that the wolf would not come, he behaved with extraordinary insight. Instead of turning away abruptly, he turned gently, slowly, trying not to startle the wolf or make it suspicious again. All his movements were eloquent with friendliness because he felt friendly. Walking softly, he went over and picked up his bow; but instead of returning to his former position near the wolf, he advanced only part way, realizing that if he covered the whole distance the wolf would flee. The wolf was still sitting, ears cocked, looking at him. Gode wanted to talk to it in a friendly voice, but the only words he could think of to say were "friend-come." "Friend-come," he said over and over, and he could tell that the wolf liked the sound of his voice.

Upon looking over to see what the hyenas were doing, Gode saw that they were about forty yards beyond the mammoth, crouching, snapping, and waiting. So far as Gode cared, they could kill and eat the beast in their own time. If there had been a vague emotion of pity in him earlier, that was gone now. His whole interest was fixed on his dog. He withdrew, making soft and reassuring gestures and calling to it; and after he had gone a little way the wolf rose and followed him.

If he had hastened at once on his long stride, he would have missed the deeper and better part of this experience; but he went slowly, turning often to look at his dog or to call to it. When he was about three hundred yards away, he was stopped by a terrible sound. It was the sound of a great beast in agony; and while he stood and listened, wondering what it could be, he remembered the mammoth and its foes. He knew that the pack had closed in.

If Gode had been the man he was before the wolf had followed him home, he would have paid no heed. Certainly he would have felt no emotion so sharply and sufferingly akin to pity. In times before, he had seen helpless old things set upon by their enemies and killed; that was life as he knew life. Among his own kind he knew that old men usually died such a death—and sometimes old women too. But after the wolf entered his life, there had been in him a slow and indefinable change. The paternal feelings in him had been dormant, with no chance to grow and ripen in the kind of family life he had, where women possessed the offspring and a man was no more than a lonely hunter in a friendless world. There had been a change; and now while listening to the agony of a helpless beast, he felt anger and an emotion very like pity. Calling to his dog he turned back and ran. After a hundred yards, he paused and looked behind him, and when he saw the wolf following, he felt reassured. He ran again and did not stop until he came in full view of the squealing mammoth and its killers. Then he began to shout, and his voice roared like thunder. His cry was a warning and a challenge, but the hyenas were too ravenously busy to pay any heed. Gode ran again, and when he was within a few yards of them he dropped his bow, poised his lance, and shouted another challenge.

On the side of the mammoth next to Gode, the hyenas had chewed through the tough old hide and entered the side wall, and now they were thrusting their heads in. Though they were eating its organs, the beast was still alive; it waved its big helpless trunk and swayed from side to side. Its squeals of agony were ear-splitting.

After shouting again, Gode glanced round at his dog and then attacked. Rushing forward, he impaled the creature nearest him, driving the lance through its breast. In the next moment he lifted the lance with the beast impaled on it and swung it round him; and the creature fell off and rolled in a ball of fur and claws and fangs. Gode's glance swept the area and saw the wolf. It had been standing about twenty yards back. When the hyena was hurled off the spear, it rolled toward the wolf and the wolf leapt on it; and in the next few moments Gode watched his dog sink teeth in the beast's throat and shake it. Something went through him then in a warm flood of joy.

He advanced to strike again, but the hyenas fled and turned their bloody faces and red mouths toward him. He rushed at them, and swiftly they slunk away. When he looked behind him, he was surprised and deeply pleased to see that his dog had come up and now stood almost abreast. It was from the wolf that the hyenas were slinking as much as from the man. "Come!" Gode shouted and ran against the pack. After chasing them away, Gode turned and saw that his dog was feeding at the mammoth, and when he came up, the wolf retreated from him, its mouth drooling.

The mammoth seemed to be dead; its trunk and curved tusks rested in the mire. Its eyes were glassy and still. In the wall of one side there was a large hole; and upon looking in Gode saw that parts of the organs had been devoured. A hundred yards away the hyenas squatted and waited. Thirty yards away in the other direction his dog sat and cocked its ears.

The emotion in Gode now was dark confusion. A few minutes ago something akin to pity had been aroused in him by the cries of agony and he had attacked. But the old bull was dead now; it was only a great pile of food. It was not the kind of food Gode wanted, and he turned away, bewildered by the realization that he had wasted time here for no purpose that was clear to him. But when he remembered that the wolf had attacked with him, that the wolf had leapt in to kill the beast he had hurled off his spear, he felt a kind of pride and, deep within him, a sense of well-being that no man had ever felt before. The world was not quite so dark or so friendless as it had been

"Come!" he called, and set out for home.

8

Two days passed before he tried again to organize a hunt. The women were angry and demanded food, and during these days he killed birds and rabbits and gathered eggs; and when one morning he had satisfied the hunger of his family, he set out to find men for a big chase.

The families of his people, each living in a cave, were scattered over a large area, no two of them living close together. Some of the men knew one another by sight, but there were strong feelings of rivalry and suspicion in them and they did not often meet in the hunt and pause to talk. If when out hunting one man saw another, he rarely called to him or made his presence known; but now and then the men did meet to hunt in packs.

Because he knew where a herd of horses grazed close by a ledge, Gode wanted help; and today he set out, not to shun men but to find them. The first one he saw he shouted to, waving his lance; and after they had come together across the distance, the man looked at Gode's wolf. Like many others, he had heard that Gode had a wolf but he was astonished nevertheless. He gave a cry of warning and raised his bow.

But Gode shouted, "Friend!"

"Friend?" asked the other.

"Yes. Friend-there."

"Enemy," said the man.

"No. Look." Gode caressed and patted his thigh and called to his dog; and the wolf advanced a little and cocked its ears. "Friend-mine." The man was speechless and unconvinced.

These two roamed the hills and forests and found other men, and they were speechless, too. For all of them the wolf was an implacable enemy, yet here was one who followed a man and seemed to be friendly and obedient. At least it seemed to be friendly toward Gode, though it was not friendly toward them, as they discovered when they spoke to it. Then it laid its ears back and showed its teeth; but when Gode called to the wolf, it cocked its ears and wagged its tail. They wanted to know where he had found it; and with words, gestures, and drawings on the earth, Gode explained that he had killed the mother and the pup had followed him home. It now spent the night close by his fire and followed him all day in the hunt. For the men the story was incredible; yet here was the wolf, following him wherever he went. Their astonishment gave way to envy, and one and another made friendly gestures and sounds to the wolf, trying to persuade it to show friendliness for them. But the dog knew its master. It distrusted the other men, and when they strove to seduce it with good will, it bared its teeth and slunk away. Gode felt triumphant. When he spoke to the wolf, it cocked its ears and looked at him with unmistakable friendliness, expectant and waiting.

When there were seven men in the party, Gode told them of the herd of horses. He had no word for horse but he drew it on the earth. He made images of several horses, and on one side he drew lines to suggest a precipice; and the men understood. They climbed to a hill and Gode pointed in the direction of the beasts; and it was agreed that the next morning they would all meet here. When Gode turned away, the men tried to persuade the wolf to stay with them. They called to it and patted their thighs as they had seen Gode do, but when the wolf turned to look at them, it snarled and bared its teeth. Then it trotted obediently behind its master. Gode felt angry and resentful and again and again he looked back to see if his dog were coming. The wolf was his property, and it was a law among his people that a man stole from another at the risk of his life.

The next morning only four of the men appeared. Two of them, unknown to the others, had sneaked away, each going alone, to find a bitch wolf with pups. For an hour the five men waited for the two. Gode's dog sat on its haunches about forty yards away, and again the men tried to woo it to friendliness. Anger grew steadily in Gode, and at last he swung to them and shouted.

"Mine!" he roared, glaring at them.

"Yes," one of them said.

Because he had to lead the way, Gode was unhappy; the men behind him were still making gestures to his dog. The most persistent of these men was a giant almost as large as Gode. He was bolder than the others and called repeatedly to the wolf; and when he could no longer endure this outrage to his vanity, this unabashed attempt to steal his property, Gode turned and faced the man. Their gaze met. The three other men drew aside. This looked to them as if it would be a fight of the kind they wanted no part of.

Two bold men, one angry, the other arrogant, looked in the eyes of one another, each taking the measure of his opponent's courage and will; and at last in a voice low and deep and menacing, Gode said:

"Mine. Friend-mine."

When the other did not answer, when there was no sign of yielding in his eyes or his bearing, Gode let his bow fall from his left hand, and both hands grasped his lance. This gesture meant that he was ready to fight. When he spoke again his voice was harshly menacing and final: "Friend-mine."

The other man did not drop his bow and grasp his lance, but he still looked at Gode, his eyes unwavering and his body tense. Then his throat relaxed, and in the next moment he swallowed. "Yes," he said.

The three others now came forward. "Food," said one, and pointed in the direction of the horses.

Gode did not lead now. He indicated the direction to be taken and fetched up the rear. The giant who had faced him now led the party, and for two miles not a word was spoken. The wolf followed twenty yards from its master's heels.

The place where the horses grazed was a long meadow of tall grass. On one side was a stone ledge, and at a right angle to it was a river bordered with impenetrable thicket. The meadow lay along the river for more than a mile. Back from the meadow on the side parallel with the river, the terrain climbed to a plateau that lay about a hundred feet above the meadow and sloped gently down to it. There were about a hundred horses in the herd. They were only a little larger than Shetland ponies, and in the tall grass they were almost hidden from sight.

When the men came cautiously across the prairie and looked down at the beasts, they understood the plan Gode had in mind. Along the prairie, beginning at the stone ledge and running back a half-mile or more, they would make a fence of fire parallel with the meadow and the stream. When they had the fires burning, they would come in from the open side, shouting and bearing torches, and stampede the horses down the meadow and over the precipice.

After taking in the picture, the sullen giant stretched an arm to the meadow and said, "Food-there." His mouth watered. Horseflesh fattened with succulent grass was the best of all meat; and, besides, there would be piles of it for everyone. For several minutes the men rested on hands and knees and looked down, studying the landscape and thinking of their problem; and then they moved silently back out of sight and set to work. They had to gather grass and wood for countless fires. They began at the ledge. Toward it the fires would have to be larger and closer together; but as they moved back from it the fires could be smaller and farther apart. And, too, the line of the fire had to converge toward the river line, so that the neck of the trap would be only a few yards wide.

They were big powerful men, all of them, and they labored for several hours without pause. They would first gather an armful of grass; then upon this they would pile brush and small dead trees. The piles near the preci-

243

pice were only about twenty feet apart, but as they moved back they made them thirty feet apart, and then forty and fifty. They had to go several hundred yards away for fuel and they gathered only very dry stuff, because the fires would have to burn quickly and brightly to serve their purpose. In the past they had stampeded beasts with fire and knew what had to be done.

For a while Gode's dog trailed him back and forth, but when it observed that its master covered the same path endlessly, it lay down and watched and waited. None of the other men spoke to it or tried to lure it with friendly gestures. They did wonder, though, if the wolf would be of any use, and they hoped it would run with them when they pursued the beasts.

It was dark when the brush piles were all laid. Agreeing to meet here the next morning, the men turned away to seek their homes. Gode was about five miles from his cave, but he went on long easy strides and covered the distance in half an hour. Marigg came forward when he entered and, perceiving that he brought no food, she howled with rage.

"Food!" she screamed.

"Food-no," he said. He went to the shelves to find something for his dog. There was nothing but bones, and when he took a bone and moved to the entrance, Marigg tore it from his grasp.

"No!" she shouted. "Enemy!"

"Friend," said Gode, and he looked round him in the firelight at the other faces. Agger and Memmee were sewing. Memmee's boy was making a lance point of a piece of flint. Gode had not eaten since morning. He was willing to go to bed hungry, but he wanted food for the

244

wolf lest the men come with meat during the night and lure it away.

"Food," he said, and looked hopefully at Marigg.

"No!"

Gode lay on a deerskin, rested his face on his left arm, and tried to sleep; but all night he was haunted by dreams. He dreamed that men were feeding juicy flesh to his dog and calling it away; and again and again he rose and went outside to learn if the wolf was there. Usually when he rose, Marigg sat up to watch him, but toward morning she slept, and he stole out quietly, taking a bone for the dog and one for himself. He thought light was coming and he decided to leave early and find a partridge or rabbit for breakfast.

When he arrived on the prairie, the other men were there. One of them had brought his fire sticks and made a fire, and the others had gone into a grove of pine and found resinous pieces to use as torches. When Gode came in sight, they were ready to move. It was agreed that four of them would go to the far end of the meadow and drive the beasts down; the fifth would light the fires and then remain near the precipice. He would be armed with blazing fagots to hurl at the horses if they tried to break through the line of fire.

After skirting the prairie and coming in at the far end, the four, including Gode, waited for the fires. The first fire awake was in the pile of wood nearest them. They could not see the fire but they could see the smoke, and they watched the smoke rise as the fifth man hastened with a torch from pile to pile. When Gode thought the torch bearer must be close to the precipice, he said, "Come!" and they moved swiftly into the deep grass, followed by the wolf. As soon as they heard the movement of beasts ahead, they began to shout, and the four voices made a terrible sound, wild and baying. They could not see the horses in the deep grass, but they could hear them running, and the four of them pursued at top speed, fanning out across the meadow and howling as if demented. Gode stopped for a moment to listen and heard the sound of hooves. Then he ran again. After several hundred yards he saw the herd ahead of him. Because the beasts were leaving the meadow and racing up to the prairie, this was the time to go swiftly; and shouting to the other men to hasten, Gode ran like a deer. The other men were long-legged runners, too, and presently the four of them were close to the flying heels, their voices wild with menace and their lances flashing in the sunlight.

On the prairie the beasts saw the line of fire and circled and turned; but behind them they saw four racing men and a wolf and heard the baying of human voices. They swung again and headed for the precipice, but the men, pursuing them, ran at unbelievable speed. Before the beasts reached the ledge the men were almost at their heels; and the fifth man rushed in and hurled flaming torches. The horses were mad with terror now. Behind them was wild outcry and waving lances and fire, and above all the clamor was the piercing cry of a wolf. Snorting with frenzy the herd stampeded toward the precipice; and if the first beast to reach it paused there, it was only for a moment. The avalanche behind hurled him over, and the next behind him and the next, until it was a cascade of hooves beating on stone and of bodies plunging into depth. Five seconds after the first beast had fallen, the entire herd had gone over and vanished, and there was only the dust they left behind and the squealing below.

The men stood on the brink and looked down. The horses had dropped a sheer hundred feet, but only the first to fall had been killed instantly. The last to fall had landed on the soft pile, and some of these now ran away, unhurt. Others had broken legs or backs, and some limped away and some strove to crawl. Those mortally wounded squealed; and the scream of a horse in pain is one of the most terrible of all sounds.

The men looked down at the writhing mass, but when they saw that some of the beasts were escaping, they ran back and forth along the precipice, seeking a place to descend. Though they had more flesh than their families could eat in months, they were greedy; if there had been a thousand horses they would have tried to kill all of them. After descending, they hastened over and with lances or stones dispatched those with broken legs and backs. Then they interrupted their labor to drink blood. Some pierced throats to the jugular vein and drank from the wounds, but Gode rolled a horse upon its back, and after making a deep incision, he reached in and tore the liver from its moorings and carried it over to feed his dog. The wolf ran when he approached, but it saw and smelled the fresh meat. Gode laid the liver in plain view and retreated, and the wolf came forward and ate. Gode returned to the carcass and thrust his head in and drank from a pool of blood.

The other men had opened bellies and were eating livers. Each man clutched a dripping liver with both hands and buried his face against it and with strong teeth bit off large morsels. The meat was so tender and juicy that they did not have to chew it; like the wolf, they tore off chunks

247

and gulped them. After they had eaten, they were thirsty again, and they spread the carcasses and thrust their heads into the lung chambers to drink. Then, with bloody faces, they looked at one another and considered what was to be done next.

Their task now was to divide the kill, to drag the beasts into five separate piles. Two men working together would each grasp a leg and drag a carcass a little way down the hill. Gode went from pile to pile to count the horses in each. He counted on his fingers, and when there were five piles with ten beasts in each, he indicated to the men that five more piles were to be made. "Here!" he would say, calling to them; or "Here!" and they would drag a horse over. When the task was finished, the extra piles contained four each except one; in that there were five. The other men had been counting, too, and they all realized that there was an extra beast. One of them indicated that the extra horse was to be divided into five portions, but Gode said no. He pointed at his dog and said, "Food-there." The brows of the men darkened. They were so greedy, so fearful of being cheated, and so vain in regard to property that they wanted their share of the extra carcass. If each of them had had a thousand horses, they would nevertheless have quarreled over the division of a rabbit.

"No!" said the giant who had faced Gode; and the other men echoed him. The four of them came together and scowled and looked at Gode and at the wolf; and their movement plainly declared that they were resolved to fight, if they must, for their share. Gode turned to the extra carcass and held up five fingers, indicating that they would divide it and each take a part.

The division resulted in very unequal portions, but none of them seemed to be sensible of that. Indeed, while dragging the horses to piles, or later in claiming piles as their own, no man had made any effort to choose as his own the fattest or youngest animals. A piece of food was a piece of food; they thought of it as a unit and not of its weight or size. From the extra beast, Gode received a hunk of shoulder with the head and neck attached, and this he carried to his wolf.

Now that the food was divided and each man had his portion, the next task was to carry it home. Gode's home was five miles away and he had fourteen horses to carry to it, each of them weighing about five hundred pounds. The men fell to with lances, each dividing a carcass into two parts. Then in turn they grasped two legs, threw half a carcass across their back and shoulders, picked up their weapons, and set off for home.

Gode was the first to go. He followed the ledge and, after he had gone a quarter of a mile, he saw a great cavern in the stone wall and paused to consider it. This, it seemed to him, would make a good home for his family; then he would not have to carry his meat such a long way. The homes of the other men were in the same direction, and when Gode saw them approaching, he no longer hesitated. He entered the high-vaulted room and laid his meat on the floor. When the other men came abreast, they dropped their burdens and looked at him, and Gode told them that he intended to live here. The notion captured their fancy and, leaving their meat, they hastened along the mountain wall, looking for other caverns.

It was a custom among them that a chamber belonged to a man and could not be invaded if a piece of his property lay within it. When, therefore, Gode laid his meat on the floor, this room became his, and he knew that the other men would not try to take it. Not even the surly giant would do a thing like that. Gode's problem now was to bring his family; but before he set off for home he hacked off a piece of flesh. This he carried by thrusting his lance through it and letting it hang from the lance across his shoulder.

He did not foresee that the women would not want to leave the home they had. It had the comforts of a dry floor and dry walls, shelves for storing, and abundant water and wood in the valley below.

"No," said Marigg when Gode explained that he had another home and much food. She folded hairy arms across her withered breasts and looked adamant.

"Come," he said. "Food," he said, and with gestures he indicated a pile as large as a hill.

"No," said Marigg. She took the piece of flesh and cut off portions for the older children and the other women. She ate a little herself; and when she realized that it was tender horse flesh her face softened. This was her favorite meat. "Much-food?" she asked, pointing at the meat.

Gode again made gestures of height and breadth; and this time he indicated that the pile was as big as the room they sat in.

"Look," said Marigg, and pointed outside. Night was coming. Already the sun had vanished and dusk was cloaking the far hills.

The next morning Gode persuaded Memmee to go with him; and when Agger understood her intent, she hastened to follow. With Memmee and the wolf willing, Gode would have cared little enough about the others.

He would have left them here to starve, and Marigg knew that. She knew that a man's devotion to his family was as fickle and capricious as his whims.

When the two women and the children went outside with Gode, Marigg began to scream with frustrated rage. She was an old and enfeebled woman and she did not like to be dragged from home to home. Besides, she was the grandmother and the queen, and her word was supposed to be law. When she screamed and stamped her feet, the others turned to look at her; and Memmee said, "Come!"

"No!" Marigg shrieked; but she was looking wildly round her, knowing well that she would have to go or live here alone. "Fire!" she cried, and pointed at the fire. That meant nothing to Gode; he had his fire sticks with him and would make another fire. But fire for Marigg, for all older women, was something that lived and needed care. For them, it was a symbol of their meaning and of their power in the group. This fire belonged to Marigg; she had been its guardian, its mother, and if she went, it would have to go with her. If she left it here to die, she would feel that a part of herself had died with it.

She threw bed pelts and garments out to the other women and then ran out to Memmee to take the stone jug and the skin pouches, including the handful of wheat and barley seed. Returning, she chose the largest piece of burning wood and followed them, but every two or three hundred yards she had to stop and build a fire and choose another torch. Gode was impatient to reach his food; he knew that flesh-eaters had probably come during the night and destroyed a part of it. But if he went too far ahead of Marigg, she would scream at him and leap up and down in a wild tantrum. Then Gode would wait until she came, bearing fire. She stopped so many times that it took them most of the day to cover the five miles; and when they reached the cave which Gode had chosen as their new home, he saw that beasts had come and eaten the flesh he had left there.

Now he fell into a rage, and when Marigg came up with fire she did nothing to calm him. Glancing round her, she saw no sign of water or of dry timber; nor did she like her new home. It smelled of wild beasts, the floor was covered with dung, and there were no shelves for the storing of garments and food. She ran about like a huge, angry insect, exclaiming with disgust or rushing at the others if they approached her fire.

Gode hastened over to his meat to learn how much had been eaten. All ten piles had been visited by wolves, jackals, and hyenas, and most of the carcasses had big holes eaten in their bellies. For several minutes he stared at the carnage. Then he grasped a leg, intending to drag a carcass home, but even for a man of his strength it was too great a burden. While he was laboring with it, two of the other men approached his cave, and Gode hastened over. One of them was the surly giant. He came up and looked boldly at Memmee, his gaze frank and covetous and without shame. Memmee was a handsome woman. He did not speak but there was no need to because his wish was naked in his eyes.

Memmee looked at the stranger and read his meaning and turned to Gode. Gode was angry. This man had wanted his wolf and now he wanted his woman. "Come," he said, and Memmee went with him to the pile of meat.

Assisted by Agger and the boy, they dragged several

of the horses to the cave and were still laboring when darkness came. Upon seeing how much food Gode had, Marigg felt a little more indulgent toward him. She laid a fire in the cave entrance and with a flint knife skinned a beast and cut off portions for the children. Memmee and Agger spread pelts on the floor. Gode stood beyond the fire, lance in hand, keeping an eye on his dog and the other men. He decided that he would have to build a fire by the remaining carcasses and spend the night there.

9

FOR several days the women were very busy. They had the animals to skin and cut up, the flesh to dry and store; and after this task was done they would have several hides to tan and to sew into garments. Soon, too, they would have fruit to pick and dry, roots to dig up and lay away, and a big pile of food to fetch up the mountain.

But Gode had little to do. Periodic idleness in the man has led him into the realms of art and philosophy; it has prompted him to reverie, speculation, and abstract ideas. In one day of genius Gode had piled up so much food that his women were almost dismayed, and now he had nothing to do but to follow his fancies and his whims. A part of the time he might have given to drawings on the walls of his new home or to the polishing and engraving of weapons if he had not been astonished again by sight of a creature that, for him, was neither beast nor human.

In coming to this mountainside he had invaded the area occupied by Harg and his people. Indeed, Harg's home was in this same mountain, less than a mile away. Returning one night after dark, Gode saw Harg's fire and warily climbed the mountain for a closer view. He recognized it as the home and the fire which he had seen once before. He recognized the stooped dwarfs in the cave. During the intervening weeks he had forgotten them, but now, staring with amazement, he was again troubled by the feeling that they were both like and unlike his own kind. But he did not accept them as fellow human beings; they were too stunted, too hairy, too stooped and beastlike for that. Because the notion persisted that they might be human, and because they outraged his vanity and self-love, he felt resentful and angry and wanted to kill them. And when at last he turned away, deeply troubled by their presence, there was in him both fear and hate.

A few days later, while hunting, not for meat but for delicacies like doves and eggs for his own and his dog's lunch, he saw one of Harg's people. It was an old stooped man who shuffled along on bent legs, a stone axe hanging from one of his long arms. He was so filthy and stupid, and moved in such a blind and awkward way, that his only resemblance to human beings, for Gode at least, was his upright posture. Gode trailed him and spied on him; and he became convinced at last that this was only a strange beast of a kind he had never seen until recently. Because Gode wanted to examine the creature, he resolved to kill it.

The old man had come out of a thicket and was crossing an open space to a grove of trees. When he came to the edge of the grove, he stopped and peered round him. He turned his whole body while he looked, because he seemed unable to turn the head on his neck. So far as Gode could tell, he had no neck. Hunched forward, with his head growing out of his chest and shoulders, he stared back at the thicket and listened. His arms hung almost to his knees, and the head of the axe touched the earth. For several moments he looked and listened as if he had heard a sound.

About a hundred yards away Gode was hiding and watching him. When the creature entered the woods, Gode came quickly out of hiding and ran softly across the open space, his wolf trailing him by a few yards. As noiseless as a panther he entered the grove. He could not see the creature now but he could hear him, and he followed, with bow and arrow ready to shoot. For him, it was like stalking a deer. Now and then he caught a glimpse of his prey, moving like a shadow in the gloom; but not until the old man had gone through the woods and reached the open ground on the far side did Gode get the chance he was waiting for. He was now only about thirty yards behind. The man stopped at the edge and looked out, cautiously, timidly, like one who sensed that an enemy was near. He presented his broad shoulders in full view. Gode drew his bowstring far back and took quick but careful aim; and a moment later the arrow was driven deep between the old fellow's shoulders.

At first he seemed paralyzed by the shock; he gave no cry and made no move. Then, like long tentacles, his arms began to explore, reaching above and behind him. Perhaps he thought he had been struck by a snake. When his hand reached back and grasped the arrow, he was still too amazed and bewildered to make a sound; but in trying to pull the arrow out he turned and saw Gode. Gode had fitted another arrow to his bow, and while the old man gazed at him with horror and astonishment, Gode shot again. This arrow entered the man's stomach and pierced his spine.

He now gave the most horrible scream Gode had ever heard. It was not a cry of amazement or pain; it was the mad bawling sound of helplessness and horror. Shaking, sweating, and never for an instant taking his eyes off Gode, he grasped the arrow in his stomach and tried to pull it out; and all the while his big open mouth squealed with naked terror. He pulled the arrow out of its flint head and hurled the stick from him. Then he reached round to the one in his back and broke it off. The stone axe had fallen from his grasp.

Gode was so upset by the awful, lonely anguish in the man's crying that he could not decide whether to shoot him again or to finish him off with his lance. He glanced round him for the wolf. This experience was building in him the quality of a haunted dream. He himself was sweating and trembling a little. Dropping his bow, he grasped his lance and went forward; and the creature's terror was now so wild and shrieking that it was heard by other men a mile away. As Gode swiftly approached, the old man sank to his knees. He was shaking terribly and supplicating with his hands; and his eyes were such big pools of horror that they were the only thing Gode saw when he stepped in and drove the lance home. He spitted the man in his soft throat above the collar bone. He yanked the lance out and stood poised, ready to strike again; but the creature collapsed with a gurgling cry full of blood. Gode stepped back.

The strange animal now lay at his feet and he could see it clearly, but he still did not accept it as a human being. Nevertheless he was troubled by the likeness to himself;

257

and he was still staring and wondering about it when two other men came in view. They shouted to Gode, and Gode called to them to come over; and they came up and looked at the dead thing, their eyes filling with amazement.

"Man?" asked one of them, using the word for their own kind.

"No," said Gode.

"Man?" the other asked again.

Gode rolled the creature over. One of the men saw the stone axe and picked it up.

"Look," he said.

It was so crude that they could hardly think of it as a weapon; for them it was only a piece of stone. Then one of the men knelt and peered·at the creature's face; and as if he were making comparisons, he looked up at Gode. Then he noted the creature's dwarfed size. "Man-no," he said, rising to his feet.

"No," said Gode.

But they were troubled nevertheless. Both their sense of sight and of smell told them that this was one of their own kind, no matter how stunted and bent and hairy; but their self-love could not accept the kinship. This dead thing had a browner skin, its eyes were farther apart, its lower jaw was more protruding, and its teeth were larger and pressed the lips outward; and though all these were superficial differences, these men looked upon the fallen one as a monster.

"Many," said Gode, and he gestured at the region occupied by Harg's people.

"Many?" asked one of the men incredulously.

"Yes."

"Enemy?"

Gode hesitated. "Yes," he said.

For the other two men, that settled it; these creatures were enemies and must be killed. They picked up their weapons and looked warily round them as if expecting attack.

Gode decided to carry this monster home. He wanted his women to see it. After returning for his bow, he grasped the dead man and threw him across his right shoulder. He climbed the mountain with his burden and entered the cave and let the dead man fall to the floor.

"Look," he said.

The women and older children gathered round to look. For the women, it was not a strange creature but a man.

"Dead?" Memmee asked.

"Yes. Enemy," said Gode. He stooped and turned the old man over so they could see the arrow wounds. The eyes had bulged with horror, and when she saw them Marigg made a sound of disgust. Kneeling, she examined the genitals, which were almost completely hidden by a heavy growth of hair. Then she rose and indicated to Gode that he was to take the thing away.

Gode seized a foot and dragged the body outside and along the mountain, looking for a crevice in which to hide it. He sensed that the women saw nothing strange and repulsive in this creature that to him resembled a human being, yet was not one; and after he had thrust the body into a crevice he examined it in greater detail. He looked at the toes and fingers and observed that the latter were very short and thick in comparison with his own. There was a wide spread between the forefinger and thumb. He observed, too, the huge lower jaw, the low withdrawn forehead, the shaggy and protruding brow-ridges, the grotesque shortness of the forearm and lower leg, and the accumulation of filth that covered the brown skin. But more than all these, it was the ungainly posture of the creature in life and its bent, awkward way of moving that convinced him of its unlikeness to himself.

Human beings, and especially men, have always felt that their own appearance—their proportions and size and color—was the norm of the race. Those who have differed sharply from them they have regarded as unhuman or at least as subhuman. And so it was with Gode. He recognized the similarities; but in spite of the fact that his women had accepted this thing as a man, he was unwilling to do so. For him it was a beast that resembled a man; and while he stood and gazed at the corpse, he decided that all these creatures ought to be hunted down and killed.

In this he was moved, wholly unknown to himself, by a deep and enveloping self-love. If he had not felt that Harg's people might be human, he would have had no wish to exterminate them. For Gode they were a kind of impostor among the beasts. They stood up on two legs instead of walking on four; they carried a hunk of stone and pretended that it was a weapon; and in some strange and presumptuous way they had stolen a part of man's physical appearance. That is the way Gode felt about it.

And that is the way the other men felt, though less deeply because they were less intelligent than Gode and therefore less vain. There spread among them news of the creature Gode had killed, and some of them came to look at the body in the crevice. Indeed, they dragged the body out where they could see it clearly and examine it and talk about it; and when Gode said that all these monsters ought to be killed, they eagerly agreed. They returned to their homes to make arrows and lance heads, and to smear red ochre on their bodies and faces. They were preparing to kill their own fellows; and though they had formulated no moral values, no concepts of right and wrong, they did feel that they had worthy reasons. They were going to kill, not for the pleasure of killing but to rid the world of a repulsive impostor who was trying to look like them. The emotion they felt was obscurely righteous in its intensity and fervor. In their simple and primitive way they were undertaking a crusade in an effort to make the world conform to their notions of what it should be.

Here were the first faint beginnings of race prejudice, born of and nourished by self-love. For the first time in the history of the human race on this planet, men were ready to go to war.

10

THEY had no traditions of war, because never before had men banded together to destroy their own kind. Of the small group now preparing to fight, Gode was accepted as the leader by right of size, prowess, and speed. The men who had helped him drive the horses over the ledge had taken homes along the mountain; and these four warriors came each morning to Gode's cave, and he led them to battle.

To say that they went into battle is an exaggeration. They hunted as a fighting unit, but there was no organized opposition to them; they might as well have been stalking any beast of the forests. Five formidable hunters, armed with bow, arrows, and a lance, and trailed by a wolf that was now two-thirds grown, would hunt down a lone man of Harg's people and destroy him. The hunted, armed only with a stone axe and a flint knife, was more defenseless against them than a deer because he was slow and awkward and unable to flee.

The first morning Gode and his men set out, they were

deeply excited. They were going out to exterminate impostors who had the effrontery to stand up on two legs and pretend to be human. In a way they had become moralists, judges of the good and the bad in the appearance of things, arbiters of right and wrong. Their vanity had been dreadfully outraged by ungainly creatures who resembled them. They resented them as they resented barren women, malformed children, or diseased old men; because all of these were a threat to their security in an unfriendly world. It was threats to the safety and future of the individual and the group that first drove human beings to conceive of moral values and rights and laws; and this morning five moralists, five crusaders, set off to rid the world of an image that was false to their notions of what the world should be.

After descending the mountain, they fanned out, going abreast across a distance of several hundred yards, with Gode in the center and the wolf trailing him. By this time they all knew where Harg's people lived. They did not know how many of them there were or how far toward the sun lay the region which they occupied.

About noon one of the men shouted a warning, and at once the five of them closed in. The man who had uttered the cry pointed to a grove of trees and said: "There!"

"Many?" asked Gode.

The man extended one finger.

With arrow fixed, Gode now led the group. When he came to the timber, he stopped and said, "There," and pointed to the right, and "There," and pointed to the left. Two men advanced on either flank. Before entering, Gode waited until they had circled the woods; whereupon, with the wolf trailing him, he moved stealthily in, holding his bow ready to shoot. The growth around him was dense, and he was unable to see more than a few feet ahead; but presently he heard excited cries and then a piercing scream, and he hurried through to the far side.

The other men had outflanked their prey and waited for it to come out. All four had shot, and four arrows had struck their victim. When Gode came up, the man was rolling on the earth in agony and clutching at the arrows. The men who had shot him stood close by and looked at him with astonishment but with no trace of pity. As the leader, Gode stepped forward and drove his lance into the soft throat; and then blood gurgled in the cries and issued from the mouth and nostrils. Twitching convulsively, the man rolled over on his back and turned glazed eyes to the sky.

This man was short, even among his people, for he was barely five feet tall; and lying on the earth he looked like a hunched dwarf with crooked limbs. The surly giant lifted him by the hair of his skull and set him on his feet; and while holding him thus he said contemptuously, "Look!" They had no word for monster but they felt that this creature was monstrous. The giant let the dead man fall and stepped back. Then four of them knelt by the corpse and tried to draw out the arrows with the heads intact; and when they were unable to do so because the arrow heads were imbedded in bone or sinew, they took their lances and hacked the dead man into pieces. In dismembering him one of the men noticed the genitals, and with a sharp lance head he cut them off and held them up for the others to see. The resemblance between them and their own was so undeniable that the giant felt fresh outrage and drove his lance into the open mouth.

Then he kicked the mutilated body, impelled by a wish to obliterate it from the earth. The man who held the organs now let them fall, but after a few moments he knelt and stared at them. After long scrutiny he turned to look at the organs of a companion; and soon all of them were gazing curiously at one another as if only now had they become fully aware of this part of themselves. But their emotion was of another kind. The genitals were, for any man, the most precious part of his body, not only because they were sensitive and exposed and sometimes wounded in the chase, but also because they produced exquisitely pleasurable sensations in conjunction with a female. That these dwarfed impostors should have a part so much like their own was reason for fresh resentment; and before they left the corpse they stabbed it spitefully, angrily, with hatred like a darkness in their eyes.

During this day they found no more victims, but on the third morning they spied a family group. There was a male, two females, and three small children. The group prowled in or kept close to wooded areas, and for an hour or more Gode and his companions trailed it. When, after looking anxiously around, the adults moved to cross an open space, the women carrying the small ones, Gode quickly sighted and drove an arrow into the man's back. The other men were drawing their bowstrings to shoot the women; but an instant before they were ready to release the arrows, the man leapt into the air with a wild scream. The two women swung around like enraged she-beasts.

Gode and his companions were now in full view, not more than thirty yards away, and the women saw them when they turned. Meanwhile their man was screaming dreadfully. In the moment of turning, the women not only saw the men but saw their drawn bows and fixed arrows. Perhaps news of these tall stalking killers and their strange weapons had reached them. In any case, they did not hesitate. From their arms three children slid to the ground, and the older woman seized the stone axe from the wounded man's grasp. The younger woman threw herself face downward to hug and draw the children under her body to protect them; and the other woman, with the axe in her grasp, rushed like a furious tigress against the men.

It all happened so quickly that Gode and his men were startled and nonplussed; they stood like men of stone while the woman rushed toward them. They were still standing like men too astounded to move or think when the woman reached them and swung with the axe. With cries of amazement, the men backed away, but one of them stumbled; and in the next moment the furious woman split his skull wide open. She struck with such force that she buried the blade in bone and was unable to dislodge it; and while she struggled with it, Gode sprang forward and drove his lance through her. She sank upon it, moaning, and her hands rose and clasped at her breast, like the hands of one in prayer.

This had all happened so quickly that the other men had not moved; but when they saw their companion with the cleft skull, and looked across and saw the other woman crawling away, they shouted and ran toward her, with lances poised. She was moving away to find a hiding place, and while she crawled she tried to keep the three children under her belly and out of sight. Before the men reached her, she had come to a depression in the ground.

266

This she crept into and pushed the children down into the hole under her; and now she hovered above them, trying to hide them from sight. The big giant reached her first, and, with a blow of his lance, he killed her almost instantly. She sank upon the children, still striving in the moment of death to shield them.

When the giant tried to withdraw the lance the head stuck and he pulled the woman out of the hole and exposed the children. They began to cry. They were only babies, the oldest of whom was not more than three. This child, a boy, looked up and saw the men standing with lances and his mother lying still on the ground. He raised his arms as if to protect himself and began to scream. The giant had torn the lance head out of the dying woman; and now he reached down and lifted the boy by the hair of his skull, held him for a moment and looked at him, and let him fall. He then shoved his lance through the child's belly and picked him up on the lance and twirled him round and round. He lowered the body to the earth and put a foot on it and drew the lance out. Then he dispatched the other babies by thrusting through them and pulling them out of the hole. The other men, standing near by, made no move to assist in the killing.

They all returned to the other woman and their dead companion. The man was lying on his back, with arms outstretched and mouth wide open. The blade of the axe had divided his skull with a fissure between the two halves an inch wide. His brains had exuded from the cleft and looked like pink fungus. His eyes were filled with amazement.

While his companions looked at him, they all had the same thought. They would have to carry him to his family, and this none of them wanted to do because his family was two or three miles away. While staring at the dead man, the sullen giant was suddenly taken by a notion. He knew this man's family. In it were two women, and the younger one was attractive. He wanted her, and now he plotted to get her. If he offered to take the dead man home, he could possess the woman and the property; and so, more with gestures than with words, he said he would carry the man home. He picked up the corpse and laid it, belly downward, across his right shoulder; and when the others handed him his bow and lance, he set off in haste.

Gode had had enough of killing for one day and indicated that he was going home, too. His dog had been sitting at the edge of the clearing, watching the murders; and Gode now called to it and turned away. He felt a little shaken by his experience. It would not be true to say that he felt shame or pity, but he did feel troubled. He had examined the female whom he killed, and though she was a dwarfed and stooped thing, he had perceived that she was much like his own women. And the cries of the children had been like the cries made by the children in his home.

Alone with his dog, he went rather aimlessly, heading in the direction of his home but in no hurry to reach it. Now and then he sat on a stone or a fallen tree, standing his lance by one knee and his bow by the other, and thought of these creatures whom he had helped to slay. Memory of their cries haunted him. After sitting a little while, he would rise and look round him for the faithful wolf; and then he would resume his journey, but slowly and aimlessly, like a man sunk in thought. He killed a rabbit and ate the organs and gave the remainder to his

268

dog. In the dank gloom of a forest he found mushrooms and by a stream he dug up and ate several wild carrots.

When darkness approached he was following a river, and he stopped by a watering place where beasts came to drink. On one side of the path he hid in a thicket to wait for a deer because he was weary of the dried horse-flesh which his women gave him. While sitting here, he heard a strange sound. It was a faintly hissing and very cold and deadly sound, and Gode thought it was made by a serpent. He crept forward until he could see the stream and the far bank. This bank was a shelf of rock with crevices in it from which water trickled, and hiding in the crevices were snakes. Partridges were coming to the stone shelf to drink. The snakes had heard the birds coming and had crawled to the entrance of their caverns; and there they lay coiled and waiting and made a chilling sound. When a partridge dropped gently down, a snake would strike and seize the victim with its fangs. Soon a dozen birds were captured by as many snakes; and Gode looked across at the scene and listened to the despairing cries of the birds and the helpless beating of their wings.

The cries recalled to him the sounds made in dying by the creatures whom he and his companions had killed. He felt a little angry. He felt an impulse to go over and stab the serpents with his lance; but he knew very well, he had known all his life, that the world was made of the killed and the killers. In times past he had seen snakes kill their prey. He had seen death so often in so many times and places that he almost never thought about it.

Tonight, however, his attitude toward it was not quite what it had been. Leaving the thicket, he waded the stream and climbed up the wet stone ledge; and when the snakes saw him coming, they drew back into the crevices and tried to draw the birds with them. Most of the crevices were too small to admit a partridge; and so the snakes drew the birds against the stone and hung on with their fangs and waited. Gode stooped and peered before one of the chambers. Then he reached in with his lance and stabbed a serpent's head. The fangs relaxed, and Gode took the wounded bird in both hands and looked at it. He felt blood on one hand and when he turned the bird over he saw blood on the feathers. In any former evening of his life he would have snapped the head off the partridge and taken it home to eat; but there was a different emotion in him tonight. He set the bird down to see if it could stand, and at once it flew away. That pleased him. He marked its flight for a few moments and then stabbed another serpent, and a third and a fourth, releasing the birds that could fly and laying the others on the ledge at his feet. All but two of the birds flew away. These two were so badly wounded that they were dying; but Gode did not pull off their heads. When he turned homeward he carried them in his arms and from time to time he stopped and set them on the earth to learn if they could fly. This was a strange thing for Gode to do, but in this evening he was a strange man.

II

DURING this night he was haunted by dreams. New emotions were reshaping the materials in his subconscious mind and his subconscious mind was making strange patterns of his recent experiences. Over and over, with almost no change at all, he dreamed the same dream.

He was out hunting, with no companion save his dog, when he came upon human-like creatures, a mother and her child. She was carrying the child, hugging it to her breast, while she walked slowly, half-bent to the earth, as if sniffing along a path. With a terrible cry he rushed toward her and struck her to the ground and beat her; and when she crawled to the child and drew it under her body, he rolled her away and thrust through it with his lance. In wild rage he killed both of them; and while he stood and looked down at them, his eyes inflamed with loathing, his whole being outraged by the sight of them, the mother moved over, even though dead, to cover the child and protect it. Thereupon he beat her and stabbed her again and again. He rolled her over and tore the child from her grasp and flung it away; and again the dead creature crawled toward it. She reached out, as before, and drew it under her belly and hid it.

She did this again and again, and in his dream he became afraid of her and went away. He was horrified by this thing which all his beating and stabbing could not make lie still—by this dead mother who crawled in death to protect her child. When he turned away, he was sweating with horror, and he ran, intent only on getting beyond sight of a beaten and mutilated body that still moved. But after he had run a considerable distance he felt that he was being followed. On looking back, he could see nothing behind him, not even his dog; and he ran again, dodging to the right or left, entering thickets, wading streams, climbing over hills and down, and crossing areas of stone to hide his tracks and his scent; but the invisible thing followed him. It made no sound, but he knew it was stalking him, softly, relentlessly. He could feel the presence of it. It was as impalpable as the air and as silent as the fire in the sky. And when at last in desperation he turned to face it, to meet it in combat and destroy it, there was nothing visible to attack. The presence was near him, but no matter whether he fled or stood still and waited, its distance from him seemed to remain constant. It was this aspect of the experience that was too dreadful to bear. He began to make a sound, a low, choked gurgle of terror that rose in anguish until it was almost a scream. The sound aroused Marigg. She left the skin on which she was lying and went over to Gode and looked at his face. His eyes were closed, but his face was distorted by awful suffering and his wet lips were making the sound that had awakened her. She prodded him with a finger, and at once he sat up and stared at her, his eyes filled with horror. For a moment he thought she was the presence and recoiled, but when she spoke he recognized her as Marigg. Then for a long moment the man and woman gazed at one another in firelight.

"Sick?" asked Marigg.

Gode stood up and looked round him, and Marigg rose, too, and laid wood on the fire. He knew now that he had been dreaming, but he was deeply shaken; and even when wide awake he felt that the presence was near. He had no word for ghost, no concept of such a thing; if he had had such a concept he would have said that a ghost was haunting him. On looking round him he felt rather foolish—because here he was, safe in his own home, yet covered with the sweat of terror.

He returned to his bed and presently he slept again; and he dreamed the same dream. This time there were more details in the experience. After he had slain the mother and she had crawled away to recover her child, she looked up at him and her eyes were sad and reproachful. And now, when fleeing aimlessly, or when turning to face the thing, he could see the eyes. They were only a pair of disembodied eyes that alternately appeared and vanished; but again and again during his flight when he turned to look behind him he could see them floating in the atmosphere. In this dream he was again overwhelmed by dread and began to make a choked sound in his sleep—a sound like that made by the creature's gasping and blood after he drew the lance from her throat.

This time he was aroused by the horror of his experience. He rose, shaking, wet with sweat, and looked at the other sleepers; and because he felt cold he went over

273

to sit by the fire. After a few minutes he remembered his dog. Going to Marigg's store of food he got a piece of horse meat and entered the night, intending to find and feed the wolf; but the wolf was gone. He went to the skin that he had taken out for his dog to sleep on and knelt and pressed the hair with an open palm, but the skin was cold. He knew the wolf had not been on it during the night. Prowling in the darkness and calling softly, he searched until morning came; and when he could see clearly he went down the mountain or back and forth under the ledge, but there was no sign of the wolf. He was still searching when the other men came over, ready for the day's hunt.

They had not been haunted by dreams and they were eager to go forth and kill the strange creatures that looked like men; but Gode was unwilling to go. He was deeply upset by the loss of his dog and he was troubled by his dreams. He told the men the wolf was gone, and they joined him in the search, exploring the mountain and down into the valley, but they found no trace of it. When again they indicated their wish to have Gode join them in the hunt, he pretended to be ill. He opened his mouth and thrust out his tongue; and they peered at him curiously, looking for signs of disease. His face was so pale and drawn and he was so sleepy and tired that they decided he was ill; and so they turned away to their hunting, and Gode climbed the mountain and entered his home.

He still felt the invisible presence of an evil and avenging thing. He did not, of course, perceive it with any of his senses, though repeatedly he tried to; he would look round him and listen and sniff the air, or he would search the earth for strange footprints. He was so plainly disturbed that the women became aware of his unusual behavior. After remaining in the cave only a few moments. he had gone outside, and when Memmee brought food to him. he refused it. She knew he was troubled and she looked at him, her eyes asking questions; and while wondering about him, she realized that the wolf was gone. She went over to the skin and touched it and looked round her for the wolf; and then she came back and gazed soberly at Gode's unhappy face.

"Gone?" she asked.

"Yes."

"Dead?"

Gode did not know whether the wolf was dead, but he answered yes to the question. Memmee thought she understood then why he was grieving, and she entered the cave and told Marigg about it; and Gode heard the women talking, but he paid no attention to what they said. He had been thinking in a confused and persistent way and he had come to the conclusion that the invisible thing haunting him had killed or stolen his dog. Soon after this notion entered his mind, it became a certainty. The fact that the wolf was gone was proof for him that an unseen thing had bothered him all night.

He did not at once arrive at his second and more significant conclusion. For a long while he sat out in the sun with thoughts and impulses and dark and elusive hints making bewildering patterns in his mind. In an effort to understand what had happened to him he stared at many objects, as if seeking beyond him for a clue. The world had become larger, stranger, more perplexing. The circumference of his mental life embraced a great deal more than the world he had always known.

He looked at the sun, for instance, as he had never looked at it before. For him and his people it was a fire because it gave warmth. But the manner of its life was utterly mysterious; it floated through space and alternately appeared and vanished. Though it was a strange thing, they were used to its strangeness and rarely thought about it. But today, because life had become more baffling, Gode looked at the sun as if to decide whether it might be more than a floating fire. After several moments of gazing at it without seeing more than he had always seen, without finding any new meaning there, he turned his eyes to the far horizon. Across the valley were scattered hills. Upon the crest of the farthest hill was the skyline. He knew that if he were to walk to the hill the skyline would advance beyond him. He did not know what it was, but he had learned that a man could never reach it.

In looking at it now he wondered how far away it was and how far it could go, and whether, if a man were to walk long enough, he could come to the end of things. He was thinking such thoughts because his world had become bigger during one night of dreams. He had been followed and spied on by something which he could not see; and if there were more things in the world around him than he perceived with his senses, then perhaps there were things beyond the skyline. He had become smaller because he was now measuring himself not only by the known but by the unknown as well. He had become more defenseless and lonely, and much less secure.

Against this invisible presence he could not use his

weapon; a man could not fight what he could not see. All day he felt that this presence was near him, and when night came and he had eaten a little and stretched out on a skin to sleep, he was haunted again by the same dream. In some particulars it was different from the dream of the preceding night, but he was still pursued by an invisible and unfriendly thing. Upon being awakened by the nightmare, he rose, as before, and searched round him for such evidence as odors and footprints. And the next day, though he took his weapons and went forth as if to hunt, he was a distracted and goaded and very unhappy man whose mind was busy with a riddle.

When the second conclusion came to him, it came suddenly and without warning out of the depths of his mind below the level of consciousness. His conscious mind was too confused, too harassed by ignorance and too darkened by fear, to draw from the known the probabilities of the unknown; but in his subconscious mind there had been intuitive reasoning. The conclusion came to him with the force of a shock; for a moment it was a stark and lucid meaning and then it was gone. It was as if it had come for an instant of terrifying clarity and then had been swallowed by all the darkness of what he did not understand. And because there was only a moment of meaning he did not grasp it. He was shocked and startled, as human beings always must be when an intuitive truth shines like a light for an instant and slips from the conscious mind's grasp.

The illumination was this: In the brief and tantalizing moment of recognition, he felt that the presence which haunted him had come from one of the creatures whom he had helped to kill. It was the human mind's first notion of the ghost. But before he could seize the truth, it was gone. He continued to walk, but more slowly, because he was deeply troubled; and the recognition in him was like a light that would flash and vanish and flash again while he struggled desperately to capture and hold it.

He did not capture and hold it during this day. Not until he slept and dreamed again, and still again, did the notion take the firm, full shape of a fact. One morning he rose with the truth in him as if he had always known it. In a few days his world had expanded enormously; it had become two worlds: the invisible and the visible. Wholly unknown to him, he had taken a great stride beyond the understanding of his people. This morning he stood erect and tall and knew there was something which his weapons had no power to kill. He was a man who felt the presence of the ghost. Not for him, and in a few generations not for any of his people, could the world again be so small as the visible world in which he had lived.

12

He became, of course, a strange man for those who knew him. He spent most of the next two days hunting for his wolf; and when he was home the women found him silent and gentle. He was afraid. He had always been afraid, but only of certain enemies that he could see; now he was haunted when asleep and when awake by a more dreadful enemy because it was invisible and constant.

Most of his time he spent thinking of this enemy and wondering how he could destroy it. He did not tell his women about it or speak of it to other men. Perhaps he felt they would not believe him; or perhaps he was silenced by a wish to learn more about the ways of this enemy before announcing its presence. At the end of several days he felt more secure and was much like his former self. His dreams were less terrifying; and during the days when he wandered off alone he did not always feel that the unfriendly presence was near him. Little by little he became bolder and at last he was prevailed on by the other men to join them in the hunt.

They had been zealously stalking Harg's people and killing them; and they had learned with astonishment that one of the creatures seemed to know how to make fire. They had found Harg and his family, who, after fleeing their cave, had moved under a ledge of stone by a river. The men told Gode of these creatures who used fire and asked him to come with them; and Gode went because it occurred to him that perhaps these fire makers by the river had stolen his dog.

The four men set out late one forenoon. Their appearance was dreadful because they had smeared their faces and parts of their bodies with red and green dyes. Down their cheeks and across their foreheads they had painted lances of red and green, with the two colors alternating. On the less hairy parts of their bodies they had painted designs. Gode was more artistic than the others; the painted areas on his body were intended to represent weapons. Down each thigh, for instance, he had long red arrows with the heads just above his kneecaps. The other men seemed to have daubed themselves without purpose. In appearance the sullen giant was the most terrifying one. He had painted his ears and nose and his big full lips. His red mouth looked like an open wound full of gleaming bone. In decorating themselves some men imitated others; but some, fiercely independent and vain, strove to be unique. The giant scorned the arrows on Gode which the other men admired. He fancied himself as the most impressive warrior of the four—and in a huge and gaudy way he was. Around his neck was a deerskin lace from which teeth and pieces of staghorn hung across his broad chest. This vain and ferocious man had even painted his genitals, using red ochre to make them brightly con-

spicuous. He wanted to attract the attention of the women
—and he did. Memmee stared at him for a long moment
and then turned and grasped Marigg's arm and asked her
to look. While they gazed at him the giant strutted about,
delighted by their interest.

Gode was as vain as any other and was busy meanwhile
painting colorful designs on his legs. He was more intelligent and he was an artist; but, if he had been more observant, he would have realized that his art was too
refined for the taste of these people. They were more
impressed by the giant's splotches of color.

When Gode was ready at last and the men turned
toward the hill, proudly bearing their weapons and admiring themselves, the giant went ahead, swaggering with
arrogance and feeling that on this day he would distinguish himself. Because Gode had no wolf now, the giant
no longer envied him. Indeed, he thought Gode was very
ordinary and unattractive. Gode had no wolf and tiger
teeth hanging across his breast; the women had not stared
at him and gasped with astonishment.

When the four men came to a stream, they stopped to
admire themselves in its mirror. The giant was more his-
trionic in his attitudes, but they all struck poses and gazed
at themselves with childlike pleasure. Now and then the
big fellow glanced over at another image in the water;
but it seemed to him that none save his own was impressive.

"Look," he said, and pointed at his image.

"Look," said another man, pointing at his; and in turn
each of them invited attention to his own reflection. For
each of them, his own image was the only one worth
looking at.

After they entered the zone of danger, they became more humble. At some distance ahead was the smoke of a fire; one of them indicated it and turned to look at Gode's face. It was not a happy face. Upon reaching the area where he had helped to slay the strange creatures, he again felt the invisible presence; and instead of striking out as the leader, as had always been his custom, he went quietly and fearfully, content to let the giant take the lead position. They all moved more fearfully now. In comparison with their prey they were formidably armed, and in all their battles with them except the first they had been easily triumphant; but these ahead of them had fire, and from this they inferred that they might be more dangerous.

Keeping to the alder and birch thickets along the stream they slowly advanced, with the giant leading and Gode at the rear. When they came within sight of the fire they stopped and hid behind bushes and peered out. They were looking at Harg's family, and present now were Harg and three women and their children. The men knew that this male had three females and they hated him for that. Among them, only Gode had so many.

Harg's family was in a deep recess under overhanging stone. They were twenty feet above the river, and from their fire at the outer edge the bank dropped sharply to the stream. While peering out, the men were considering the approaches. Attack would not be so easy here, because these creatures were in a kind of fortress to which there seemed to be only one, and a rather difficult, way of approach.

They moved stealthily forward until they were about fifty yards away. Peering out, they now had a clear view of the little table above the river. The females were squatting by the fire. Just beyond the fire was a huge pile of wood. Back in the recess, but visible, was the male, who also squatted, and he seemed to be busy. All these details the men noted while wondering how to attack.

Between them and their targets were birch tops. The giant slipped forward to a better position, whereupon, crouching, he fixed an arrow to his bow, aimed at Harg, and pulled back the string. In this moment Harg moved and the man waited; and the others watching him could see him moving his bow a little as he sighted. Then he sped the arrow, and all of them stiffened; they expected a yell of terror. But the arrow missed. It passed a few inches to the right of Harg and struck the stone wall.

The men were surprised by what happened next. Harg and the women heard the flight of the arrow and the impact of the flinthead against the wall; and they all moved swiftly, as if they had been expecting attack. Harg leapt back and out of sight, but Kayah ran to the fire and seized a torch. She stood by the fire, waving the torch and looking round her for sign of an enemy; and almost at once the other two women ran to her and grasped fagots. The three were embattled and ready. Kayah screamed at the children, and they vanished into the recess where Harg was grasping his stone axe and looking out at the women.

When she saw no sign of an enemy in the river woods, Kayah, carrying the torch with her, went to the wall and picked up the arrow. From the three women there was an angry and anxious outcry. It should have been clear to those hiding in the thicket that these creatures knew they were being hunted not by beasts but by men; but the four of them only looked at one another, their eyes asking questions. They had not expected these people to use fire as a weapon. They had expected them to flee; but there the women stood, armed with fire and waiting.

The giant had crouched out of sight after shooting the arrow, but now he rose little by little and put another arrow to his bow. He was visible now, and Memm saw him and pointed at him and screamed. The scream unnerved the man, and again he missed; the arrow went between two of the women and above the stone wall and out of sight. Kayah, gazing in the direction of Memm's extended arm, saw the man just as he ducked out of sight. She knew now where the enemy was. Shouting commands, she seized a fresh torch and went back into the cavern, and the other women clutched wood and followed her. None of them were now visible to Gode and his men. There was only the fire which the women had left and smoke from a second fire which they could not see.

"Come!" said the giant, looking back at his companions. He felt cheated. He felt that these creatures, like certain beasts of the prairie, had disappeared into a hole in the earth. But he remembered that all things that lived in holes came out if a man waited long enough, and he moved forward, intending to close in on his prey. The others followed, with Gode still in the rear. He was haunted and frightened. The wild cries had recalled to him those in his dreams; but he was also troubled by the fact that these creatures made fire and used it as a weapon. He refused to recognize them as human. Nevertheless, their use of fire suggested kinship even more than their upright posture and the quality of their voices; and he had little desire to join in this attack.

The giant followed the stream, with the others trailing, until he was close to the cave. He then crawled forward on hands and knees, resolved to look round the stone ledge and see, if he could, where these creatures had gone. He never suspected that they might be watching him and waiting. He was so convinced that they had disappeared into a hole that he went recklessly to the very edge of the cavern. Kayah had peered out and had seen him coming; and grasping the largest of the flaming fagots she waited. The moment his head came round the ledge of rock she thrust the burning torch into his face, driving it with such power that fire was shoved into his mouth and eyes. Never before had Harg's family, never had the other men, heard such a thunderous bellow of astonishment and rage. The man recoiled like a beast; but before he could recover, Kayah was upon him, beating his skull with the chunk of flaming wood. Then she vanished. She ran back for another torch to resume the attack and she screamed to the others to join her; but when she appeared again at the edge of the cave, the man was gone.

Blinded, maddened, convulsed by anger and terror, the giant had lost his footing and rolled. Like a mortally wounded beast, he had fallen over a shelf of rock and pitched head downward to the river; and there in the thicket he was threshing like a bull mammoth. The dreadful sound of his rage and fear could have been heard for two or three miles. Gode and his companions ran back, out of sight. They were so terrified that they were sweating and trembling; never in their lives had they heard such wild clamor as now came from the river bank. One ember had burned the giant's tongue and the whole inside of his mouth, and other embers had destroyed his sight. He had lost his bow, his arrows, his lance; and he could not see where he was or know how close his enemies were to him. He was furious, but he was horrified by the fact that he could not see.

While the other men hid and waited, and the giant clawed at the brush and attempted to climb the ledge, Harg came forward, grasping his axe. He had sensed helplessness in the cries of the man. When he looked over the ledge, he did not realize that the giant was blind but he did perceive that the man was weaponless; and he crouched on the shelf and waited. His enemy was trying to climb, clutching about him with huge hands; and while waiting for him to come within reach, Harg saw the man's eyes. They were red and weeping and looked sightless. Feeling bolder, Harg descended, raising his axe as he went; and when he swung the heavy blade downward he buried it in the giant's skull. The man sank without even a moan.

Gode and his companions had seen Harg come out. They were fixing arrows to shoot when Harg raised the axe; and upon seeing the blade descend they came quickly to the ledge and looked down. Ten feet below them Harg was staring at his fallen enemy, and a moment later three arrows entered his body. He screamed, and his scream brought Kayah out, a firebrand in her grasp. Gode saw her coming and shouted a warning, and the three men fled, with Kayah pursuing them. Like deer they vanished into a thicket, and Kayah returned and looked over the ledge to see what had happened to her man. She saw the giant with his skull laid open. She saw Harg lying close by him and she knew that both of them were dead.

She was still gazing at them when she felt a sudden blow

and a sharp pain in her side; and a moment later a second arrow pierced her throat. This arrow she seized angrily and tried to tear out. The head of a third arrow was buried deep in one thigh, and a fourth struck one of her ribs and fell to the ground. She uttered no cry. Like one attacked by bees she stood and fought. She tore the arrow from her throat; and while blood spilled down over her she grasped the one imbedded in her thigh. Other arrows now struck her, and furiously she seized them, tearing them out or breaking them off. Not until Gode's powerful arm buried an arrow deep in the chamber of her heart did she sink to the earth; and even then she continued to fight these things that tormented her. She fought them desperately until she died.

The other women had listened to the fighting and the screams and had crawled to the far wall with the children. Gode and his companions came up and looked at the dead around them. Remembering then that others in the cave still lived, they crept to the ledge and peered round it. In the gloom they could see the women. One of the women saw the men peering in and left the children and rushed, screaming, toward them. When she turned to the fire to seize a torch, one of the men leapt into the cave and impaled her with his lance. She sank to the earth, moaning, but she tried to crawl to the fire; and now the man picked up a stone and crushed her skull.

The other men had entered behind him. Back in the gloom, Memm was on hands and knees, hugging an infant against her belly. Near her were the older children. When she saw the men advancing with lances poised, she sprang up and ran past them, clutching her child. Gode and one of his companions pursued her. Memm left the cave and ran but she stumbled and fell and then crawled; and in her frenzied effort to escape she came to a fissure in the stone ledge and crept into it. She thrust her baby down into the crevice as far as she could and then hovered above to hide and protect it. When the men came up, only her back was exposed to them and it was three feet below the surface of the stone on which they stood. Down in the fissure she was like a beast pretending to be dead and hoping its enemies would pass it by.

Gode looked at her, but he made no move to strike. The other man jabbed her with his lance and slowly cut her to pieces; but Memm made no sound. Desperately she tried to thrust her child farther down and to cover it completely so that it would be hidden; but the repeated stabs of the lance in her back and neck brought from her no cry of pain. She died there, silently, with her hands reaching down to her babe until her hands were stilled. When he knew she was dead, the man who had slain her went back to his companion; but Gode stood and looked at this mother. He knew that her child was under her.

Never had a man been self-conscious, and it cannot be said that Gode was self-conscious now. Nevertheless, the emotion in him was akin to self-consciousness and to shame. In a way, he felt spiritually naked. Kneeling, he grasped the bloody mother and pulled her out of the crevice; and then he looked into the depth and saw there, on its back, with short legs crooked up to its belly, a living child. It was staring up at him, its eyes blinking in the sudden strong light, its tiny hands clenched. It was stained with the blood of its mother.

Gode knew very well that the mother had been trying to save the life of her young one. Without a murmur, she had died, to save it—and she had saved it; because there it lay now, squinting up at him, unharmed but helpless, and making no sound at all. The babies of many animals were very quiet when in time of great danger their mothers hid them. Gode knew that. He had seen the young of grouse hide in tall grass and refuse to move even when he reached out to touch them.

This one seemed to think that it was hidden and safe, though something was looking down at it and it was looking up; but when Gode reached down into the crevice and touched the infant, it began to cry. He drew it up and set it on the earth by its dead mother. At once it smelled her, and its cries were hushed; and after a moment it explored her and found a breast and began to nurse. It was a tiny thing only a few months old.

Leaning on his spear, Gode looked down at the babe sucking its dead mother; and while he stood here, his mind troubled and wondering, the two men came over. They had slain the children back in the cave. When they saw this living child, one of them moved to strike it but was stopped by a sharp cry from Gode.

"No!" he said, and waved the man back.

He could never have explained why he wanted to spare the life of this thing. He did not accept it as a human child or its mother as a human mother. Perhaps he was remembering how he had killed a bitch wolf and the young one had followed him home and had become his faithful friend; or perhaps he was feeling a little shame that men so strong and well armed should attack and slay such defenseless creatures. Whatever it was, he waved the men back.

"Kill?" asked one of them.

"No," he said.

"Enemy."

He gave no answer to that. The other men went away, and Gode stood for several minutes, watching this thing try to draw nourishment from dead breasts. He had been wondering whether to kill it or take it home. He decided to take it home.

13

For Gode's women it was a human child. They did not ask Gode where he had found it; they supposed that some mother had died and left it, and for them that was enough. Because Memmee was pregnant her breasts were full of milk and she nursed the orphan. Then she and Marigg examined the infant, not for unhuman differences but for vermin and wounds. Gode was amazed.

He had not known what response his women would make to the child, but he had thought they would ask him to take it away. When he saw them fondling it and making motherly sounds, and, a little later, when Memmee sat and cradled it and gave it a nipple, he could hardly believe his eyes. For him, it was not human. It was only a little animal that had a strange resemblance to his own kind. Recovering from his astonishment, he advanced to Memmee and looked at the babe and pointed.

"Enemy," he said.

Memmee looked up at him. In her eyes there was at first only the gentleness of a mother; but when she realized that Gode was vexed and was calling this babe an enemy, her calm gaze clouded. Before she could speak, Marigg came over and faced Gode.

"No," she said. "Baby."

Well, yes, Gode was willing to admit that it was a baby; animals had babies, too. "Enemy," he said, speaking like a very stubborn and unreasonable man.

That Gode should call a human child an enemy was an incredible thing for the women. They looked at one another. The older children came over to gaze at the nursing infant, and after a moment they looked up at Gode.

He was confused and angry. When he moved to take the infant, Marigg cried sharply and pushed him away. She was angry, too. It was strange of him to bring a baby home and then call it an enemy. "Enemy-no!" she cried, and menaced him. Their gaze met. In Marigg's eyes there was disgust and anger; in Gode's there was only bewilderment. He withdrew beyond the fire and looked in. Marigg now took the babe in her arms and hugged it, keeping an eye on Gode all the while as though he were an unfriendly beast.

He was a deeply perplexed and unhappy man. The women did not know that he was haunted by ghosts—indeed, that ghosts had stolen his dog. They did not know that his world had become enormous and dreadful. For them, the world was what they had always known and was no more than they could see. For them, Gode was their man who hunted food and drove enemies away. Lately he had behaved strangely, moaning and crying out in his sleep or rising to prowl in the darkness; but they were not thinking of that. They were happier tonight

292

because they had another child. That it had not been born to one of them made no difference at all; if Gode had fetched home a dozen babies they would have tried to nurse and mother all of them. Children were the meaning of their life, and its richness was measured by the number of small ones they cared for.

They did not understand their man, and he did not understand them. For the most part they lived in different worlds. His was a world of killing and of death; theirs was a world of birth and of life. He slew their enemies, but the women took one of them in and nursed it; and even now Marigg was turning to her needles and pieces of skin to make the new child a garment.

Of course, Gode would never have brought the strange thing home if he had not been a haunted man. He had been afraid, but he was bolder now; and if the women had fetched the child to him and said, "Enemy," he would have slain it. And now he was baffled. If this creature was human, then he had been killing human beings. He felt no repugnance to the killing of human beings, and especially males; but it was not his way or the way of his kind to hunt them down merely to kill them. It was not his way to kill anything except for food or the safety of his people.

Gode and his companions had been driven to murder because of outraged self-love. Other men would go on killing the bent-legged and stoop-shouldered dwarfs until they had exterminated practically all of Harg's people; but Gode would not. Never again would he join them in hunting these creatures. It was not disgust that restrained him; it was not conscience nor a sense of wrong. It was fear. He was convinced that his arrows and lance did not entirely kill these animals; there was something in them that still lived, even after they were hacked to pieces and all the blood had run out of them. He felt this because he was haunted by their voices after they were dead. And besides, his wolf had been stolen and perhaps it had been killed. If the ghosts had power to kill his dog, they had power to kill him.

In thinking of the matter he did not come to such clear and definite conclusions. He knew only what he felt; but after an emotion dwelt in him for days with no relaxing of its intensity, it took on the force of logic. He would have dismissed the idea of the ghost if he had been able, but it had persisted night after night in his dreams and day after day in memory of the dreams; and now for him it was a fact.

While watching the women fondle the child he was deeply troubled because in him, transformed by an alchemy that lay below thought, the ghost that had been only that of an animal was becoming that of a human being. In his dreams the cries had been animal cries. Tonight, after Gode slept and dreamed, they became human cries, and when he stood up the next morning, he was a man haunted by a human ghost. A night of dreams had convinced him of what he had refused to believe. Now when he looked at the orphan he accepted it as human; there was no longer a struggle to reject it nor any wish to kill it. This was so because in his dreams he had again tried to slay a creature protecting its child; and though it was a bent and stooped dwarf it had cried to him in a voice that was human.

The moment he left his bed, Marigg rose also, not knowing what murderous intent he might have; but Gode surprised her by looking at the child he had brought home and saying calmly, "Enemy-no."

"Enemy-no," said Marigg.

"No," he said, and looked at the child. Then he ate a chunk of dried meat and took his weapons and went down the hill.

He thought at first to search for his dog because, though he believed it was dead, he hoped it still lived; but after he had gone some distance there pressed upon him a strange and enveloping loneliness. It was not the emptiness of a world in which he walked alone but the fullness of a world hidden from his senses. Nothing today was what it had always seemed to be, yet the difference eluded him. The trees were trees, the river flowed with its familiar murmuring sound, the hills around him stood in the deep silence of the eternal and the changeless. Birds he recognized by their cries or sometimes by no more than the sound of their wings in flight; and from the lazy breeze that moved across his path he picked out the odor of juniper and birch and pine, or the bloom of whortleberry and wild apple. All these sensory impressions, and many more, were as familiar to him as the image of his face in clear water; but there was a strangeness about them, too, because their richness and variety bore upon him as the innumerable smells and sounds of a world of which he saw only the surface.

Today he was like a man possessed by a nightmare that would neither take hold of him completely nor set him free. As he walked, aimlessly, without any purpose at all, he would feel himself clouded and obscured by anxiety so intense that he would stumble over objects or against trees; but again the world would suddenly open before him, bright and clear like a full morning, and he would know himself as a man armed and alert and ready to face his enemies. Then the world became the old and familiar world; he loved it and felt happily alive and secure.

But in his subconscious mind a wild and intuitive logic was busy. Into his consciousness it lifted, not concepts or fancies but only shadows, only tantalizing intimations of danger and horror. When hunting, it was a man's way to look behind him; his eyes were to the front and many enemies had learned to attack from the blind side. But also it was a man's way to feel reassured if he glanced behind and saw no skulking foe. Today Gode looked behind him often; and though he saw nothing, he felt nevertheless that he was being followed and watched. He was so sure of this that dread was a tingling sensation in his scalp and down his spine. Sometimes he would turn and face back on the way he had come and wait and watch for sign of stealthy movements among trees. In his dreams the ghost had become visible, and he believed that the ghost would be visible in daylight if he were alert enough to catch it out of hiding.

After a while he resolved to try to lose his pursuer; and so he ran swiftly across open places, or in forests dodged from tree to tree like a crazy man, hiding for a moment behind one before hastening to the next. On coming to the edge of a grove he quickly circled it and entered from the far side, hoping to overtake and surprise the ghost; but all he got from his violent exertion was a deepening conviction that he was followed. There was nothing to see and nothing to hear save the sound of his own running. Nevertheless, that his pursuer was noiseless was no argument against its existence. There were certain birds that made no sound in flight; there were animals with padded feet that made no sound when they walked. And there were beasts like the panther; sometimes a man knew that this creature was close by, even though all his maneuvering did not enable him to catch a glimpse of it.

And so it was, Gode believed, with this ghost that trailed him hour after hour, patiently, relentlessly, no matter where he went. He thought it was a mother ghost because the cries in his dreams had been a mother's cries. Because in his dreams she wished to kill him, he knew that she followed him now with the same purpose. If he were to throw his weapons away she would attack.

Until late afternoon Gode wandered from place to place, a haunted and terrified man. He had no conscious wish to find the spot where Harg and his family had been slain, but his subconscious mind guided him to it, and he was surprised when he found himself there. He looked round him to be sure that this was the place; and then he slowly advanced, hanging his bow by the string over his left arm and grasping the lance with both hands. He came in on the side where Memm had been killed; and here by the crevice he found her bones. Beasts had come to strip the flesh, and birds had flown down to eat her eyes and pick the bones after the beasts had gone. Gode knew this was the skeleton of the mother whose child he had taken because the bones were scarred with lance marks from the base of her skull to her rump.

Standing with his feet far apart, and grasping the lance in the way of a man ready to attack, he stood for a long moment and looked at the skeleton. From time to time he glanced behind him for sign of the ghost. While gazing at the bones of this mother he felt an impulse to thrust her into the crevice and hide her; and this he did, moving the skeleton with his feet. After it was down in the fissure, it was still painfully visible; and now Gode laid aside his weapons, looked round him for sign of enemies, and then quickly piled rocks on the bones. When this task was finished he felt deep relief. With the unreason born of desperate and terrified action, he felt that he had buried the ghost.

He went next to the river ledge where the family had lived, and saw the bones of a woman and several children. After searching vainly for crevices into which to thrust them, he perceived that he could take these skeletons back into the cave and cover them with stones; and this he did, laying them in a pile by the rock wall and then bringing materials to hide them. Though he could see no sign of them when the task was finished, he nevertheless felt that they were not securely hidden; and while he was searching for stones and wood to add to the burial mound, he came upon the skeleton of Kayah. After gazing at it, he looked over the ledge and saw the remains of Harg. The body of the giant had been taken home by his companions.

Nowhere could Gode find a natural grave large enough to hold the two, and while thinking of the matter it occurred to him to dig a hole in the earth. Taking his weapons with him, he descended the ledge to the river bank where Harg lay and, using the point of his lance as a spade, he began to dig a hole. The earth was moist and friable; he loosened it with the lance and then scooped it out with his hands. This was the first time a human being had ever dug a grave; and instead of shaping it as a rectangle Gode dug a round hole. It was three feet deep and about two feet across. When he put Harg in the grave and saw that the skeleton was unable to lie down, he felt dismayed.

Sitting by the hole he thought of the matter, and there came to him another thought. He wondered if a person would not prefer to sit rather than lie—because, though he knew Harg was dead and had been stripped by beasts, he felt that he was also alive in a mysterious and unhappy way and was looking on, helplessly, to see what would be done with him. Climbing the ledge, Gode picked up Kayah's skeleton and brought it to the grave. He tried to set her in the hole with Harg but there was not room for the two of them, nor even comfortably for one; and so he grasped Harg gently by his skull and lifted him out. He now made a big hole; it was five feet across and a little deeper than it had been. It received the two skeletons easily and allowed them to sit side by side with their leg bones extended. The skulls were a foot below the earth's surface. It seemed to Gode that they looked comfortable, and he was rather pleased with himself. His burial of the other bodies had been crude, but he was an intelligent man who quickly improved his handiwork. While looking down and wondering what else he could do before piling earth on them, he remembered that this man had had a weapon; and the conclusion that came to him now was so sharply intuitive that he looked round him quickly for the axe. When he found it, he knelt by the grave and set the axe by Harg's right hand. He thought it was Harg's hand, though he was not sure now which was the man and which was the woman. After staring at them vainly for sign of genital or breast, or anything else that would mark them as male or female, he let the axe stand where he had set it and rose to his feet.

He now piled earth on the skeletons. After this was done, he looked at the grave and drew a deep sigh of relief. Now all the members of this slain family were buried. They were held down by earth or rocks and could not rise and wander over the earth or come to him in his sleep and cry with terror. He felt the deepest peace he had felt since the first of the mothers was killed. To be sure that he had missed none of these, he climbed the ledge and explored in the cave and the area around it; and when convinced that they were all securely imprisoned, he turned homeward.

He felt such deep, warm relief that physical hunger, until now overwhelmed by dread, excited him and sent him searching through the woods for something to eat. He found wild fruit and shot a rabbit and sat by a berry patch to make his meal. Taking the rabbit by its hind legs, he tore the creature apart and ate first all the more tender portions. Laying the carcass aside, he rose and fed on the berries and leaves of the rosebush and then returned to finish the meat. It was a day of lazy sunshine and tranquil sky. Looking round him while he gnawed and sucked the bones, Gode felt warm sensuous happiness and a belief that all was well. To express their joy in life his people sometimes made tuneful sounds; when Gode rose and took up his weapons, his delight was a wordless murmuring. The world for him was again the kind of world he had known—a dangerous and unpredictable world but with nothing in it that he was afraid to face. He went homeward, his senses alert, his lance poised to kill.

14

On his homeward journey nothing disturbed his tranquillity, and when he entered the cave the women observed that he was in an indulgent mood. He went over and stood his weapons against a wall. He fetched some twigs laden with berries and these he gave to Marigg; and then he sat on a wolfskin and stretched his long legs and relaxed. Looking round him he saw the strange child; it was lying on its back on a skin with its short crooked legs drawn up against its belly, with fascinated eyes watching the movements of its hands. It was the mother of this child, Gode supposed, who had haunted him during the previous night; but she was hidden now with stones piled on her and she would haunt him no more.

Not since the last day of his hunt with the men had he put on war paint. Now, feeling again his strength, his power to kill, his right to triumph over all things, he rose, intending to find his pigments and adorn himself; but while searching for them he saw on a wall a drawing of a wolf which he had made several days ago. The crude image turned his thoughts to his dog which some un-friendly being had stolen or killed; and while thinking of the dog he remembered the graves. Taken by a wish to draw one and to explain to the women what he had done, he got charcoal and faced the wall.

To indicate a hole in the earth he made a big U, and in this, with their backs to one side of the U, he tried to draw two skeletons. His picture of them was no more than circles for the skulls, lines for the torsos, and lines attached to the torso to represent arms and legs. He was at a loss to know how to draw the grave so it would seem to be covered with earth; but at last he did this by making a charcoal smudge across the top of the U. Around the U he made other smudges to represent earth. When he had finished, he looked at a hole with one side out of it and two skeletons within. For him, it was clearly the pic-ture of a grave with bodies in it, but when he called the women over they could make no sense of it at all.

"What?" asked Marigg, and pointed.

Gode had no word for grave nor any word for corpse. He touched the lines of a skeleton and said, "Dead." By making a circumference with his arms he tried to suggest the pit he had dug; and by running outside and returning with a handful of earth and then calling attention to the smudge over the U, he strove to make them understand that he had filled the hole with earth. Marigg thought he had planted something and she went outside to look at her new seedbeds of wheat and barley; but Memmee thought this was only another of his idle fancies, with-out worth or meaning, and altogether too foolish to bother with. She was bored and she turned away; and Gode was left to improve his drawing or to stand back and contemplate it with murmuring delight. Still devoted to his art, after darkness came he fetched a burning stick and set it up to use as a candle; and for what seemed to the women a long while he labored over his picture, grunting when annoyed, exclaiming when pleased, and trying with all the genius he had to make the U look like a real hole in the ground.

It was later than his usual time when he went to bed, but he had not stayed up because he was apprehensive. He felt deeply that all was well with him. When at last he stretched out on a skin, he sank into slumber as effortlessly as a child and was soon snoring with the women and children. At the cave entrance the fire burned brightly and talked in its flames. Beyond it was a world of half-light under a round moon.

But Gode took to sleep with him the problem of the drawing, and after a while he began to turn and moan or to strike out with violent arms. The skeletons were emerging from the grave and he was trying to restrain them. Indeed, many ghosts were haunting him tonight, the ghosts of all the people he had buried. In his earlier dreams they had been little more than a presence that he could feel; tonight they came with their bones. Each of them was an invisible presence of which the bones in one moment seemed to be the supporting framework and in the next to be detached, as if a skeleton were wandering in search of its flesh. They made a terrible nightmare of his sleep. He fought them; and because they were visible and corporeal tonight, he could seize and hold them. He grasped one after another and thrust them back into the grave, but always when he looked at the grave it was empty; and his dream became a frenzied and futile effort to force them into the hole and keep them there.

Then their number seemed to multiply and he became lost in a forest of skeletons. Close by each was an invisible and sinister presence, directing the bones in their attempt to rise and escape. Such terror overwhelmed him that he choked in his sleep, as if strangled; and at last he sat up with a yell of anger and fright that awakened everyone in his home. The women sat up, too, and looked at him, and Gode stared at them, and anxiously Marigg asked: "Enemy?"

If Gode had had a word for the dreadful things that haunted him, he would have spoken the word. "Yes," he said. He had no words to make them understand. He wiped the sweat of horror from his brow and rose slowly to his feet like a man cautiously trying out atrophied muscles. The moon was down now, and the earth had darkened. The fire had burned low. Marigg left her bed and laid wood on the embers; and then she came over and looked at Gode's eyes. They were such eyes as she had never seen. She had seen fear and rage but never eyes so stricken and terrified. She had had bad dreams in her life, and her children as well; and she supposed that Gode had been aroused by unhappy dreams. But she could not imagine what kind of dream would make a man shake all over while the sweat dripped from his face.

"Dream?" she asked, still peering at him.

"No," he said.

For him, it had not been a dream. Ghosts had come and had struggled with him here in this room; and he was so convinced of this that he looked round him for sign of a grave. Memmee now left her bed and came over, and the two women gazed at their man and marveled that he could tremble so.

"Dream," said Marigg to Memmee; but Gode heard the word and cried sharply:

"No!"

"No," said Memmee, and looked at Marigg.

For women, whose minds were practical and who believed only in what eyes could see, it was strange if an enemy had come and they had not known it. They searched for footprints or signs of struggle. Meanwhile Gode had gone outside and stood looking across the world. He was looking toward his graveyard and thinking of it; and the women, who knew nothing of all that, thought an enemy must have come, else why was he out there as if looking for one? They went down the hill, searching in the gloom for footprints, and they spent quite a little time before turning back, convinced that no enemy had come here. They went to their beds, and presently Gode came in and sat with his back to a wall, but he did not sleep again tonight. He suffered the kind of shock a man must feel when, having solved a dreadful problem and made himself secure from a malign power, he learns that he has not solved it at all. The human mind tries to simplify the complex and give an appearance of commonplaceness to what it cannot understand. In explaining his dreams, Gode had come by the idea of a ghost; and though he knew that this horrible thing was invisible, nevertheless it lived, and like all living things it could be restrained by physical force. Now, sitting by the wall and gazing at the fire, he decided that the ghosts had left their graves. If that were so, he had not piled enough earth on the two, or enough stones on the others. His reasoning was so plausible that he felt relief.

When daylight came he took his weapons and, without eating, went down the hill. It was several miles to the graveyard, but this distance he covered quickly, trotting in long easy strides, one hand swinging his bow and the other his lance. He went first to the grave he had dug; and there he saw a part, even if not all, of what he had expected to see. The grave was open and both skeletons were in plain view. If Gode had not been the victim of his own logic, he would have looked round him and discovered signs that beasts had come during the night. He might easily have seen and smelled their footprints; he could have found unmistakable evidence of their digging. But Gode was not thinking of anything like that. He was completely obsessed by a preconceived notion, and he looked for evidence that would support and not deny it. The grave was open. The ghosts had pushed the earth off and had emerged and toward morning had returned and were now sitting there. At least the bones were there, and it was with these that he had fought in his sleep.

He now climbed the ledge and went to the grave back in the cave. He expected to find the stones scattered over the floor and the skeletons in plain view. He was bewildered when he saw nothing of the kind. So far as he could tell, the stones had not been moved; and, dropping to hands and knees, he crawled back to examine the mound. The stones were large and the thought occurred to him that perhaps the ghosts had been able to crawl out. To learn if the skeletons were there, he removed so many of the rocks that he was able to see the bones. Then he went to the grave of the mother whom he had thrust deep into a crevice. This grave, too, was undisturbed. Perplexed, he returned to the pit.

He remembered that several ghosts had visited him, yet only two seemed to have escaped. While with simple logic he was trying to reconcile the matter, he heard a shout, and, looking across the river to the woods beyond, he saw a man on the summit of a hill, waving his arms. Gode recognized him as one of those with whom he had hunted Harg's people. He called to the man and beckoned him over; and a few moments later he could hear him coming through the woods and then he could see him wading the river. Wet to his waist, the man came up the bank. When he saw the two skeletons in the hole, he looked at Gode, his eyes wide with amazement.

"Look-there," said Gode.

"Yes," said the man, and stared at the bones. "Dead."

"No."

Gode gestured helplessly. He was tormented by want of words to explain his new vision of the world. He tried to tell the man that these were enemies and, though dead, they still lived—that they lived as things that could not be seen or killed. As enemies they came to him at night when he slept, and screamed and fought with him. All this he strove to explain with gestures and pantomime and a few words; and though the man by no means understood all of it, he did sense a part of Gode's meaning. He was frightened. His eyes were bleak and chilled when he turned to Gode.

"Dead-no?" he asked in a low voice.

Again Gode tried to explain that these skeletons were not alive, no, but that something which had been part of them still lived and wandered invisibly over the earth. It was, he wanted the man to understand, a phantom, a living thing without substance; you could thrust a lance through it and not kill it, and it would scream and fight you all night long. Sometimes you could see it, but you saw nothing really that you could take hold of, nothing that you could grasp and feel. You would be asleep and it would be screaming at you and trying to kill you; but when you moved to seize it, then it was not there.

While explaining, Gode acted the part of both man and ghost. He would move quickly and clutch at the air and close his hands on emptiness; and opening his palms wide he would say, "There-no." And this man who, like all men of his race, had a notion of the soul, of the part of him that wandered while he slept, did understand at last that these creatures were both dead and alive, that their souls lived after their bones and flesh were killed. He became a haunted man, too. He was neither so intelligent nor so sensitive as Gode, but Gode's recital vividly summoned all the nameless terrors of the world. The man looked round him anxiously as if the earth had become peopled with invisible things.

To bury these skeletons so deep that their ghosts could never get out was Gode's task now; and in this the man eagerly assisted. Falling to his knees, Gode scooped away earth until he could lift the bones out. Then he stood in the hole and squatted and removed the loose earth; and when this was done he spaded with his lance. While working, the thought came to him that he ought to make a hole large enough to receive all the skeletons; and so he told the man to dig, and he climbed the ledge. He crawled back in the cave and rolled the stones away and carried out the remains of the woman and children. Then he went to the crevice and exhumed the bones of Memm. All these he took to the grave and laid by the skeletons of Kayah and Harg.

When the hole was large enough to admit both men, Gode entered it too, and together they loosened the earth with lance points and tossed it out with their hands. Now and then they would pause in their labor and Gode would measure the width and depth, using his lance as a measuring rod. Not until the hole was five feet deep and six feet wide was he ready for burial. He indicated that the hole was large enough and told the man to climb out. Then the man took the skeletons one by one and handed them down, and Gode set them around the bottom, with their backs to the earth wall and their legs extended. When they were all placed Gode asked for the weapons, and the man handed him the stone axe. Gode looked at the bodies, wondering which was Harg's. He could not be sure because there were four adults, and they all looked alike. In turn he pulled the skeletons forward and looked at the spines and found the one scarred by the lance point; this he knew was the mother whom he had thrust into the crevice. But among the other three he had to guess, and after he had guessed, he set the stone axe between bony knees and rested the right claw on the handle.

"Weapons?" he asked.

"No," the man said after looking round him.

Placing his hands palm down on the edge of the grave, Gode leapt up, resting for a moment on his arms before throwing a leg up and over the edge and completing his ascent with a quick roll. Getting to his feet, he looked into the grave, wondering what he could do to make these creatures more comfortable. In a later time it would occur to his people that those buried would like to have not only their weapons and other property but food also.

The two men were quite a while rolling and shoving the earth in. When the bodies were hidden, Gode gathered stones, many of them small but a few so large that he had to roll them over and over. All these he put into the grave, and then more earth; and when the hole had been filled level with the surface, he fetched more stones. The man did not understand why he was doing this; soberly he watched Gode make a mound of stones, but he asked no questions and he did not assist him. He was deeply disturbed. All the while he had labored he had been thinking of the ghost and trying to understand it. He supposed Gode was piling stones to keep the ghosts in, but it seemed to him that the earth on the creatures was enough to hold them down.

When the work was finished, the two men looked at one another. There was dread in their eyes, there were questions, but there was more than all that. There was a faint and elusive hint of human fellowship. Often men had labored together in the hunt but without any sense of companionship; today two of them had labored like brothers to imprison their enemies. Because Gode knew more fully the malign power of the ghost, the hint of fellowship was more manifest in his eyes. There was in him a feeling of friendliness for this man. He did not slap him on the back or shake his hand or exchange a bit of banter. He did nothing except to gaze at the man for a long moment, but in his eyes there was a human warmth that was new in a man's eyes. Then he took up his weapons, and the other did so, and they moved away without speaking, going together for a little distance and then separating to take the paths to their homes.

The man would go to his family and try to explain the ghost; and during this night he would dream and be haunted in his dreams. But Gode felt secure because the task had been well done, though when night came, and he slept, he was not wholly untroubled. There were unfriendly presences in his dreams but they did not invade his home and shout and try to destroy him. Somehow they were far away and wraithlike and lost. They were only the shadows of ghosts that wandered abroad in their loneliness and whispered to themselves and returned at daylight to the grave where the ghosts slept.

15

THE next morning Agger was sick. She had been ill for many days, but nobody had paid any attention to her. Because she was very unclean and stupid and sluggish, she had always been, for the others, a little less than human. If Marigg and Memmee had lived in a later time, they would have said of Agger that she was afflicted with evil, that there was a malign spirit in her; but they had no concepts of these things, and so for them Agger was simply unlike themselves and not altogether human. The woman had an offensive smell about her, even for persons accustomed to bad odors.

The people of this time felt disgust and contempt for sickly or malformed adults or older children. Many generations ago they had killed and eaten the weaklings when driven to it by famine; but now when diseased persons became intolerable they forced them to go away. Save in a mother, and in her only for the younger children, there was no pity in these people, no sympathy for the less fortunate, no compassion for those in chronic ill-health.

Perhaps Agger was sick with cancer or tumors. When sitting, she sometimes pressed palms to her belly and distorted her face as if in pain; or when sent by Marigg to fetch wood or water she walked with a hand pressed to her groin. She was a dull woman but she had sensed long ago that nobody liked to be in her presence. Instead of becoming a tantrum person, as was usually the way with the unwanted, and especially the men, she had withdrawn into the silence of martyrdom. Day after day during this summer of war against Harg's people, she had sat back in the cave by herself, with hands clutching her belly, with eyes mutely appealing for help. More recently the other women had not allowed the children to go near her. Agger was simply thrust back, as the leper was to be in a later time; and the disgust which Marigg and Memmee felt for the woman became more manifest as the foul smell of Agger grew steadily more offensive. Now and then Marigg gave her a little food and water, but that was all.

And now Agger was dying. The disease deep in her bowels filled her with unresting pain; and on the morning after Gode had buried the ghosts, Agger did not rise with the others but lay on her bed and moaned. At first her moans were so low that the others were not annoyed; but after a while they became loud and prolonged, as if the woman were trying to choke back a scream. Marigg went over and looked down at her with hard unpitying eyes; and Agger looked up with eyes stricken and pleading. Then Memmee went over, and the two hale women looked at the sick one; and Gode, observing what they did, joined them.

For Marigg and Memmee, the woman was only a foul and disgusting female who was moaning probably to draw attention to herself; but for Gode she seemed to be much more than that. She would not have been more than that a few weeks back, but now, as he stared at her, he remembered the ghosts and wondered if ghosts were tormenting her. To him her cries suggested more of terror than of pain.

After gazing at Agger for a long moment, he turned to the other women and tried to make them understand that there were ghosts in the world. With gestures and a few words he acted for them the part of one haunted by invisible enemies and fleeing; and presently he seized his lance and engaged in mock attack, charging an invisible enemy and running it through, trying to explain to them that he had not killed it, that it still lived, that it was immune to any kind of force he could bring against it. He went to a wall and with charcoal drew a grave with skeletons in it, and, with smears, he tried to suggest that he was burying the creatures. Then up through the smudge he represented a skeleton in the act of emerging, and then grasped his lance and pretended to attack it. Setting his lance aside, he spread his palms helplessly and pointed to his drawings and said, "Dead-no."

The women were confused by his astonishing behavior. They did not understand what he was trying to tell them but they did sense that it was weird and terrible. They saw clearly the passion, the anger, the fear in his face as he acted the part; and because again and again he pointed to Agger, and even menaced her, they knew that in some mysterious way she was related to the drawings. But instead of arousing in them any sympathy for the woman, Gode's pantomime convinced them that she was utterly loathsome. Bored, they turned away to give breakfast to the children and to build the fire.

Gode knelt by Agger. After looking at her sick eyes and seeing unmistakable pain and fear there, he asked: "Enemy?"

"Yes," she said.

"Enemy-where?"

Agger pressed hands to her belly. Gode was mystified. The part of her which she pressed was for him the chamber in which a baby lived before birth. He wondered if Agger meant there was a child in her. Was she suffering the first pangs of child-giving?

"Baby?" he asked, using their word for child.

Agger shook her head negatively and moaned. Gode continued to kneel by her, excited, perplexed, and resolved to understand. The eyes of these people could communicate many things which their tongues had no words to tell. Gode wanted to look into her eyes, but she turned away, and again and again he said, "Look!", repeating the word with such sharpness that at last she met his gaze. For a long moment their eyes met and neither spoke. In Agger's there was only abject misery, mixed with fear, but in Gode's there was the curious probing interest of the scientist.

"Baby?" he asked again.

Agger's "no" was almost a scream. He rose to his feet; for him, at least, the matter was solved. If it was not a baby, then it was something else; and what else could it be except a ghost? There was something in her belly. While kneeling he had perceived that she was swollen; and thinking of this he knelt quickly and moved a hand over the rounded part of her. When, like a physician, he

315

began to probe with a finger, Agger screamed and bared her teeth.

Gode now accepted the breakfast which Marigg offered and sat on a skin by the fire, to eat. While he ate, his intelligent mind was busy with innumerable fancies. He could not accept, at least, not at once, the notion that a ghost had entered Agger, because his experience with ghosts had not suggested any such behavior as that. They had come to him while he slept, and had yelled and fought and tried to kill him; but they had not tried to enter him.

After finishing his meal, he took his weapons and went down the hill. Hastening to the grave, he found it undisturbed. There was no sign at all that a ghost had emerged or had tried to; but while gazing at the pile of stones he remembered that men had killed other creatures of the kind imprisoned here. There were other ghosts, which no one had buried. This realization frightened him, and he turned homeward with the belief that there was a ghost in Agger. How or why it had entered a woman he could not imagine, but he had no doubt that its purpose was to destroy her.

During the remainder of this day he behaved strangely. It was the way of people then, as with most of them it is still, to reflect on the world and their relationships in it only when unhappy. When they were well fed, warm, secure from enemies, and free of pain they were indolent and self-indulgent. It was threat to their security or pain in their bodies that forced them to think—to think of dangers and how to avoid them, or of their miseries and their possible causes. Gode's discovery of the ghost had stirred him to extraordinary mental activity. After deciding that a ghost had entered Agger and was tormenting her, and perhaps making some of the sounds that issued from her mouth, he was faced with a very grave problem. He would have to drive this ghost away.

For a little while he stood and looked at Agger; and then, suddenly, he startled the women by dropping to his knees and grasping Agger and squeezing her. He thought that by pressing on her belly he could force the ghost to come out. Agger screamed with pain; and the other women, seeing the agony in her face, cried out with protest. Gode was a little nonplussed. He had not expected such angry outcry; and now he moved back and stared at Agger with the perplexed intentness of a primitive scientist who wondered if his experiment had been successful. Plainly it had not been; Agger writhed in pain, and Gode, eying her with professional interest, perceived that the swelling in her had not diminished at all.

He rose to his feet, still determined but momentarily baffled; and, observing that Marigg and Memmee were looking at the prostrate woman, he again strove to make them understand that an alien and unfriendly presence had entered this woman. When he indicated Agger's swollen belly, Marigg thought she understood what he meant.

"Child-no," she said.

"Child-no," said Gode. He pointed to the wall where a crude drawing represented a skeleton emerging from a grave. He went over and touched it and to Agger he said, "Look." Marigg and Memmee gazed at one another, both thinking that their man was very strange. They had never seen him behave with such unpredictable foolishness; they wished he would take his weapons and go for fresh meat.

But Gode continued to divide his interest between

317

Agger and his drawing, trying to make her understand that an unfriendly thing was housed in her and must be driven out. As he became more baffled he became more afraid, until at last he was overwhelmed by dread. It had been terrible when these enemies invaded his home and fought with him while he slept; it was horrible to realize that one of them had crawled into the baby-chamber of a woman. Other ghosts might come and creep into them all. This thought filled him with such anxiety and terror that he resolved not to sleep during this night but to stay awake and watch; and this he did. Marigg and Memmee and the children slept; but all night Agger moaned and clutched her belly, or now and then she would give a low scream and try to sit up. Sitting near by and watching her, Gode could see the sweat on her face and the bitter suffering in her eyes. The cries she made were like those of the mother who had come to haunt him. Again and again he felt an impulse to leap on Agger and try to force the thing to leave her, but he did no more than to sit and stare at her, curious, baffled, and frightened.

The thought did not come to him as a stark and sudden recognition. It was something that grew in him during the long hours of the night as if his mind were a secret laboratory below the level of consciousness. Out of it from time to time came a vague hint, a brief intimation that made him tense for a moment, an elusive something that flashed and vanished. In the restless depths of his subconscious mind, the elements of his recent experience were being gathered into intuitive logic. A conclusion was being born there. And when at last it rose to consciousness, Gode was not excited, because repeated hints had made it seem familiar. It came to him with the aspect of an old and commonplace certainty. He did not think, "I have solved it, I know what to do." On the contrary, it seemed to him that he had known from the first what to do and was only waiting for daylight.

When daylight came, he took his lance and a long, flint knife and left the cave. He looked to the right and the left along the mountain wall, but he knew that the earth under the stones would be full of rock; and so he went down the hill and to the river. There, in a birch grove, the earth was soft and moist; and there he dug a grave. He dug a hole almost as deep as the one he and his companion had made, and when it was finished, he went to the mountain and gathered many stones and carried them to the pit. Before the task was completed, he was weary from hunger and loss of sleep; but he was goaded by fear, and fear drew on his store of strength. The sky was dark, and in the air was the smell of rain. Like all his people he was afraid of anything that seemed threatening; and often while laboring he looked up at the black clouds or down into the valley, where the morning was somber and gray.

It was almost noon when he climbed the mountain to his home. The women thought he had gone hunting, and when they saw that he fetched no food they were disappointed and annoyed. Marigg offered him no breakfast, and he asked for none. He was hardly aware of her because he was obsessed by what he must do and the need to do it quickly. He went to Agger and bent over and gathered her in his arms; and if the other women made any protest, Gode was not aware of it. Agger screamed and slapped him and tried to sink her teeth in his breast, but he moved like a man in a trance. He carried her outside and down the hill, never pausing or looking back; but when he came to the grave, he did not rudely hurl her into it. There was in him, there had been in him for some time, a kind of wish to propitiate the ghosts who were angry with him and wanted to kill him. He was gentle, not with Agger, but with the presence inside her; and gently he slid down into the hole, carrying her with him, and set her on the bottom. Then he leapt out.

Before the woman could realize where she was or what he intended, he was raining boulders and earth upon her. She screamed and fought, but he was only dimly aware of her cries or her struggle. Using his powerful hands as shovels he poured the earth down; and when he looked in and saw that Agger was hidden, he floored the earth above her with a layer of stones before adding more earth. He did not pause until the grave was level with the surrounding surface; and perceiving then that he needed more rocks, he went to the mountain and gathered them until the grave was hidden under a mound of stone. Only then did he pause to draw a long breath and wipe the sweat from his brow.

Thunder now cried at him from the sky above, and lightning there was like a dance of white arrows.

16

THE season of rain had come again. Of the violent and threatening phenomena of nature Gode and his people were not so afraid as his long-ago ancestors had been; but because of his recent experiences, and especially because he had just buried a ghost, he was anxious and fearful. When large angry raindrops struck him, he quickened his stride and became vividly aware of the tumultuous sky overhead.

It was a dreadful sky in its darkness and fury. A wild wind was rolling and heaving the storm clouds in convulsed and hurrying masses; and upon their black bellies the lightning played in quivering tangled arrows. Thunder was a deep and strangled muttering far away. Huge drops stung him like the hawthorn briar.

At the cave entrance he paused, drenched and trembling, and turned to look behind him; and on glancing up at the tumbling violence of the sky, he saw a great profile. Unmistakably he saw the dark brow with a mane of hair streaming back from it, the curve of the nose, the mouth

321

and chin, and one large malevolent eye. Down from it hung the wraithlike mass of body with the legs bent as if in flight. The whole thing changed swiftly while he stared; it was dissolved and overwhelmed by the dark moving world that pressed upon it; but almost at once he saw other faces.

Indeed, he saw the shapes of both men and beasts, as if a part of the earth's life had ascended to race before the wind. Of some he glimpsed only a hint—a face that was soon gone, an arm outstretched and then enveloped and lost, a mouth that opened and melted and vanished; but also from the rushing darkness he saw beasts emerge and move softly, soundlessly, as if trying to escape, though in a few moments they were engulfed by the overturning hills.

Gode called to the women, and Marigg and Memmee came and stood beside him in the rain. "Look!" he shouted, and pointed to the sky. Their imaginations were not so vivid; they had not spent a part of their lives studying the shapes and habits of animals or drawing their likenesses on stone walls. Nevertheless, they did see familiar shapes in the sky.

"Look!" cried Gode, and they looked and saw a face. It was high above most of the storm-mass in an area wanly bathed in sunlight—an enormous and softly golden face, with hair falling to the shoulders like a pile of warm cattail-down. The eyes were far apart and distorted, but they looked straight ahead; the cheeks were pale and sunken; the mouth was closed. It was a serene face, looking down from above, and it did not race with the storm. It faded slowly until only one eye was visible, and this one in a few moments disintegrated and spread in a radiance like that of firelight on stone; and then where the face had been there were floating scarves of golden hair.

Down below was a multitude of constantly changing shapes; and presently the women were shouting with excitement and crying, "Look-there!" and "Look-there!" Gode saw the mammoth, the boar, the wolf, the horse, as well as birds, trees, hills, and valleys, all hurrying in wild confusion. The women saw only a few beasts where Gode saw many, but now and then they perceived an image that he missed. It was Memmee who saw a baby, and in a voice shrill with mother-hunger she cried, "Child! Child-look!" She was so overcome by sight of it that she took a few steps forward, her arms reaching as if to clasp it.

The clouds had been moving toward them, and vast black hulks were now passing overhead. Off to the right the darkness had come down to clothe and hug the mountains; and to the left the blackness thinned in valleys of pale light. It was on the edge where dark and light met that Gode saw the greatest number of beings and the most bewildering change of form. Lightning was dancing there like white birch twigs, and thunder was baying from deep and hidden throats. And it was there that he saw the ghosts.

The women were straining their necks to look straight above, with rain beating on their faces, when Gode cried to them in a voice shaken by awe and terror. They looked in the direction of his pointing finger but they saw only a little of what he saw. Gode saw a mother with cavernous eyes and an open suffering mouth, the whole of her cloaked with the kind of misty unreality that had haunted his dream. A moment later a sheet of lightning fell. It lit the sunken eyes, and they awoke like flame, and in this moment he was convinced that the creature looked down at him—looked down and through him with the blinded eyes of one struggling with death.

With a choked cry he recoiled. All the anxiety and terror of centuries, all the dread of his heritage stored in his soul for countless generations, all the great burden of darkness and the deep—all this now filled him with the utter intolerable passion of a man's loneliness and a man's fear. He slunk backward with a hand to his brow, backward into the cave; and there he sank to his knees and crawled to the far wall and bent forward, afraid to look any longer at the terrors around him, afraid to think of them. The visible world had been all that a man could face; the invisible world was more than he could bear.

He knelt, shuddering, with his head bowed; and he began to sob. The women came in and approached and looked down at him; and the older children, sitting on their skins and shivering, began to whimper. Gode was weeping, and it was the first time a woman had ever heard her man weep. He was not weeping with tears; he had no such blessed relief as tears can give. He was making the dry and terrible sound of a man choked by terrors, of a man driven by unutterable dread to abase himself in the strangled and heartbroken humility of what in its own way was the first human prayer.